Also By Rebecca Massek

The Bell Tower Series

Truly & Deeply: A Bell Tower Novel

Utterly & Madly: A Bell Tower Novel

Slowly & Surely

A Bell Tower Novel

Rebecca Massek

To everyone who has ever wondered if they could have it all –
yes you can!

"Perhaps some detours aren't detours at all. Perhaps they are actually the path." — Katherine Wolf

Content Warning

This book does deal with some things that may be uncomfortable for some readers.

Topics Include:

Strained parent/child relationship

Stalking

Car accident & recovery

Public Humiliation

Please, if any of these are topics that would affect your mental health to read, don't read this book. While they are not covered heavily, the last thing I want is for anyone to have a negative experience while reading my books.

Always put your mental health first.

Chapter One

Justine

First Semester, First Year

The loud banging on the wall by my bed matched the banging inside of my skull. I sighed and rubbed my eyes.

It was nearly two in the morning, and while everyone else in my dorm was either partying, having sex, or both, I was neck deep in textbooks.

I was only two days into my freshman year of college, but I already had more homework than I'd ever had in my life.

I'd always been good at school. It was the only thing I was good at, really. I'd excelled in my advanced placement classes, done every extra credit assignment, and I'd been student body treasurer my senior year. I wasn't popular enough to be president, but honestly, I hadn't wanted to be.

I liked numbers. I knew numbers. Numbers were constant. They were predictable. They never changed.

People were exactly the opposite. I had never been a people person. Not that I didn't know how to talk to people. I wasn't socially inept. In fact, I could be rather charming if I put my mind to it. I just *preferred* not to engage with most people.

My parents had tried desperately to teach me how to interact with the general public. They'd put me in sports from the time I could waddle – soccer, dance, gymnastics, softball, martial arts, volleyball, tennis – nothing stuck. I'd liked tennis the best, when I didn't have to play doubles. I didn't do well on teams.

My mother could never understand why. In her eyes, I was beautiful, intelligent, and sweet. There was no reason I shouldn't have been wildly popular.

The problem was my father. A highly competitive man, he had been born into a fractured family. His parents had divorced when he was young, his father getting full custody because of his mother's tendency to disappear. When my father was twelve, my grandfather had broken his back at the factory he'd worked at, leaving him unable to work. My father had become the sole breadwinner, taking care of the bills and putting food on the table for himself and his father. It wasn't an easy childhood, and more nights than not he'd gone to bed hungry and exhausted, only to have to wake up a few hours later to go to work before school.

He was a determined man. A stubborn man. Incredible intelligence and emotional distance allowed him to push himself through high school, but he still couldn't afford college, even with scholarships. So, he'd worked menial jobs, determined to make a better life for himself, but unsure how. Then he'd met my mother.

She was the daughter of a politician, and they met when he was a server at an event at Mother's childhood home. He fell in love with her instantly and knew that he would do whatever it took to be her husband one day. He'd pulled himself up from nothing when he fell for her. Started taking business classes at night, worked his way to a manager position at a popular local restaurant. He'd wanted to make sure he was worthy of her and could give her the life she was accustomed to. He invested his money. Worked every hour that he could. He finally saved enough to start his own restaurant, and it became a wild success. My father's life had proven to him that with hard work and determination, nothing was unachievable.

His standards were impossible to reach. As his only child, his expectations for me were high, and he wasn't one to give praise lightly. My entire life he had never once said he was proud of me. I'd wanted to hear those words so badly that I only did things I knew I was going to be good at. Only things I knew he would approve of.

Over the course of high school, these "things" had solidified into a razor-sharp wit and a distaste for social interactions. I'd figured out that the problem wasn't necessarily that I didn't like people. It was that people were inherently problematic. They asked stupid questions and wanted to be coddled. Nobody wanted to be told the truth, but the truth was the most important thing to me. My father, for all his lack of outward affection, had always told me the truth.

The few friends I'd had in high school hadn't wasted any time removing me from their lives after graduation. I'd realized I didn't need them.

I'd shown up at college hell-bent on finishing my degree as fast as possible and taking over the world.

I wanted to be a business consultant. My father had hired one when he was first opening his restaurant, and they'd become quite good friends over the years.

Roy Chestham. A decidedly middle-aged man with a shark's smile and barbed tongue. He was good at building businesses from the ground up for a share of the profit. He could choose who he wanted to work with, help launch business ventures that he believed in, and he lived extremely comfortably. Given my affinity for numbers, that career path just seemed to make sense. And, if I was good enough at it, I wouldn't even necessarily have to be nice all the time. I'd asked Mr. Chestham why he'd chosen to be a business consultant, and he'd told me, "I get to make money, foster good business ideas, and help people succeed – all without having play nice and smile at some idiot who thinks he's right all the time."

When I'd told my father my plan for college, he'd looked the happiest I'd ever seen him outside of interacting with my mother. I knew that the faster I started my career, the faster I became successful, the happier I would make my father.

Which was how I'd ended up with a migraine on a Friday night, listening to the person in the dorm next door to me chanting "shots, shots, shots" with all his buddies. I'd applied for one of the best business programs on the East Coast and I'd gotten in. I was dedicated to finishing my degree as quickly as possible and starting my career right away. I wasn't going to let anything distract me.

When something banged sharply against the wall, I lost it.

I slammed my book down and growled. Shoving my glasses up my nose, I marched into the hallway and rapped on the door next to mine. I didn't stop knocking until the door swung open, revealing the noisy culprit.

He was laughing as he opened the door, which made his green eyes glint in the dim light. His blond hair flopped in his face, and my fingers itched to cut it off.

When he finally focused on me, his slight grin turned into a megawatt smile. I assumed he was trying to be charming, but I was so far past annoyed that it only added to my frustration.

"Hey," he drawled. His Southern accent was so thick I could hear it with just one word. "Wanna come in? We've got a party goin' on."

I rolled my eyes. My arms crossed over my chest defensively.

"Absolutely not," I snarled. "I came over here to yell at you. You need to keep it down. It's two A.M."

"Oh, are we keepin' you up?" He had the gall to look genuinely concerned as he glanced over his shoulder.

4

"No, I was awake. I'm studying and you banging on the walls is distracting."

"You're studyin'? At two in the mornin'? On weekend?" His face quirked in a small smile that revealed a set of dimples that made him immediately look innocent. Unfortunately, dimples weren't enough to sway my bad mood.

"In case you hadn't noticed, we're at college, not a discotheque. It's meant for learning, not drinking and debauchery."

He whistled sharply and raised his eyebrows. "Well, now, those were some mighty impressive three-dollar words there, ma'am."

I opened my mouth to protest being called 'ma'am', but before I could say anything he held up his hands in surrender.

"We'll keep it down, I apologize for the noise," he grinned. "Have a good night. Ma'am."

My nostrils flared as he shot me one last cheeky smile before closing the door quickly.

To his credit, and my further annoyance, the music volume went down and so did the level of chatter from the other side of the door. I stood there fuming for a moment before stomping back to my room and reopening my textbook. After staring at the page for fifteen minutes without absorbing anything, I gave up.

As I lay down, I could hear faint laughter on the other side of the wall. The boy's playful green eyes danced in my head and a fresh wave of anger flashed through me.

He was distracting.

I would have to request to move.

And that just pissed me off more.

Chapter Two

Justine

Business 101 was such a cliche name for a class. But here I was, bright and early, my laptop out and ready for the first class that was going to launch me on the path to success.

I was rearranging the pens on my desk when I heard a loud laugh from behind me. It made me jump, and my pens scattered across the desk and onto the floor. As I reached down to get them a pale hand beat me to it. I looked up to say thank you and was caught by two startlingly bright green eyes. They seemed to dance, even though the boy who owned them was simply looking at me. It gave me a moment to take him in.

He was cute. Not threateningly handsome, but there was a boyish charm to his face. His blond hair flopped over his forehead, and his slim shoulders carried a confidence I'd never had naturally. He smiled at me and his dimples came out.

It took me a beat, but suddenly a memory of the weekend before raced into my mind.

This boy, standing in a doorway at two in the morning, smiling impishly.

Calling me ma'am.

"Careful there, darlin', don't want you to lose anythin' before class even starts, now do we?"

I was struck again with how thick his accent was. I still couldn't place it, and I could barely understand him. His eyes twinkled, and I could tell that he recognized me as well. But he didn't say anything else, just watched me.

It took me a moment to process the whole interaction, but once I did, I simply said, "Right, thanks."

His lips quirked in an easy smile, and he pretended to tip an imaginary hat as he started to walk up the stairs. "Well, good day to ya, ma'am."

Immediately, I felt my back stiffen. I swore he'd done that on purpose.

"Don't call me ma'am," I snapped before I could stop myself. He stopped and I felt those green eyes on me.

"Didn't mean to offend." His voice was easy, but cautious. He put a little laugh in it and said, "I'm from Alabama, we call everybody ma'am. Or sir."

"Well, I'm from Connecticut, and ma'am is reserved for my grandmother - if she's behaving."

He laughed and it was light and buoyant. It made my chest tighten in a strange way. "Point taken, ma- Miss," he quickly corrected himself.

When I glanced at him, I saw that he had a big, goofy grin on his face, and his eyes were doing the dancing thing again. Anger bubbled beneath my skin. This boy was infuriating. How was he so happy this early in the morning? And why was he still talking to me? I needed to get my notes prepped and my desk arranged and honestly be doing anything but talking to this goofy, cute boy.

I turned back around and stared resolutely at my computer. "Class is about to start. You should go back to your seat."

"What if I wanted to sit next to you?"

I blinked at my screen before saying primly, "That seat's already taken. Find another." Because the last thing I needed was for him to be distracting me the entire class.

I wasn't watching him, but I felt him start to move away and my shoulders relaxed a little. Just for a moment though, because then he was sliding into the seat behind me and leaning forward, his voice just behind my ear.

"See, this way I can copy your notes."

I whirled around angrily and was about to lay into him when the professor walked in.

"Good morning, good morning," he chirped. He was a small man with wire-rimmed oval glasses that wanted desperately to fall off the tip of his nose. "I'm Professor Clemons, and this is Business 101!"

I heard a quiet, "Shit" from behind me. I couldn't help my smirk. He was in the wrong class.

"We'll start with roll call. See how many of you managed to make it out of bed today."

The professor made it through the entire class, and never did I hear, "Here" from the Alabama boy behind me. Professor Clemons noticed this too, because he looked up at the boy over the tops of his glasses.

"Wrong class, young man?"

The boy stood up and rubbed his hand behind his neck. "Yes, sir. I was s'posed to be takin' Econ 101 with Professor Miller, but I guess I got the wrong building."

"Very well, you may be on your way then. Although, I will say that Miller is not tolerant of latecomers."

"If it's all the same to you, sir, I'd like to stay for your class," the boy said. He was all confidence. "We could call it an audit?"

Professor Clemons assessed him and then smiled tolerantly. "Welcome to Business 101. What's your name?"

"Gregory Hudson, sir."

He sat back down with a satisfied smile.

I sighed and rolled my eyes.

Things were so easy for people like Gregory Hudson. They could walk into a room and have people eating their bullshit out of the palms of their hands within minutes. I'd just watched it happen. They had no respect for rules or procedures because they didn't have to. They could choose to randomly stay in one class to avoid getting in trouble in another, and nobody batted an eye.

Professor Clemons started his lecture, and I shook my head to clear it enough to focus.

That turned out to be no easy task. Gregory insisted on whispering his thoughts about the class to me throughout the lecture. Not just on what we were being taught, but his opinion on the way the textbook was structured, why Professor Clemons had decided to lean into the traditional tweed look instead of going for something more modern, and who he thought would end up hooking up before the semester was over.

None of which made it into my notes, but unfortunately neither did much of the lecture.

By the end of class, I was distraught.

Almost pulling my hair out in frustration.

And on the verge of tears.

The last was something that had always made me ashamed. Tears flooded my face no matter what emotion I was feeling. I hated it. It made me look weak, and weakness was something I rarely tolerated. Especially from myself.

It took every bit of my self-control to pack my things quickly and storm out of the room without stopping to tear into the boy behind me.

Unfortunately for him, he decided to follow me.

"Hey, wait up!" he called as he jogged across the quad to catch up to me.

I stopped in my tracks so suddenly that he knocked into me, scattering my armful of books to the ground.

"Oh, shoot! I am so sorry; I didn't mean to do that." He fumbled as he knelt to pick up my books.

"Leave them," I snapped, my hands curling into fists.

He looked up at me like a hurt puppy. "It's not a problem, really. I truly didn't mean to do that. You just stopped so –"

"Shut. Up." I growled.

He blinked and stood up, staring at me in confusion.

"Did I do somethin' wrong?"

I rolled my eyes so hard I thought I heard them hit the top of my head.

"You mean, other than bugging me so much during class that I couldn't get any proper notes down? Or how about partying so late into the night that I can't study? Or how about running into me and knocking my shit all over the ground?" I was fuming, and my words were coming out laced with acid.

"What are you talkin' about?" He looked so confused it was almost adorable. If I wasn't so angry, I would have noticed that people were stopping to watch us.

"Just leave me alone, okay?" I snarled, crouching to pick up my books.

"I was just tryin' to be friendly, that's all."

"Well, I'm not here to make friends."

"Look, I honestly don't know what you're so upset about," he said. His tone was trying to be light, but it was lined with anger. I almost relished the fact that I could make him angry. I wanted him to feel what I was feeling.

"I'm upset because your two-bit antics in class made me miss most of the lecture."

"You took better notes than anyone else in there," he snapped. "I saw you. And I'm sorry for tryin' to be friendly. I was tryin' to make up for the other night when I was bein' too loud. I wanted to show you that I'm not a bad guy."

"You could be the best guy in the world," I said stiffly as I stood, gripping my books to my chest, "but I don't have time for friends. Especially not with someone who clearly doesn't take any of this seriously."

With that, I turned and stormed away, leaving him sputtering and red behind me.

Chapter Three

Greg

First Semester, First Year

By the end of the first semester of college, I knew business wasn't really for me. But my Daddy'd told me that the most useful thing to learn is how a business works.

He'd said, "Son, you never know where your career path is gonna wind up, so it's always good to have a head for business."

Two years after that he'd lost the farm.

I'd started working at the auto shop in town after school, savin' up money so that I could go to college and learn how to run a business. I didn't have a clue what I'd do with a business degree. Especially since we didn't have a farm to run anymore.

What I did know was that I was an average student, a hard worker, and everybody's friend. I had no idea how to turn any of that into a career that'd take care of my folks, me, and my future family. But I was good with my hands, and friendly with the customers, so the owner of the auto shop took a shine to me. He saw that I was bright and curious, and he said I was destined for more than just a mechanic job. So, he taught me about his side business.

Brewin'.

Now *that* I'd loved. The whole process of it. Pickin' out the grain, settin' up the distillers, comin' up with different flavor combinations. It wasn't something you had to be a genius to do, but you still had to get creative and problem solve. No two batches of brew would come out the same.

My boss took me to his barn where he had a whole distillery set up, and in a single afternoon I'd found it. My path. What I wanted to do with my life. I figured, people were always gonna wanna drink, so there was job security. And I'd never be bored. And hell, if I planned it right, I could make some decent money.

So here I was, in one of the best business programs I could find that would give me a good enough scholarship.

I'd managed to set up a micro-microbrew station in my dorm room and, so far, the friends I'd made loved every batch that had come out of it.

Bell, in particular, was my biggest fan. We'd met in that Business 101 class I'd accidentally taken at the beginning of the semester. Well, more accurately, we'd met after.

He'd come up to me after my dressing down from Justine. The most interestin' girl I'd ever seen in my life. He'd offered to buy me a cup of coffee and listen to my girl troubles.

"That's the problem, bud," I'd said. "She's not even my girl."

We'd gone to the coffee cart, and I'd filled him in.

How she'd shown up at my door the weekend prior, eyes wild behind her big glasses, furious at me for interruptin' her studyin'.

How I'd nearly forgot how to breathe standin' there starin' at her.

She was at least two inches taller than me, with legs that seemed to go on for miles. Her skin glowed in the dim hallway light, and her short hair highlighted her high cheekbones and full lips.

She'd stunned me.

And I wasn't easily stunned.

The spots of dusty pink that had framed her cheeks when I'd called her ma'am had haunted my dreams for a few days after.

Seein' her in that class felt like fate. It wasn't even the right class, not that I knew that at the time. But there she'd been. Fastidiously organizin' her desk in the second row, her face free of glasses and touched up with a little makeup, but not hidin' her natural beauty.

Then she'd dropped her pens, and I couldn't help myself. I'd had to talk to her.I wasn't sure why I'd stayed, only that I wanted to get to know her better. But clearly, she didn't want to get to know me. It seemed a downright shame that such a stunnin'ly gorgeous girl would be the prickliest pear I'd ever met.

Bell and I were inseparable after that talk.

We spent all our free time together. He was the first friend that I didn't have to hide anythin' from. That I could fully be myself with. We just clicked. And we were on pretty much the same path. At the school for the same reasons.

He wanted to open up a restaurant. It'd been his dream since he went to some backwoods barbecue place with his pops when he was a kid. Said it was the best meal he'd ever eaten, but what had really stuck with him was that people came from miles around and the owner knew them all by name. It was the place to be for every town in a hundred miles. Bell wanted to open a place like that.

So, I introduced him to my brews, and over the course of the last semester we'd formed a very loose business plan. One day, we'd own a brewpub together. I'd make the brews and he'd sell the food. We'd make it the place that everyone would go.

Which was what brought us to the library on the day before the Business 101 final.

Yes, I'd decided to stick with the class. Mainly because of Bell. Definitely not because of Justine. Only problem was, neither me or

Bell had stellar grades, so we needed to do well on this final to pass the class. Hence, the library.

That's when I saw her again.

She'd managed to avoid me all semester, choosin' to sit on the opposite side of the classroom from me, never bein' in a group with me for projects, and high tailin' it out of class as soon as the lecture was over.

But there she was. Sittin' all alone at a big, round table with piles of books stacked around her. She had her glasses on, and every couple of minutes she used her shoulder to push them back up her nose.

Before I could stop him, Bell gave me a shit-eating grin and called out, "Hey, Justine!"

She startled so bad she dropped her pen. It was like she'd thought she was the only one using the library. She looked around for a moment, confused, until she saw us approaching her.

Her eyes shuttered when she saw me, and she turned to address Bell directly.

"Hello, Jackson, how can I help you?"

I snickered hearin' her call Bell by his actual name. Her gaze shot over to me and froze me to my toes.

"Something funny, Gregory?" Her voice dripped with icicles.

I wasn't about to let her talk to me like that, but I knew my answer would be mean. So, I chose not to respond. If you don't have anythin' nice to say, and all that.

Bell let the stony silence hang for a moment before jumpin' back in.

"He was probably just laughing because it's pretty rare for someone to call me Jackson," he explained with a charmin' grin. "I usually go by Bell."

She blinked. "I don't understand how Bell is a derivative of Jackson?"

"Oh, it's not," Bell laughed easily. "When I was a kid, I ran up the bell tower at our church and decided to ring it. With my head. Everyone called me Bell after that."

A small smile stole over her face. "Oh. That's funny." She bit her lip and then cleared her throat. "How can I help you, Bell?"

Bell threw me a victorious glance, and anger bubbled in my chest. Here she was, offerin' to help Bell after one little conversation, and she wouldn't even look at me. This girl made me furious. She had no genuine reason not to like me.

"Well, you've probably noticed that Greg and I aren't the best business majors you'll meet," Bell started.

"Shocking," she muttered under her breath, her eyes flickin' over to me before settlin' back on Bell's earnest face.

"You're the best in the class, Justine," he said eagerly. "We really need to pass the final tomorrow, and we were wondering if you'd maybe help us study?"

My eyes slid over to Bell in shock. I hadn't been thinkin' that he wanted to ask her for help. I'd thought he was just fuckin' with me for kicks. But, lookin' at his face, he was dead serious.

The anger that had started as a little bubble in my chest threatened to explode.

But there was another part of me that desperately wanted to hear what she'd say. I couldn't deny that havin' her help us would almost guarantee we'd pass the class. She'd helped some of the other students when they had issues with certain topics or concepts, and after workin' with her they excelled.

From somewhere deep in my head, a little voice reminded me that I also wanted to spend time with her. I wasn't sure if that was just my people-pleasing tendency to want everyone to like me, or if

16

it was somethin' deeper, but either way it made me want her to say yes.

I felt her tense. I looked back at her and watched her retreat into her head, obviously weighin' her answer carefully. Finally, after almost a full minute, her eyes refocused and she glared up at me.

"I'll help you both, on one condition."

"Name it," Bell said, right as I said, "Fuck me," under my breath.

"In your dreams, Hudson," she bit out.

My cheeks had the decency to heat.

Bell smacked my arm before turnin' to Justine. "Whatever your condition is, we'll do it."

She gave him a small smile and the bubbles were back.

"You both have to take this seriously," she said, her tone somber.

"I mean, of course we will," Bell said, confused.

Her warm brown eyes found mine and somethin' else blossomed in my stomach.

"I need to hear you say it, Gregory."

"Call me Greg."

"Say you'll take this seriously, and I'll think about it," she snarked. "Gregory."

My jaw clenched and I managed to hiss out, "I promise to take this seriously, ma'am."

Her eyes flashed and her nostrils flared, and I remembered how much she hated bein' called ma'am.

"Sorry, sorry, I didn't mean that," I backpedaled. "The ma'am part, not the takin' it seriously part. Obviously, I'll take it seriously. I just, I know you don't like being called ma'am. I didn't mean to, I just –"

She lifted a hand to stop my babblin'.

"Just…don't do it again and we'll be fine," she said softly.

I nodded and gave her an easy smile. "You got it."

She sighed and began clearin' books away, makin' space for us to sit with her.

"So, what exactly aren't you understanding?"

***

It was well past midnight by the time Justine let us go. She'd poured over every bit of material that we were confused about, not lettin' up until we knew the theory behind each concept and could put it into practice.

She'd been civil to me, but downright warm with Bell. Every time I saw her smile at him, or watched her lips quirk at what he'd said, somethin' hot and slimy slithered inside me. It was a feelin' I didn't particularly care for.

As we left the library, Bell bid us goodbye and started walkin' to his dorm, which was on the other side of campus from ours.

That left me and Justine standin' next to each other awkwardly until she cleared her throat and looked at me sideways through her glasses.

"I guess we should go."

"You want to walk together?" I'll admit, I was surprised she hadn't just taken off as soon as we were out the door.

"Well, it's dark, and as much as I'm loathe to admit it, it'll be safer for both of us to walk across campus together," she shrugged.

"Right," I nodded. Then I swept my arm out for her, tryin' to break the tension. "M'lady."

She looked down at my arm, then back at me, and rolled her eyes as she started walking.

I laughed out loud and jogged to catch up with her. "Come on, m'lady is better than ma'am, right?"

She sighed heavily and looked at me. "Doesn't trying to be charming all the time ever get tiring?"

"Darlin', I don't have to try to be charmin'," I grinned at her.

She rolled her eyes again, but a hint of a blush colored her cheeks at the term of endearment. "Trying to make people like you, then."

"Well," I thought for a moment as we walked. "I guess it's like this. Have you ever heard the phrase, 'you catch more flies with honey'?"

She shook her head. I didn't miss the way she was trying to stare resolutely ahead, but her eyes kept track of me as I walked beside her.

"Well, my momma always told me that. You catch more flies with honey. Basically means, you can get further in life if you're nice to people. So, I try to be nice to people."

"It's annoying," she said bluntly.

My eyebrows raised and my blood pumped a little harder. I wasn't used to people bein' so forward with their thoughts. And I definitely wasn't used to people hatin' me for no reason.

"That's a new take on an otherwise harmless personality trait," I grumbled. Then, I jogged in front of her and turned around, walkin' backwards to keep pace with her while bein' able to look her in her face. "Why do you find that annoyin'?"

"I find people who have a pathological need to be liked annoying," she smirked.

"I wouldn't say it's pathological," I said defensively.

"Well, you clearly have a problem with the fact that *I* don't like you," she pointed out.

I blinked at her. It was one thing to assume she didn't like me, but it was another thing entirely to hear her say the words.

"You know, you don't even know me," I snapped. Somethin' about this girl drove me up the wall. How in the hell could she justify being so judgmental to a guy she knew literally nothin' about?

"I know guys like you," she said, her tone dark.

"Guys like me?"

She huffed a sharp breath and stopped walkin', her eyes on the pavement between us.

"Can we just drop this?" she snapped. "I don't like you, and I don't have to. Let's leave it at that."

"No. No way!" I took a step closer to her. "You don't know anythin' about me, and it's rude of you to assume that you wouldn't like me before even botherin' to learn."

"Look, I get that you aren't used to being told no," she said, her tone dripping with sarcasm, "but I don't owe you an explanation. I don't owe you my time, my energy, or my attention. And if you can't accept that, then we're done here."

She shoved past me, stormin' away to our dorm building. But I wasn't done. I knew that I shouldn't push her. She was right. She didn't owe me anything. We barely knew each other. But I was pissed, and my logical, laid-back brain was gone.

"What do you mean, guys like me?" I called as I jogged after her.

She let out a frustrated, honest-to-God growl and whipped around to face me. Her eyes were fiery and glitterin' with what looked like tears. But that couldn't be right, considerin' the rest of her face was set in an angry snarl.

"Fine. Fine! You want to know what I mean by guys like you?"

"Please, enlighten me," I snapped.

She took a deep breath and straightened to her full height, holdin' her books to her chest so tightly that her knuckles paled. Like they could shield her from any counterattack I might launch.

"I mean guys who think they can get whatever they want if they flash a cute smile and a wink. Guys that have never been told no in their entire lives. Guys who have been handed everything they could ever want on a silver platter, so they don't feel the need to take anything seriously. Guys like you who can just walk into a random classroom and then enroll in the class with no regard to the fact that there might be students on the wait list that *need* this class to graduate. Guys who charm their way into successful degrees, careers, lives, with no actual effort put into it. It's sickening to me, and I don't have time for it."

My eyes were wide as saucers after her little speech. She stood there, not two feet away from me, pantin' with the anger that I could feel burnin' inside of her. And my own anger matched hers for a moment before settlin' into something quiet.

Our eyes were locked, searchin' for a name for what we were feelin'. I watched as the tears that had been wellin' in her eyes threatened to spill over.

I dropped my eyes and blew out a long breath. "Feel better?"

She sniffled angrily. "Not really."

I looked back up at her and then reached over to take her books out of her arms. She was so stunned that she let me.

"I'm not that guy," I said softly. "My life ain't been easy. And if you got to know me, you'd see that I'm actually just a decent guy who might make a pretty good friend."

I started walkin' back to our dorm, pausin' after about ten feet to make sure she would follow. It took her a moment, but she finally found her feet and trotted after me.

We walked in silence until we reached her door. I offered her books back to her and she took them reluctantly. I waited for her to say somethin', anythin', but she just stood there. Watchin' me curiously.

I rubbed the back of my neck awkwardly and then let out a sigh. "Goodnight, Miss Justine."

I walked next door and when I closed my door she was still in the hallway. Still watchin' me.

Chapter Four

Justine

In the days following my little impromptu study session with Gregory and Bell, I couldn't stop thinking about the look on Gregory's face after I'd laid into him. He'd been so angry, almost on the verge of losing his self-control. And then, in one breath, he'd looked so broken. So sad. His eyes didn't sparkle, and his lips weren't turned up in the corners. His face had fallen, and he'd simply stared at me.

And then he'd taken my books.

I'd been horrible to him. Said things that were crazy generalizations because he made me so angry with his happy-go-lucky attitude and I was sick of him trying to get close to me.

He'd just taken it. And then held my books all the way back to the dorm.

Maybe it was a little too fifties era chivalrous, but it had honestly shocked me.

People didn't shock me often. I truly hadn't expected this Alabama hick to be the one that did.

***

Eight Years Later

I sat in the café and twirled my coffee around in my hands nervously. I wasn't usually nervous when it came to business meetings. Since graduating, I'd built a rather successful reputation for being no-nonsense and straightforward. Negotiating contracts with grace and discipline. Never wavering.

But, as I lifted my cup to my lips, my hand shook a bit. I sighed angrily and reminded myself of my success, admonishing myself for the twist in my stomach. I couldn't fathom why I was so on edge. Then again, my business meetings weren't usually with old acquaintances who hadn't seen me since college.

I closed my eyes and took a deep breath.

If I were being honest, Bell was more than just an acquaintance. He's someone that I once considered to be something of a friend. He was always kind to me, at least. Never judged me, never tried to sleep with me, and never made fun of me. So, as close to a friend as I'd ever had.

I suppose my nerves were coming from the fact that I wasn't sure if it would be *just* Bell coming to the meeting, or if his hanger-on of a best friend would be accompanying him as well. I don't know what I'd do if Gregory Hudson showed up in this café in little Hartworth. I hadn't seen him since… well, at any rate it had been a long time, and I wasn't itching for a reunion.

The chime of the door made my eyes open, and I was greeted with a warm smile from the mountain of a man that had just entered. He dwarfed the café.

"Justine!" Bell boomed. His voice had deepened since I'd seen him last. And I could swear he'd grown another four inches. He was a wall of solid muscle, which should have been intimidating but the way that he held himself was still the gentle, kind soul that I knew in college.

"Jackson," I said, standing and offering him my hand to shake.

He stopped in front of me and looked at me for a moment before taking my hand in his massive paws and shaking it lightly, a smile on his face. The gesture made me remember why I'd liked Bell. He never pushed for more than what was offered to him. He was respectful, always.

"You've gotta call me Bell, Justine," he laughed as our hands dropped and we sat down.

"Bell, right," I laughed. "Apologies, I had just been reviewing the documents you'd sent over and 'Jackson' is the name on everything."

"Well, yeah, when you're starting a business you've gotta use the name on file with Uncle Sam. But friends slash business partners call me Bell."

"Fair enough."

He leaned back in his chair and studied me for a moment.

"So, how've you been, Justine?"

I paused and took a sip of my coffee, letting the heat settle my nerves.

"I've been well," I finally said. "Building my business has been challenging but quite rewarding. And yourself?"

"Good, good," he laughed softly. "Been a little bit of a ride trying to get to this point, but we're here now and finally ready to put some plans into action. Which is why I called you."

I nodded, processing his words. He'd already told me a bit about the business he was wanting to start. A restaurant and brewery that would provide a place for people from all over to come and enjoy a night out in an upscale casual atmosphere. The perfect date, celebration, and night out spot for Hartworth. It was a solid idea. That wasn't what made me pause.

"And who exactly is 'we'?"

His smile faded and he leaned forward, his eyes blazing. "Justine, now look. I know that you and Greg had some sort of fallin' out towards the end of school, but he's a good guy and we've been working to build this business together. I think we've got somethin' really special, but we can't do it alone. We need help. And the only person in this world that I would trust to help us with this is you. You're amazing at what you do, you specialize in restaurant business management, and you know us."

"I know you," I said softly. "I never knew Gregory."

"But you did. You knew him just as well as I did," he pleaded. "I don't know what happened with you two, and I don't expect either of you to tell me. But this won't work if you don't help us."

It had always been difficult for me to deny a request from Bell, and with the way he was practically begging me, I knew there was only one thing I could say.

"Fine, I will help you. Both of you. On one condition."

"Name it." His relieved smile seemed to light up the room.

"I want as little interaction with Gregory Hudson as possible," I said, my voice deadly serious. "I will be cordial and professional, but I am not his friend."

Bell was silent for a moment as he considered me. "Are you *my* friend?"

I rolled my eyes, but my lips quirked in a small smile. "As much as I'm friends with anyone, yes."

"Then we'll make it work," he beamed, thrusting his hand out across the table.

I looked at him over the top of my glasses and then couldn't help but smile as I took his hand. He shook it excitedly. I wasn't sure what I'd just gotten myself into, but if it was in the service of helping Bell achieve his dreams then I could handle seeing Gregory every so often. I would be a steadfast professional. There was no reason for anything more than that.

At least, that's what I kept telling myself.

Chapter Five

Justine

End of First Semester, First Year

I was sure I'd passed the Business 101 final, and I only had one more to take before winter break. As I left my dorm on the way to my last final, I ran into Gregory coming out of his room.

"Oh, hi," I said, mainly out of surprise at seeing another person there. Most of the other students had already gone home for the break.

He looked up at me and offered a small smile before walking away. I blinked after him. He'd never done that before. We'd had a whole range of interactions varying from outright hostility to mild flirting, but he'd never just glanced at me and walked away without engaging in conversation of some sort.

I shook my head. I couldn't worry about that. I needed to focus so that I could pass my test and then start in on the work for next semester.

But my head was clouded the entire walk across campus. I couldn't stop picturing those green eyes looking at me. So hurt. He must've been genuinely pained by my words when we'd fought last. That didn't sit well with me, for some reason.

I'd never much cared about people's reactions to the things I said to them. Mostly because it was usually in response to some horribly inaccurate vitriol they were spewing about me, so I felt justified. But I'd been thinking a lot about the conversation Gregory and I'd had that night. He was vexing, no doubt, but it seemed to be coming from a truly genuine place.

He simply wanted to be my friend.

That was the most perplexing realization I could have come to at the most inopportune moment.

I growled to myself as I sat my bookbag beneath my chair and pulled out my pencils. This class wasn't difficult, of course. It was arguably the easiest class that I was taking, so, of course, it was the last final of the semester. All I wanted to do was finish this test and get on the train back to Greenwich. Back to my admittedly stuffy house with my uptight parents.

I wasn't necessarily looking forward to spending the holidays at home, but without any friends on campus and no classes to attend there wasn't much for me at school. And there was comfort in knowing exactly how my break would play out.

We would open one present on Christmas Eve. I would get socks, my father would get a commemorative tie pin from wherever they'd vacationed that fall to add to his collection, and my mother would get a very nice bottle of wine. We would have ham and various seasonal assortments for dinner, and then go to bed after a nightcap by the tree. Christmas morning, we would exchange exactly five more gifts, all very practical in nature, before going our separate ways for the day. Father and Mother would go to either the Club or a museum for a Christmas date, and I'd go to the huge library on the second floor of the house and start on my studying for the upcoming semester.

Christmases had been like that for as long as I could remember. We used to visit my grandmother when I was younger, but she'd passed before I'd graduated high school, and I had no other relatives. My parents were both only children, as was I, and I'd only had the one grandparent left. So, holidays were solitary affairs.

To be honest, I think my parents preferred it that way. They were used to living very solitary lives. All they seemed to need was each other, and, even then, they didn't need to be with each other every waking moment. They'd been that way my entire life. I'd never met a more compatible and attentive couple than my parents. Every anniversary, every special occasion, sometimes even on random weekdays they would surprise each other with gifts and mementos. Every night before bed, my father would bring my mother a glass of water because he knew she would wake up in the middle of the night thirsty. They had pet names for each other. They genuinely were best friends.

But they were very independent people before they met and continued to be that way after they were married. They didn't rely on each other to survive. They were true partners, and they valued their time apart as much as their time together.

I thought it was rather healthy, but then again, I'd never known differently. I could see how devoted my father was to my mother, and how much she adored him in return. And I knew they loved me.

They'd divided my rearing evenly, Mother taking over the more feminine aspects of my life – how to be a good hostess, how to sit upright at the dinner table, how to cook and clean (even though she rarely did it after Father's restaurant chain had taken off, she thought it was important for me to be a well-rounded person). Most importantly, she'd taught me how to subtly manipulate the men around me who would inevitably underestimate me based solely on my sex. She was the more affectionate of my parents. When I was young, she'd loved brushing my hair. She would spend hours sitting with me, talking and brushing. Once puberty hit, I had wanted to cut my hair short. Typical teenage rebellion. I knew it must have killed her, but she'd booked me in with her stylist and gushed over the pixie cut I'd been sporting ever since. I loved my mother, and I knew she was proud of the woman I was becoming. She told me so before I'd left. She was warm and affectionate, but not smothering like some of my friends' mothers had been.

Father taught me more traditionally masculine things. Money management, education, how to command a room, how to be a leader, how to keep my golf handicap under ten. He knew that the world could be cruel and difficult to navigate, and he wanted me to be prepared so that I could maneuver through it successfully. He pushed me to be the best at everything, and I desperately wanted his approval. It lived in my gut, a constant source of tension that drove me to excel. He was a man of very few words, and nothing I did ever felt like it was good enough for him. I knew he loved me, but I wasn't convinced that he liked me much. I think that I was simply a biproduct of the intense love he and my mother shared, so he loved me for that at the very least.

I had a good childhood, and we were a happy family. I know it sounds like my parents cared more about each other than me, and that might have been partly true, but when I say I know that they loved me it's because they always took the time to make sure I was happy. We would take vacations to New York every year, seeing Broadway shows and walking around Central Park. We went ice skating one year when I was about ten, and they both held my hands as I wobbled unsteadily on the ice. I had many fond memories of them.

They were good parents. I'd missed them while I was away. And even though our Christmases weren't the idyllic TV-show warm and fuzzy type, I knew what to expect and I knew I'd enjoy it.

I wanted to be home. Done with these tests and away from the pained green eyes of a certain Alabama bumpkin.

I somehow managed to focus enough to finish the test before everyone else, earning me some sidelong glares as I dropped the stack of papers on the professor's desk and gathered my things to leave.

I stopped at the coffee cart as I made my way back to my dorm. As I was waiting for my small latte, I happened to glance across the quad into the student store and saw Gregory holding a book in his hands.

I watched as he flicked through it, a grin on his face. Then, he flipped it over. The smile immediately faded as he sighed heavily and set the book down, walking out of the store.

I quickly turned back to the coffee cart, hoping he hadn't seen me watching him. I thanked the vendor for my drink and surreptitiously looked around to make sure Gregory was gone before walking over to the store and picking up the book he'd been looking at.

Homebrewing: The How, The Why, The Where.

My forehead scrunched in confusion. Why was this book even in this shop? It's not like they encouraged underage drinking on campus. Then I looked at the section it was under and saw that it was for prospective restaurateurs. Did Gregory want to open a restaurant? A brewery?

I couldn't imagine him actually running a business. To run a business, especially a restaurant, took a steel backbone and the perfect blend of compassion and ruthlessness. You couldn't be a people-pleaser and run a successful restaurant. I knew from watching my father build his from the ground up. It could be a disheartening industry for even the toughest of people.

I ran my fingers over the vintage-looking cover art, confusion swirling in my head. Was he really trying to do something with his degree as risky as this? Every business major knew that restaurants were one of the most volatile and unpredictable ventures to undertake. When they worked, they worked, but there were so many variables to overcome.

I supposed, if he started planning now and worked extremely hard, he could probably pull it off. Hell, he could probably pull it off on charm alone.

I flipped the book over. Twenty-five dollars. It wasn't the cheapest book in the store, but it wasn't a bank-breaker either.

My mind conjured up Gregory's face as he had flipped through the pages. The incessant sparkle in his eyes glowing a little brighter, his lips quirking up a little more than normal. He'd been so excited to see this book. And so disappointed when he'd seen the price.

I don't know if it was lingering guilt over our argument or the faint spirit of the holidays that took over my body, but before I could stop myself, I was at the checkout counter asking them to gift wrap the book.

I tucked it into my bag carefully and made my way back to my dorm, sipping my coffee and feeling conflicted. I'd never bought a present for someone outside of my family before. And for that first time to be Gregory? It's not like we were friends. After the other night, I was convinced he never wanted to speak to me again.

Never in my life had I felt regret about laying into someone the way I was feeling about Gregory. Sure, I'd had tiffs with my friends growing up, but those were usually dismissed and never spoken of again. I sure as hell had never apologized for them.

I stopped in my tracks as I realized that was what this was.

An apology. Not a very good one, but an attempt.

I growled in frustration.

This was *exactly* what I hadn't needed going into my college career. Gregory Hudson was proving to be a horrific distraction.

Grumbling to myself, I stormed up the stairs to our hallway and propped the wrapped book up against his door. I knocked twice and then fled into my room.

I leaned back against my door, listening for him.

I heard his door open.

The book falling to the floor.

I heard the crinkle of the paper as he picked it up.

I could imagine his confusion as he turned the parcel over in his hands before the door clicked shut.

I pictured him sitting on his bed and opening the book. The sparkle in his eye coming back. That stupid grin, too.

I felt my cheeks heat as a small smile stole across my own face.

I sighed and rubbed a hand over my mouth, rolling my eyes at myself acting like a lovestruck schoolgirl instead of the determined college student I was.

I needed to get home.

Away from campus.

Away from distractions.

Away from Gregory.

Chapter Six

Greg

Second Semester, First Year

I hadn't seen Justine since Winter Break had ended. Not that I'd been lookin' for her or anythin'. God's honest, I hadn't.

But we lived right next to each other. I figured I'd see her when she got back from Connecticut, assumin' that's where she went for Christmas. But I didn't.

I had a feeling she was avoidin' me on account of the book that I was ninety-nine percent sure she'd bought for me.

When I first found the book outside my dorm, I was confused. But it was addressed to me. My first thought when I'd opened it was that Bell had bought it for me. But if it had been Bell, then he woulda stuck around to see my reaction to it. I thought it mighta been one of the other guys that was a part of my friend group, but they'd already gone home for the holiday break.

There was only one person my mind came up with. Justine.

I don't know how she knew I'd wanted this book more than anythin'. I don't think she even knew about my brews or that Bell and I wanted to open a restaurant. How could she? We'd never talked about it in front of anyone but ourselves.

But my gut told me it was her. And even more than that, it was her best attempt at an apology for the way she'd treated me a few nights before. I had a feelin' that she didn't apologize often, but as far as they went this was a pretty good one.

It had made the start of what could have been a lousy break pretty good. I hadn't gone home. Ma and Pop couldn't afford to fly me home, and I didn't have a car to drive. Sittin' for hours on end on a crowded bus to spend a few days at home and then turn around and spend another hundred-odd hours on another crowded bus didn't sound the most appealin'.

Bell lived pretty close, though, so he'd invited me to come back home with him. He lived in a little town about an hour away from the university called Hartworth.

It was cute.

And I don't use that word lightly.

I mean, it was picture perfect. Small-town charm, magnolia trees on every corner, pure Southern perfection. Cute.

His old man was fun. A carbon copy of Bell, but with a little more gravitas and a bigger belly. He'd been an engineer at a big auto company, designin' their new engines and makin' sure there weren't any problems when they were manufactured and put in the cars.

So, smart guy.

He'd immediately asked what I was studyin', and when I told him business so that I could open my own brewery, he lit up. He knew that Bell wanted to open a restaurant, and when we told him we were drawing up some loose plans to go into business together he got real serious.

"Now, boys," he'd lowered his voice and looked at us over the top of his glasses. "You may be good friends, but going into business together is something serious."

"We know, Pops," Bell had sighed.

"I know you know, but I'm going to say my piece anyway," he'd said evenly. Bell had the decency to duck his head. "As I was saying, business is tough. It'll chew you up and spit you out if you're not prepared. So, take it seriously. Make a good, concrete plan, and execute it well, even if that means hiring someone else to help you. Don't be afraid to look outside of yourselves for help. Your ego can't be in charge of your business, or it'll be doomed from the get-go, you hear me?"

"Yessir," we'd both mumbled.

After that, Bell's Pops had offered us each a beer and launched into a story about Marigold Withers from his readin' group and the drama she was having with her ex-husband.

I don't know when he'd had time to, but he had also bought me a present to open for Christmas. It was a snazzy wallet; leather and imprinted with my name.

They'd made me feel real welcome, and my Ma had insisted on thankin' Bell's Pops for about an hour over the phone Christmas mornin'.

After that, we'd come back to campus and watched as our classmates slowly filtered back in. But the one person that I was itchin' to see had yet to make an appearance.

Bell's big ass hand waved in front of my face, gettin' my attention back on him. We were sittin' in the cafeteria because it was colder than a witch's tit outside, and I'd been watchin' the door waiting for her to show up.

"Bud, you've got to get your head on straight," Bell laughed as he dug into his nachos. "You don't even know that the book was from her."

"It's the only thing that makes sense," I grumbled, crackin' open my orange juice and takin' a swig.

"Except that it doesn't," Bell chuckled.

"My gut says it does," I sniped back. "And if she would ever show up, then I could at least find out for sure."

"Well, look what happens when you stop watching the pot." Bell nodded over to the door where Justine had just walked in.

The cold had made her cheeks and nose an adorable deep rose, and her eyes glittered behind her scarf. Even bundled up against the weather, she was still the most gorgeous woman I'd ever seen. Crazy to me how someone so pretty could be so damn closed off to the world.

I took a deep breath and then made my way over to where she stood in the food line.

"Can I hold your tray for you?"

She jumped at my voice and audibly sighed. I'll admit, that dampened my mood a bit. I'd hoped she'd at least gotten over the 'disappointed to see me' phase of our relationship, but I guess not.

"Gregory," she said curtly. "I can handle my tray on my own, thank you very much."

"I never said you couldn't, darlin'," I drawled, fallin' into step beside her. "I just offered to take it for you."

"Why?"

I almost rolled my eyes. "Because it's the gentlemanly thing to do."

"I don't need a gentleman, thanks," she huffed and moved forward in the line.

I gave myself a beat to sigh and regroup before steppin' next to her again.

"Thanks for my present." I decided to jump right in.

She stiffened and then blinked before a clipped, "Present?" fell from those perfect lips.

That's how she wanted to play it?

I grinned. "Yeah, my book. I don't know how you knew I wanted it, but it made my holiday. So, thank you."

I watched her face carefully. Her eyes flicked down towards me and a small smile pulled at the corners of her mouth before she caught herself and refocused on the food options in front of her.

"I'm honestly surprised that a book could make you that happy, but I'm glad. Whoever bought it for you must know you well," she said softly.

"Oh, I don't think they actually know me that well," I laughed. "I think they must've seen me lookin' at it and then bought it for me when I wasn't around."

"So, it wasn't Bell, then?" she said with a little laughter in her voice.

My heart stuttered at the sound. She'd never had that lightness in her tone with me before. I didn't want to screw this up now.

"No, definitely wasn't Bell," I said thoughtfully. "I'm thinkin' it might've been an apology gift from someone."

"Piss off a lot of people lately?" she asked. Now her tone was borderin' on teasing, and I was about to start jumpin' in victory.

"Not as many as *you* might think," I joked back.

We were at the end of the counter, and I waited while she paid and then turned to me.

Her eyes were serious but warm as she looked at me. Our gazes held and there was so much unsaid between us. I didn't have the words for it, but I wanted her to know that we were good. I wasn't holdin' onto anythin' from our fight. I wanted us to be able to move forward and be friends. And, lookin' in her eyes, I hoped she understood that.

I think she might have, because after a moment a small smile graced her lips and her eyes dropped to her feet.

"Merry Christmas, Greg," she said softly before walkin' away.

I turned to watch her, my mouth probably hangin' wide open. She'd called me Greg.

***

Four Months Later

Nothin' about this goddamn semester had been easy. And it was only gonna get worse, so they kept tellin' us.

Still, Bell and I were managin' to pass all our classes with high enough grades that we were feelin' pretty good about startin' a business eventually.

Justine had been distant after Christmas. Not icy or hostile, like before, but she was busier than a beaver in spring. I was pretty sure she was takin' more than the recommended maximum number of classes, and when her nose wasn't shoved into three different textbooks, it was pressed up against her laptop screen. I'd hear her door open at about five in the mornin' and again after midnight. I didn't know how she was survivin' on such little sleep, but every time I saw her across campus she was just as put together as ever.

Spring was fadin' off into hotter summer days when I finally got a chance to talk to her again. I was walkin' back to my dorm after my last final to start packin' my things to head home for the summer.

She was sittin' by a fountain around the back of the science buildings with a large book in her hands. Her glasses kept slidin' down her nose and she would absentmindedly push them up with her shoulder, so she didn't have to move her hands. She was wearin' shorts and a tank top, and her legs seemed to stretch for a country mile. The sunlight caught her hair and it shimmered with warm honey browns.

She didn't look up as I walked up to her and stood there. I waited a full minute before clearin' my throat, which startled her. She looked up at me with wide brown eyes.

I swear my heartbeat couldn't have skipped harder if it were a six-year-old schoolgirl. Why it kept doin' that whenever we made eye contact, I wasn't exactly sure, but I didn't hate it. We just stared at each other for a moment, neither of us quite knowin' what to say.

"You're not done with finals yet?" I asked, tryin' to break the strange tension that was between us.

She cleared her throat and glanced down at her book. "One more. My stupid math requirement class. I took Calculus, for some godforsaken reason."

"Eh, you'll ace it," I drawled.

She smiled softly at me and pushed her glasses up her nose with a finger.

"Goin' home for summer?" I asked.

She nodded. "I'm interning with a friend of my father's. He's a business consultant. Actually, he's the reason I chose that as a career to pursue, so it'll be good experience."

I blinked. I hadn't even thought about internin' somewhere. To be fair, I didn't quite know what my career was gonna look like outside of the vague business plan Bell and I were puttin' together.

"That's mighty impressive, then." Was all I could come up with to say.

She blushed lightly and ducked her head. "I wouldn't say impressive," she said dismissively. "It's right on track with my five-year plan."

"You've got a five-year plan?" I blew out a long breath. "I've barely got the next twenty-four hours mapped out."

She looked at me seriously, any trace of laughter drainin' from her face. "I told you from the beginning. I'm here for a reason. I can't afford any detours from my plan."

I pursed my lips as I considered her for a moment. "Sometimes detours are the best part."

"Detours are wasteful," she sniffed, snappin' her book shut. "I have a plan and I'm going to follow it to the letter. Just you wait, in five years I'm going to be making a name for myself as the most successful business consultant in the tri-state area."

Then she stood. When she stood to her full height, she looked like a goddess put on Earth for my own personal torture. A goddess who hated me and then sometimes didn't. A goddess who I wanted to be friendly with more than I'd ever wanted anythin'.

"Have a good summer, Gregory."

I bristled a little at my full name and spoke without thinkin'. "You too, ma'am."

I knew it bugged the bejeezus out of her to be called that, but I couldn't help it.

She stiffened and glared at me. "You live to make my life hell, don't you?"

"Well," I pulled the word out and flashed a cheeky grin.

She rolled her eyes, but as she walked away, I saw a small smile on her lips. I watched her go with a smile of my own.

Somethin' in my chest pulled when I realized I'd be going a whole three months without seein' her. I don't know why but becomin' Justine's friend was somethin' I needed to do.

Chapter Seven

Justine

Eight Years Later

Bell had a surprisingly modest apartment in Hartworth. I suppose, with what I knew of Bell, I shouldn't have been shocked that it was fairly barren. He wasn't a flashy guy. But I had expected a little more than a few pieces of furniture and a bookshelf after having seen his earnings statements.

"Justine, please have a seat." He ushered me over to the dining table where a pitcher of lemonade and a pitcher of water were already set out, along with three folders each in front of their own chair.

"Thank you, Bell," I said as I looped my purse over the back of my chair. "I take it Gregory will be joining us?"

Bell had the decency to blush a bit before offering me a small smile. "I know you wanted as little to do with him as possible, but it's our first official business meeting since hiring you and I felt it was important that he be here."

"No, no," I sighed. "You're absolutely correct, all managing partners should be present at all meetings."

"There is one thing I should probably mention –"

Bell was cut off by the front door opening and a surprisingly deep, Southern voice drawling, "Bell, bud, how many times have I told ya, you can't just leave your door unlocked. Any maniac could walk right in."

Gregory had grown a bit since college. He was probably my height now, if not a little taller. His blond hair was short, trimmed and styled neatly. And he'd... filled out, for lack of a better term. Where he'd once been all skinny arms and elbows was lean muscle trapped beneath a flannel shirt that was almost too small, with the sleeves rolled up to show his veined forearms. His chest had broadened, and he cut a fine figure as he stood in the doorway.

As much as I wanted to admonish myself for being caught off guard by the physical transformation, I couldn't bring myself to.

My eyes drifted from his torso up to his face and were immediately caught in the summer green that I remembered so vividly. In my memory, though, they were angry and hurt. As our eyes locked now, they were simply shocked.

"Justine?" His voice was soft, but it shook me out of my staring.

I cleared my throat and offered a small, professional smile. "Gregory. Good to see you."

"I...what...how?" He seemed lost. Then he looked at Bell and clarity settled over him. "You didn't."

"I had to," Bell said firmly. "We talked about it, and both agreed we needed to bring on a consultant to help us through this process."

"But you never said anythin' about-"

Bell cut him off and crossed his arms. "I knew that if I told you who I was thinking of you'd never go for it. And she's the best."

"But-"

"Gentlemen, if I may," I said softly, standing up. I looked pointedly at Bell, who gave me a short nod, and then turned my attention to Gregory.

"Gregory, I understand that I was probably not the person you were expecting Bell to hire. While I believe he should have told you who he was considering, I do understand his hesitation in doing so. We have a complicated history, but rest assured that will not affect my professionalism or management of your restaurant as we move forward with making it a reality."

Those green eyes simply blinked at me for a moment before closing in concentration.

"So, how exactly is this gonna work?"

I took that for what it was. He wasn't necessarily happy about us working together, but he would accept the help. We would have a professional relationship, nothing more. That was fine by me.

I smoothed a hand down my blouse and sat back down.

"Why don't we start by going over your proposal. We'll take it section by section and make any adjustments if needed."

They settled on either side of me, grabbing their folders. Bell looked as happy as I'd ever seen him, his eyes sparkling. Gregory looked as uncomfortable as I felt on the inside.

For a moment, a vague feeling of familiarity settled over me. Something about sitting at a table with these two sent me right back to college. And with that came an unsettling bubble of anxiety in my chest and my eyes started to sting with tears.

I shook my head and focused on what Bell was saying about their combined assets.

This partnership might be more difficult to navigate than I'd thought.

***

End of First Semester, Second Year

I was late.

Horrifically, catastrophically, apocalyptically late.

To the most important test of the semester. With the professor that I had been planning to ask to be my advisor for the next year and a half.

I was on track to graduate a year early. I'd taken what was usually a four-year course and had been successfully doubling my class load to finish it in three. I was now at the end of my third semester and passing this class would keep me on track. Not taking the final, which was fifty percent of the final grade, would put me in danger of having to repeat the class. Which was only offered in fall. If I didn't pass this, I'd have to switch to another class next fall, and I needed every class on my schedule to graduate early.

Which was why I was now racing through two-day old snow (read: ice) and slipping across the concrete. It didn't normally snow in this part of the country, but an untimely arctic freeze had dropped six inches of snow that was taking its sweet time to melt.

I ripped around a corner and my left foot slid out from under me, dropping my ass straight to the ground. Pain exploded from my hip and elbow, and I groaned. I tried to get up, but my arm wouldn't support my weight.

"Justine!" A familiar drawl met my ears.

I groaned again.

Look. It's not that I didn't like Greg. In fact, I did like him. A little too much. When those stupid green eyes danced at me it made my stomach flip. And even his atrocious accent was becoming more and more endearing.

We hadn't had any classes together this semester but whenever he saw me around campus, he made a point to come over and talk to me. Outside of my lectures, it was really the only time I talked with the other students because whoever he was hanging out with would usually come with him. I was taking so many courses and had so much work that I didn't have time for a social life. Greg, on the other hand, was the king of campus.

Everyone loved him. He was never without at least Bell, but it was usually a large group of coeds that were laughing at his every word. Which I didn't fully understand.

From what I could tell, Greg was kind of nerdy. Not in a bookish way, like myself, but in a comic book, Dungeons and Dragons, fantasy world way. And yet, there he was, surrounded by adoring fans, day in and day out.

He understood people. I didn't. We were diametrically opposing personalities. We didn't fit.

And I really didn't have any spare time to put towards cultivating a friendship with someone I didn't fully understand.

So, we were acquaintances at best. But he was still the last person I wanted to see at that moment when I had literally just fallen on my ass.

"Justine, are you alright?" He sounded worried as he kneeled next to me.

"I'm fine," I bit out. I was angry and embarrassed, and tears threatened to slide down my cheeks. "I need to get to my final."

"Are you late?" he asked, holding out a hand to help me up.

I stared at his hand for a moment too long.

"You didn't hit your head, did you?"

I scoffed and gripped his hand tightly, hoisting myself off the treacherous ground.

"Yes, and no."

"You did hit your head?"

"No," I sighed as I tested my weight on each foot. Nothing hurt too badly, so I started a fast pace towards the lecture hall. Greg kept pace easily, his eyes watching me. "Yes, I'm late and no, I did not hit my head."

"Oh," he said softly. "Will your professor let you in?"

"He has to." My voice was desperate.

Greg walked with me all the way to the classroom door. When I pushed it open, he held it so that it didn't slam shut.

Professor Sparks looked up from his desk, his icy blue eyes glinting disapprovingly.

"Miss Wilkson," he bit out, "you're late. You must leave."

46

"Please, Professor Sparks, I have to take this test," I said.

I was deeply aware of every set of eyes in the room on me, and I willed myself not to cry. This was too important to cry about.

"Professor, if I may," Greg started, "it's all my fault."

I whipped around, my eyes wild. "What are you doing?" I hissed.

"Trust me," he said in a low tone that only I could hear. Then he moved further into the room with a pronounced limp in his step.

"Sir, Justine here is only late because she was helpin' me off the ground. See, I took a corner too fast and landed on my hip and could barely walk. I thought I was bound to freeze to death before anyone found me, seein' as it's a veritable icebox out there, but just when I was about to give up all hope Justine found me. She was gonna make it to your test on time, but we made molasses-speed progress on account of my bum leg here. So, instead of takin' me to the infirmary I made her come here first so she could take your test. It's awful important to her, and I'd hate for her to miss takin' it because of me and my stupidity. Sir."

I held my breath as I watched Professor Sparks consider this story. Normally, I wouldn't condone lying under any circumstances, but if Greg could use his insane charisma for my benefit, I wasn't about to stop him. Finally, after a long moment, the professor sighed and held out a test sheet.

"Miss Wilkins, come get your test. You do not get extra time."

I bound down the stairs and took it before he could change his mind. "I don't need any. Thank you, sir!"

"As for you, young man, I will have my TA take you to the infirmary." He waved a hand and a mousy brunette stood up from the corner of the room.

I glanced at Greg, and he flashed me a wink before addressing the professor. "Much obliged, sir. I appreciate your generosity and understandin'."

I heard Professor Sparks scoff, but he didn't say anything more.

Greg shot me one more grin before putting his arm around the small girl who was supposed to be helping him.

I felt a smile pull at my lips as the door clicked shut and I focused on the first question.

***

I didn't know why I was so nervous approaching Greg as he sat on a bench in the weak sunlight. In a lucky turn of events, he wasn't surrounded by giggling sycophants.

"Hey, Hudson," I called when I was a few feet away.

His head whipped around, and a breathtaking smile stole across his face. His green eyes glittered as he waved.

At me.

He was smiling like that for *me*. He was genuinely happy to see *me*. I couldn't say that I understood why, but it made my stomach flip either way. Not many people in my life had ever seemed actually excited to spend time with me, but Gregory did. He kept trying to break down my walls, and I was both nervous and curious to see if he eventually would.

"Hey, Wilkson." His accent lilted my last name and heated my cheeks. He stood and closed the distance between us.

"I wanted to thank you for earlier," I said, fiddling with the books in my arms. "I was able to finish the test, so I'm still on track to graduate early. So…thanks."

"Anytime," he laughed. "It was fun. Did you see the look on ole Professor Blue Eyes' face towards the end of my monologue there? Priceless."

I found myself laughing with him. "I don't think Professor Sparks has people fib to him very often. And you were quite convincing."

"I even managed to shake the TA after a few minutes," he grinned and shook his head. The sunlight caught his floppy blond hair.

"Ah, so you didn't have to keep up the charade for the nurse, then?"

"Alas, I did not," he said dramatically.

"Pity," I tutted. "I've heard that Nurse Helms can see right through most fake injuries."

"Yeah, I'd heard that too." He rubbed a hand across the back of his neck. "That's why I really didn't want to see her."

I chuckled softly and we fell into a comfortable silence. Finally, after a long moment, he blew out a sigh.

"So, you're graduatin' early?"

I swallowed around the lump that was suddenly in my throat. "Yes, as long as I can stay on track."

"Why's it so important to you to finish so fast?"

I shrugged one shoulder. It was too much to try to explain. What could I say? Because I wanted to prove to my father that I was someone he could be proud of? Because his approval was the most important thing in the world to me?

"I just want to get my life started."

The corner of his mouth twitched, but his eyes were serious. "Your life's been started, Justine. Don't forget to enjoy yourself now, too."

"Well, I wouldn't expect you to understand," I found myself snapping. My defenses were raised. I didn't have time to enjoy myself right now. I was on track. Setting out on a path that would define my entire future. I couldn't waste my time.

His eyes grew cloudy. "Right," he snarked back. "Because I don't take anythin' seriously, so how could I possibly understand wantin' a better life for yourself?"

He huffed and grabbed his backpack off the bench.

"I'm not sayin' to abandon your goals, Justine. I'm just sayin' that there's more to life than books and business."

"Maybe for you, but not for me."

He slung his backpack over his shoulder and looked at me for a long moment. I couldn't tell what was going through his head, but he looked disappointed. He looked sad. I swore I saw a thousand emotions flash across his face, but he just stood there silently. Finally, grinding my teeth, I shook my head.

"You don't understand, I knew you wouldn't," I muttered. "I'll see you around, Gregory."

As I turned to leave, I felt a hand on my arm. I didn't turn around, but I stopped.

"If you'd open your eyes, you'd know that more is waitin' for you to see it," he said softly.

He squeezed me quickly before letting go.

I heard him walk away, and tears welled behind my eyes.

As I stormed my way back to my dorm room, they fell. Streaming down my face, which burned in embarrassment. Luckily, I was wearing a scarf, and it was cold enough to justify wrapping it around the lower half of my face.

When I finally made it back to my room, I slammed the door shut behind me, locked it, and launched myself onto my bed.

The tears refused to stop as I got myself more and more worked up.

My father had worked his way up from nothing to provide a comfortable and, I'll admit, somewhat privileged life for me, his only daughter. And the one thing he wanted to see was for me to succeed. To excel in life. To make him proud.

I was intelligent and goal-oriented and ambitious, and there was no reason that I shouldn't achieve everything that I wanted and more. I didn't want to work for another person. I didn't want to have my life dictated by someone else's schedule and goals. And I *knew* that I could succeed. I had to stay focused.

And someone like Gregory wouldn't understand that. He had no idea why I wanted to do everything I wanted to do, and he had no idea the lengths I was willing to go to get there. The things I was willing to sacrifice.

Besides, I'd managed to get along without extraneous people in my life so far. What was one more? One more person that didn't understand me. One more person that I disappointed by not being friendly enough. One more person that would never think I was normal.

As a sob wracked my body a thought flashed across my mind. I'd never cried for the loss of someone before. And it wasn't that I had lost Gregory. It was that I refused to let myself get close enough to have a chance to get him. I'd never wanted somebody to stay in my life like this before. I'd never cared if people thought I was strange or unapproachable. That's where this pain, this feeling of loss was coming from. From that fact that I wanted him but couldn't let myself have him.

In any capacity.

I let myself cry for another few moments before sternly sitting up and wiping my face aggressively.

"You don't have time for this, Justine," I whispered harshly.

I rose from the bed and grabbed my suitcase from the closet. I needed to pack to go home.

As I threw clothes into my open bag, I tried to clear my mind of all thoughts of Gregory. I focused on how happy I was to be going home, and that I'd be able to show my parents the hard work I was doing. I could start working on my business plan for after graduation. I was going to graduate early, no matter what happened.

I was feeling better, more centered, after thinking about everything that I could get accomplished over the break, when I heard Gregory's door open and then slam closed.

My hands paused as I heard him shuffling some things around. Then his music turned on and I heard the deep twang of a steel guitar float through the wall. It sounded sad.

My heart ached thinking that he was listening to sad music because of me. I felt another round of tears welling in my chest and immediately tamped them down.

I grabbed my headphones from my bag and turned on my own music, continuing to pack with a new course of anger running through me.

Next semester I'd just have to focus more. That was the answer.

Chapter Eight

Greg

Seven Years Later

"You didn't wanna give me at least the teensiest heads up that you were gonna be asking the Ice Queen herself to be our business manager?" I huffed at Bell as he cleaned up after our meetin'.

Justine had left after walkin' us through the few changes we'd need to make to the proposal before takin' it to a bank to get the loan we needed.

We'd built a sizeable savings. I'd been sellin' my brews to local breweries and bars, and Bell was the manager of one of the nicer restaurants in the area. Plus, he'd started playin' around with the stock market right out of college and he'd been fairly successful. And by fairly, the boy was more than comfortable. We just needed a loan to make sure we could afford to buy the space that would do our vision justice without completely bankruptin' ourselves.

We'd set up a meetin' with a loan officer that Justine recommended for the next week. That would make two weeks in a row of seeing the woman who'd effectively torn me up and thrown me away before she graduated.

When I'd walked into Bell's apartment that afternoon and locked eyes with her after so many years...boy howdy. My stomach dropped out, along with the ground beneath my feet. I felt twenty-one again, starin' into that face.

She was somehow even more gorgeous than I'd remembered. Fiercer, sharper, deadlier. Stunnin'.

And, for the briefest of moments, I'd seen somethin' in her eyes that looked like longin'. But I must've imagined it, because when my brain finally focused, she was cool and collected. Professional. All business. Like I was nobody more than a stranger. A new client.

I suppose that's all I was to her at this point.

"Look, bud," Bell's voice broke through my thoughts. "I knew that if I told you, you'd throw a tantrum."

"I beg your pardon, sir," I said dramatically. "I have never thrown a tantrum in my life."

"A hissy fit then," he chuckled.

"I still don't know why you thought springin' it on me was the way to go," I grumbled.

"Because I know that Justine is the best person to help us succeed. But you're too blinded by whatever happened in college to even bring up her name in passing, let alone agree to see her face to face."

I knew my mouth was twisted like I'd been chewin' on a lemon, but he was right. Over the years Justine's name would get brought up in random conversations. Sometimes it was someone from college wonderin' how she was doin'. Other times it was her name in a headline in the newspaper toutin' her business success. But any time I'd seen her name a new wave of sadness, anger, confusion, and whole buncha other emotions would hit me and I'd clam up. I couldn't say why she'd affected me so much, but she did. Well, if I'd thought about it hard enough, I probably *could* say, but I didn't wanna go there. And now we were workin' together.

"Just give her a chance, Greg," Bell sighed as he started washin' dishes. "I think everything's gonna work out exactly the way it's supposed to with this."

"You're lucky you're my best friend," I grumbled. "But fine. Let's hand her the match and the gasoline and hope she doesn't light us on fire."

***

"We can approve you for a four hundred-thousand-dollar business loan," Mr. Heller said with a smile on his face.

A low whistle escaped Bell and my jaw dropped a bit.

"Please, boys," Justine sighed, though her tone bordered on amused. "Thank you, Josiah, that will be more than enough. And I can assure you, it will be paid back in no time at all."

The older man laughed and winked at Justine. "I'm sure it will, with you at the helm, Miss Wilkson. In all honesty, you boys have put together a very thorough and well-thought-out business plan. I, for one, am very excited to patron your establishment when it's all ready."

I blinked and my senses came back to me. "Thank you very much, Mr. Heller," I said, standin' and extendin' my hand to him. "We'll make sure to reserve you and your family a table on openin' night."

"I'll hold you to that," he laughed as he gave me a firm handshake.

He left to go get everythin' printed out and I took a moment to step outside.

I needed some air.

It was surreal.

This dream that Bell and I had cooked up in college and spent the next seven years workin' to bring to reality was finally becomin' just that. Real. We had four hundred thousand dollars to use to make this restaurant everythin' we could ever want it to be.

There was still a shit ton of work to do, but we were so close I could taste it.

"You realize you've stopped in the middle of the doorway?" A bitin' voice broke my thoughts.

I immediately started to apologize as I stepped aside, but my voice died when I locked eyes with Justine.

"Sorry," I managed to mutter once my voice came back. "I just had to take a minute."

Her eyes softened for a moment. "Four hundred is nothing to sniff at. I think you boys will do something quite extraordinary with it."

I blinked at her. "Well, that sounded mighty close to a compliment, Miss Wilkson."

"I've never begrudged your and Bell's vision," she said stiffly, her eyes locked on somethin' over my shoulder.

We were silent for a moment. Everythin' from the past felt like it was hangin' on a line between us, heavy.

"Justine," I started.

"Don't." Her voice was small. I'd never heard it like that before. Nothin' like the confident professional she'd been inside. "Whatever you want to say, I don't want to hear it."

"I just-"

"It doesn't matter," she sniffed. When her eyes met mine, they were closed off again. Her strength was back, and she was all shuttered up. "Let's get back inside so you and Bell can sign the documents, and we can start looking for property."

She turned quickly and walked back inside. My chest felt tight as I watched her walk away, and suddenly I was angry.

She acted like I was the bad guy. Like *I'd* fucked up our friendship and ruined everythin'. Like I was in the wrong.

Suddenly I was right back in college. No one in my life was able to make me angry the way this woman could. I was fumin', standin' there in front of that bank. It took me a full minute to compose myself, so I didn't march in there and start arguin' with her.

I sent up a quick prayer that we'd be done with each other as soon as earthly possible.

Chapter Nine

Greg

Second Semester, Second Year

It had taken me awhile to figure out what to major in. Everyone had kept askin', and this far into college it was better to know than not. And I'd finally chosen.

Business Administration and Management.

Bell was majorin' in the same thing, so that we could both feasibly run our own business someday. I had to admit, it was nice havin' someone going through it side-by-side with me. Someone that I knew I could count on for anythin'.

I'd had a few friends growin' up, and a helluva lotta acquaintances, but I couldn't ever really remember havin' a best friend. From the time I was knee high to a grasshopper I'd been working for my Pops on the farm. Between school and work, it didn't leave a lot of time for hangin' around causin' trouble, which is what my Ma'd always said the other boys were doin'.

Bell was a true friend. We spent most our spare time together, plannin' our brewery, talkin' about girls. Guy stuff. We also talked a lot about the difficulties of college. Bell had his own slew of problems; his mom left when he was little, his Pops worked a lot, and he'd had to work real hard to get good enough grades to get into this school. He was smart as a whip and had big dreams, but he didn't always know how to work things out in the right order. He tended to skip right to the end, bypassin' everythin' between go and stop.

As we narrowed down our major, it also narrowed down the group of people that were in our classes. We started seein' a lot of the same faces and becomin' chummy with a fair amount of them.

Bell was just a friendly guy. People didn't necessarily gravitate towards him, like they seemed to do with me, because of his size and all. Bein' a big guy, people were always a little cautious of him at first. But as soon as they talked with him, they realized he was just a big ole lug.

Turns out Justine was also majorin' in Business Administration and Management. Which didn't fully surprise me, because she'd told me last semester about her plans for after school.

I still didn't understand how she was fit to be graduatin' an entire year early when I could barely keep up with the minimum number of credits I was takin'. But every time I saw her, her nose was in a book and her eyes looked a little more haggard, so I figured she was hell-bent on it.

We were comin' up on the first test in our Logistics course, and Bell and I needed to pass this one. And, like the little hell-raiser he was, Bell insisted that we ask Justine to study with us.

"You can't," I sighed when he asked for the tenth time over breakfast.

"I'm gonna," he grinned, takin' a big bite of his cereal.

"Please, don't."

"Whatever happened between you two anyways? Last semester you couldn't stop talkin' about her, and now you won't even look her way."

"We had a tiff, that's all," I sniffed and poked at my eggs sullenly.

"Y'all have tiffs every time you talk, but it's never stopped you from going back."

"This one was…different."

"How?"

"I don't know, man." I pushed my plate away, no longer hungry. "It just was. It felt different. Still feels different. Like…somethin' changed between us this time."

Bell was quiet for a moment as he chewed. His dark eyes looked at me, seein' past what I was sayin' and right to the truth of the matter.

She'd rejected me again, and I didn't know how many more rejections from her I could take.

Bell finished his bite and set his spoon down. He folded his arms across his chest and cocked his head. He always looked like that when he was about to lay down some truth on me.

"You can't force people to be who you want them to be, bud," he finally said slowly. "Justine's wound tight. You're not. Doesn't mean that just 'cause you're different you can't get along."

"Tell that to her!" I snapped. "Every time we talk she's flip-floppin' between bein' nice to me and hatin' my guts. I don't know how to be around her, let alone be friends with her."

Bell laughed out loud at that. "Greg, I think it's high time you finally admit that the last thing you want to be with Justine is *friends*."

I opened my mouth to protest and then snapped it shut. What was that supposed to mean? All I'd been tryin' was to be friendly with the girl. I could see how wrapped up she was in her studies, and I knew that spendin' time away from that could be good for her. I just wanted to hang out with her, get her out of her shell a little. Okay, and see her smile. She had the prettiest smile I'd ever seen, but it was so rare. And sure, she was the most gorgeous girl I'd ever seen, but a guy could think that and still be just friends with a woman. Right?

Bell raised an eyebrow as my silence drew on.

"I just want to be friends with her like I am with everybody," I said defensively.

"Greg, look, I know you know that you don't have friends," Bell sighed. "Other than me, of course. You're a nice, funny, open guy, and people gravitate towards that. It's what's going to make our business so successful. But you and I both know that you're not really friends with a lot of these people that hang out with us. You're friend*ly*, sure, but not real friends."

"I've just always been like that," I shrugged. "But with Justine it's different. I want to be her friend. Get to know her. Get her out of her head a little bit."

"Get into her bed a little bit," Bell twanged, a laugh on his face.

"What?" My eyes whipped up to his. Heat crept up my neck as an unwanted image of Justine laid out on my shitty dorm bed popped into my brain. I tried like hell to get it to leave, but it stuck around for a moment too long.

"You never shut up about how gorgeous the girl is. How smart. How clever. How insultingly funny. You're clearly in love with her."

"Absolutely not," I huffed, shakin' my head to clear the vision that was lingerin' there. I pierced Bell with a no-nonsense glare. "A guy and a girl can just be friends, you neanderthal. And that's all I want to be with Justine. Her friend."

"Fine," Bell conceded with a wicked smile. "Then you won't have a problem with me asking her to study with us?"

I blinked. I'd forgotten where the conversation had started.

This sonofabitch had played me. Played me good. And now he was sittin' there, a stupid grin on his stupid face, lookin' like that cat that got the cream.

"Ooooh, you're good buddy-boy," I glared at him. "Very good."

"Great, I'll ask her next time I see her." Bell stood and clapped me on the shoulder. "Oh, look. She's right over there."

I watched in disbelief as the man I was unfortunate enough to call my best friend sauntered over to where Justine sat at a table by herself, surrounded by textbooks as she shoveled food into her mouth without seemin' to taste it. She took a minute to come out of her focus when Bell approached her.

I couldn't hear what he said to her, but she processed for a moment before a small smile lit up her face. Then Bell said something else, and her eyes slid over to me, her smile fadin' a bit with apprehension. Whatever Bell said next had her relaxin', and she looked back at him with a softer smile and nodded.

Bell turned back and gave me two big thumbs up with a shit-eatin' grin on his face.

As he made his way back to our table, I felt someone watchin' me. When I looked back at Justine our gazes locked. I watched as her eyes widened and a faint blush crept up her neck and blotted her cheeks. I felt my own cheeks heatin' but didn't break the eye contact. Tryin' to telepathically let her know that we were okay, that whatever disagreements we'd had in the past were water under the bridge. Strangely enough, I thought I saw tears start to well in her big, brown eyes before she abruptly looked away.

My heart was beatin' erratically in my chest, and my brain was runnin' in circles. Had she really been about to cry, or was it a trick of the fluorescent lightin' in the dinin' hall? And why, if they were tears, would she have started to cry just from lookin' at me? Did she really hate me that much? But no, because she wouldn't have agreed to study with us if she really hated me.

As Bell finally got back to the table and we packed up our things to go to class, I realized that maybe this little study group was the best thing that could happen for me and Justine. We could finally move past this weird stage we were in and become friends. That's what I allowed myself to hope, anyway.

***

Justine had asked us to meet her in the library at seven that night.

I'd never admit it, but I tried on every pair of jeans I owned and a few dozen shirts before settlin' on my favorite jeans and a well-worn Crimson Tide t-shirt.

When I met Bell outside of the big brick building, he looked me up and down and smirked to himself.

"Shut up," I grumbled, shovin' him. He barely moved, the behemoth, and his stupid grin widened.

"I didn't say a word."

"Shut up anyways."

Justine was waitin' for us at a big round table at the very back of the library. The space was filled with stressed coeds crammin' for various finals. Bell and I were the most relaxed out of everyone there, but after seein' the mountains of books next to Justine I knew that wouldn't last long.

"Gentlemen," she said crisply.

"Hey, Justine," Bell drawled. "How are you?"

Her face softened a little as Bell sat next to her. "I'm fine, Bell. Yourself?"

"I will be much better after we get crackin' on studyin' for this test," he said with a chuckle.

Justine laughed lightly along with him, and my heart stuttered in my chest as I sat on her other side. When she heard the chair move, her attention turned to me. I watched her eyes shutter a bit and a blush warm her cheeks.

"Gregory." Some greetin' I got. At least she was speakin' to me. Then she turned and started distributin' books and papers.

"So, the test tomorrow is on what we've learned in the first month and a half of the course," she said, all business.

She kept talkin', but I found myself gettin' lost in listenin' to the crisp way her lips moved around her words. Her Atlantic twinge was so different from my Alabama drawl. It captivated me, watchin' her mouth movin', seeing the way her eyes were sharp and focused as she discussed the finer points of the basics of business logistics. I was so caught up in watchin' her talk that it took me a moment to register that I'd been asked a question.

I looked up and saw that both Justine and Bell were watchin' me, but with very different expressions. Bell looked about to bust a gut. Justine looked like she'd just caught me with my hand in the cookie jar. She wasn't that far off.

I laughed awkwardly and rubbed a hand on the back of my neck. "Sorry, I got distracted."

Justine heaved a long-sufferin' sigh and fixed me with a pointed look. "Gregory, this isn't going to work if you can't focus. I have other things I could be doing than studying with you."

"I know," I bristled. Her eyes flashed and I took a deep breath. "Sorry, I do know. I appreciate'cha takin' the time with us."

Her eyes watched me carefully, widenin' in surprise and then meltin' into a look I'd never seen on her before. Warmth.

"Okay," she finally said softly. "Then let's start again."

As I watched her turn her attention back to the book in front of her, I was hit with an overwhelmin' thought. I'd do anythin' to see that look on her face again. I sighed internally as I realized Bell might've been more right than I'd thought. I wasn't sure friends would be enough for me.

Chapter Ten

Justine

Second Semester, Second Year

I studied with Bell and Gregory every Wednesday throughout the rest of the semester. From our time together re-teaching them what we'd learned in class, I found that I came to know them pretty well.

Bell was charming and gentle. A true gentleman at heart. But he didn't have girlfriends. He wasn't by any means a womanizer; he was just upfront about what he was willing to give and never gave more than he promised. I knew that this had left more than a few girls brokenhearted, but for the most part it seemed he was good at finding women of similar interests and inclinations. He was very intelligent but lacked patience.

He was always nice to me, too, which was a pleasant change. Not that people weren't nice to me, but Bell seemed to go out of his way to be nice to me without flirting or innuendo or anything other than just being a good person.

He was also an excellent buffer between Gregory and me. Whenever disagreements between us began to escalate, Bell would pointedly step in and refocus the conversation. This saved more than a few study nights from dissolving into complete verbal cage fights between Gregory and me.

There was something about Gregory that got under my skin. But at the same time, he was just…fun.

It surprised me, but it was the truth.

In between everything about him that irritated me, he was full of life and laughter. He told lame jokes and laughed at them as though they were the peak of comedy. He used roundabout logic to remember various facts and lessons. Logic that would make no sense to a sane person but seemed to all work out in his head. He spoke in complicated riddles that Bell understood but made me question my sanity. I was told they were common Southern colloquialisms, but there were times I was sure Gregory was just trying to mess with me by inventing them.

He was whip-smart, too. When he wasn't goofing around, he picked up on the concepts we went over quickly and could repeat them back to me flawlessly. More than that, he actually understood their application. But, for some reason, getting him to focus was almost impossible.

This was usually what led to our arguments and cemented my belief that Gregory was more of a hindrance to my five-year plan than not.

I had to remind myself of this every Wednesday, because every Wednesday he and Bell would walk into the library and his electric green eyes would find mine and my breath would leave my lungs. I hated my body's physical reaction to him almost as much as I hated my heart for wanting to spend more than one night a week with him. He was a distraction. A cute, sweet distraction, but a distraction, nonetheless.

It had taken me some time and introspection, but I'd realized that I was, in fact, ridiculously attracted to the straw-haired hillbilly with the emerald eyes. And that a part of the reason I'd been so hesitant to form any kind of relationship with him was because I wasn't sure what kind of relationship I'd eventually want.

I knew he couldn't feel the same way about me. He was the same way with everyone. Joking, flirting, jovial. It was just his personality.

I wasn't a special case.

But sometimes when our eyes would meet, something in his would make my stomach drop.

I couldn't afford to be distracted by a relationship with someone I was attracted to. Someone I could develop real feelings for.

There were so many stories I'd heard growing up. Women who'd had goals and ambitions and plans, and then fell in love and found all of that disappeared. Ending up a stay-at-home mom with two point five kids and an alcoholic husband. I wasn't even sure I'd ever want children, and I certainly wasn't going to forgo my plans because of some starry-eyed Alabama boy.

I couldn't let that be me.

So, I tried like hell to keep some distance between Gregory and myself. However, after spending six consecutive weeks with them, I found that I thought of Bell and Gregory as my friends. And, even stranger than that, I enjoyed their company.

Which made leaving for summer break particularly difficult.

It was our last study session of the semester, and we were sequestered in our little corner of the library.

"So, Justine, what are your plans for the break?" Bell asked, slinging a gigantic arm over the back of his chair.

"Probably plottin' out world domination," Gregory mumbled.

I caught his eye, glaring at him, to which a grin broke out on his face and his eyes sparkled.

"I'm working at a business consulting company for the summer," I said.

"The same one you interned at last year?" Gregory asked casually.

I blinked at him and felt my cheeks heat. I was surprised he'd remembered.

"Yes, actually."

He nodded and then looked at me for a long moment before grinning. "You don't have to sound so surprised. I listen when you talk. It's common decency."

"It's not common," I said quietly. "It's nice."

We fell silent as we looked at each other. I couldn't read his face, but I could feel the blush worsening on mine, so I refocused on my nailbeds.

"What about you, Bell? Any summer plans?" I asked after an awkward pause.

When I looked up at him, his eyes were flicking between Gregory and I with glee.

"Greg and I are going to spend the summer writing out draft one of our business plan," he said, his deep voice warm and light.

"Business plan?" I asked. This was the first time I'd heard of this.

"Greg hasn't mentioned? We're goin' to open up a brewery and restaurant after college, once we've figured everything out."

"A restaurant?" I blinked. I had thought briefly that Greg might have wanted to do something like that after the book I'd caught him reading, but I hadn't heard him or Bell talk about it, so I'd dismissed it from my thoughts. "That's risky."

"Not too terribly," Bell chuckled. "Our winning bet is that Greg's brews are going to make us rich and famous."

My attention turned to Gregory, who was sitting with an embarrassed look on his face.

"Brews?"

He rubbed a hand across the back of his neck and flicked the hair from his eyes. "Yeah, it's somethin' I got into in high school. I make brews in my dorm room. I'm surprised you didn't guess that, considerin' you bought me that book last Christmas."

"I didn't know it was something you were actively pursuing," I mumbled, trying to logic out exactly where he would have the space to brew beer in his dorm room.

Suddenly, Gregory slapped the table and stood up, making a noise from deep in his chest that I'd never heard before. I would have called it a whoop, but I wasn't quite sure. It was loud enough that it startled me and drew attention to our table.

"I *knew* it!" he shouted.

Bell looked just as shocked as me at Gregory's outburst.

"What on Earth are you hollerin' about, boy?" Bell asked, his voice a little sterner than usual.

Gregory looked at him and grinned and then turned that megawatt smile to me. "I knew that you bought me that book, you were just too stubborn to admit it."

I inhaled sharply.

Shit.

I don't know why I didn't want him to know I'd bought him a present, and something he'd wanted at that, but knowing he'd just found me out was unsettling.

"Well, are you gonna say anythin'?" Gregory asked, spinning his chair around and plopping down, his arms folded over the back. He rested his chin on his wrists and his eyes glittered at me.

I sniffed and picked an imaginary piece of lint off my shorts.

"Even if I did buy you some ridiculous book - that shouldn't have been for sale in a college bookshop, by the way - I still don't see why I would have made the leap to you brewing beer in your dorm room."

He smiled goofily at me. "So, you don't know everythin' after all."

My eyes narrowed and I opened my mouth to retort back when his laugh stopped me.

"Calm down, you crazy Yankee," he chuckled. "What I meant to say was thank you."

It sounded like he sincerely meant it. Like it had been killing him not to be able to thank me. The look on his face was soft and warm and made my toes curl. Then, my brain caught up with my raging libido and registered what he'd called me.

"Yankee?" I scoffed, folding my arms across my chest and looking at him over the tops of my glasses. I wasn't actually upset, but I had never been called that before and for some reason it ruffled me. "Did you seriously just call me a Yankee?"

He blinked at me and his eyes flashed with mirth. "So what if I did? It's true, ain't it? That's what you are?"

"I am no more a Yankee than you are a Confederate, so I'll ask you never to call me that again," I glared at him, playful but serious. I wasn't really offended, but it was just too easy to drop into a verbal battle with him. Besides, we'd been dangerously close to friendly for far too much of this conversation.

He glowered right back at me and opened his mouth to retort when Bell suddenly stood.

"Well, this has been, as always, an interesting match to watch, but we're veering into dangerous territory here that some of us," he looked pointedly at Gregory, "might not want to get into with those present."

He was right. While this was still borderline polite banter, Gregory and I had a nasty habit of spiraling into truly terrible arguments that left us both angry and sweating. While Bell could usually moderate them, there were times, like now, when he chose to avoid the growing tension altogether.

Gregory looked at Bell and then at me and deflated.

"You're right," he sighed. "Apologies, Justine. I didn't realize it'd rankle your feathers so bad. I won't call you that ever again."

"Thank you," I said primly. Then I gathered my bag and stood as well. "Bell's right. I've got one last final in an hour, and you guys are done, right?"

"That we are," Bell said happily.

"What are you going to do with all your free time, now that you don't have to sit here once a week with me and suffer?" I laughed lightly.

"I'd hardly call it sufferin'," Gregory mumbled, so low I almost didn't catch it. But I did, and it made my heart stutter.

"I don't know about Greg, here," Bell said loudly, drawing my attention back to him, "but I could go for a cold beer and a football game."

"Sounds good to me." Gregory cheered right up, a goofy grin plastered across his face as we made our way out of the massive library.

I shook my head and laughed to myself. "You boys have fun, then."

"You too," Bell waved. "See you, Justine. Have a good summer."

He moved away and I started in the other direction when a hand on my wrist stopped me.

I turned around and saw Gregory, who was watching me with cautious eyes.

He held onto my wrist without saying anything, so after a moment I glanced down at his hand and then back to him.

"Did you need something, Gregory?"

He groaned and dropped my hand. "How many times do I have to tell ya to call me Greg?"

"Depends on the day," I smirked.

I expected a snappy retort, or perhaps an eye roll, but instead he just looked at me for a long moment, his green eyes serious.

He stared at me for so long, and so intensely, that I started to worry.

"Are you okay?" I asked. "Is something wrong?"

He blushed and looked down. "No, nothin's wrong, per se," he mumbled. "I just…"

This pause was just as long as the other one, and I tried not to get annoyed. I did have to make it all the way across campus to get to my last final, and he chose now to think through his words?

I fidgeted a little, trying to keep my tongue in check, and he noticed.

"I'm sorry." He blew out a long breath. "I guess, what I'm gettin' at is this: I've really enjoyed spendin' time with you this semester."

I blinked.

"Well, me too," I said honestly. "Surprisingly."

A small smile from him made the summer heat a little more intense for a moment.

"So, we're friends then, right?"

Now it was my turn to think through my words.

"You and Bell are probably the closest I've come to having friends in a long time," I said slowly.

"I'll take that," his smile grew. "Next semester then, we'll hang out? Outside of our study group?"

I could picture it. The three of us, twenty-one and heading into the popular bar right by campus. Going to trivia nights or going for them to watch some inane sports game while I pretended to be interested. I could see our study sessions turning into hangouts. I could even see spending time trying some of Gregory's brews and finding out more about the business they wanted to start.

A part of me desperately wanted that.

But the reality of my situation was this: I was going to be twice as busy next year as I was this year. I would be graduating at the end of next year. I couldn't let anything distract me from that. And, as I'd been saying and knew deep in my soul, Gregory was a distraction.

But then I looked at his face. His stupid, hopeful face, and I couldn't just outright tell him no.

"I'm going to be really busy next year," I started. I saw his smile start to fall, so quickly hurried on. "But, and I'm not making any promises," I warned, "I can try."

Weeks later, sitting in a cubicle in a stuffy office, I could still feel the heat from Gregory's answering smile.

Chapter Eleven

Justine

Seven Years Later

How Bell had managed to convince me to come downtown on a Friday night I still couldn't understand, but he had, so here I was.

Looking around, it would be a perfect spot for the restaurant. There was an old warehouse building at the end of the row of shops on the main street that was sitting empty, so Bell had invited me down to look at it with him.

Downtown was bustling with people. There was a nice lawn that ran along the backside of the buildings, with a fountain, an amphitheater, and plenty of benches. It was a place where you could spend hours on a warm night. There were twinkling lights wrapped around the trees and they glowed warmly as the sun dipped below the rooftops.

I was early, per usual, so I had a bit of time to wander. Families played on the grass, the smaller children doing cartwheels and the older ones throwing a football back and forth. Laughter and chatter and joy filled the air, creating a comforting buzz of humanity in my ears. People sat at chairs on patios behind the only other little restaurant on the strip, drinking cocktails and unwinding after a long week.

Bell and Gregory's restaurant would fit beautifully in this space. It would create another place for the community to gather. It would attract a younger crowd, but not a rowdy one. I could see it thriving here.

"It's a cute little area, even I can admit that." Greg's tell-tale twang made my shoulders tighten.

I turned around, my lips already pursed.

"I'm supposed to be meeting Bell."

"Bell had somethin' come up." Greg's lips quirked in that irritating half-smile of his.

"Likely story," I grumbled under my breath.

Greg and I stood looking apprehensively at each other for a moment before he let out a long sigh and rubbed a hand over the back of his neck.

"Look, I know you don't like me, and I'm not one hundred percent sure of the reason why but I know it's probably my fault-"

"It is your fault," I snapped, suddenly feeling like the twenty-one-year-old girl I'd been the last time I saw this infuriating man. "And if you don't know why then you're dumber than you sound."

"I'm not dumb, and I'm tired of you tellin' me I am." His face darkened.

That stopped me for a moment. Greg was usually too upbeat to be bothered by anything, but the way his face fell in that moment had me almost feeling bad for what I'd said. Almost.

"Regardless," I sniffed. "You know why I don't like you. Luckily for us, there's nothing that says you must be friends with your business manager."

"Yeah, but we at least have to tolerate bein' in each other's presence."

"I can be an adult about this if you can."

"Darlin', I've been bein' an adult. You're the one actin' like a you're too good for your own mud."

I blinked at him. "I understood about thirty percent of that sentence, but the sentiment stands." I clasped my hands in front of me and turned sharply away from him. "So, that's the warehouse we're looking at. It's in an admittedly great location, and I peeked through the window and the inside doesn't look like it needs much structural work. It was recently renovated per the city's ongoing historical building update plan, so the work was done well."

"I've got the keys from the owner, if we wanted to take an actual look inside." Greg flashed a grin as he jangled a set of keys in front of my face, his sour mood seemingly forgotten.

I swatted them away and he simply laughed. It infuriated me. He never took anything seriously. Everything was such a game to him. But I'd worked hard to get to the position I held in my life, and regardless of the way he was going to act, I could be professional.

"Fine, let's go inside. Let's make sure you're getting your money's worth with this space."

Greg offered me his arm. I looked down at it, looked up at him, rolled my eyes and took off in the direction of the warehouse. I heard him chuckle lightly before following me.

I waited, facing the door. When Greg finally caught up to me, he stopped barely an inch away. I could feel the heat of his chest on my back, and it made the hair on my neck stand on end. I'd been right. He was maybe half an inch taller than me now. And the arm that reached around me to unlock the door had more muscle. He smelled of something vaguely sweet, and I closed my eyes as I took a breath. I heard the lock click, but he didn't move. I glanced over my shoulder and saw that his eyes were watching me intensely.

76

I don't know why I didn't move. Gregory was an idiot. A charming idiot, who got everything he wanted out of life without ever having to lift a finger. He'd been a relentless pain in my side in college, caused me to almost fail a class, nearly derailed my life plan. And he'd strung me along. Made me think he was my friend and then humiliated me. He was everything I had no respect for.

But I didn't want him to move. His body heat surrounding me made me calmer than I could remember being in years.

I felt him move slightly closer, so that his shirt skimmed my bare shoulders, and goose pimples blossomed on my arms.

"Justine." His voice was soft in my ear.

It jolted me back to reality and I cleared my throat and moved forward.

"The door's unlocked, let's go inside," I said stiffly.

He sighed so quietly I was almost sure I'd imagined it. Then, he turned the handle and the door swung open.

The space was huge. The warehouse had been cleaned well when the renovations had been completed, so the only thing that would really have to be done would be moving in the brewery equipment and then setting up a kitchen and restaurant. There would be plenty of space for everything they wanted to do. There was a small pile of old lumber and pipes in one corner, but no deep cleaning would be necessary.

"Hello!"

I jumped as Greg's voice echoed off the exposed beams of the ceiling.

He laughed loudly. "A little jumpy, huh?"

"Well, when you scream right next to someone, it startles them," I snapped.

"Oh, calm down," he chuckled. "It was just a little shout that's all. I wanted to hear if I was really as dumb soundin' as you say."

"The verdict?"

"I'd say half as dumb."

"Still pretty thick then," I sniffed, but a quick smile flashed across my face when he laughed at my joke.

"So, what do you think? It's perfect, right?" He sounded like a kid in a toy store. "We were thinkin' that we divide the space in half. We're not going to need a whole warehouse full of brewin' equipment, just enough to keep our specialties going through the seasons. We can always stock the bar with some other brands to keep everyone happy, but we're really gonna try and push our stuff."

"As well you should, if you want this business venture to succeed," I said drily.

"Well, yeah, that," Greg shrugged. "Also, my stuff's the best. Always has been. And it can only get better once we've got actual equipment and not plastic jugs and PVC pipe."

"Jesus."

"So, one half for the brewery, and then we were thinkin' we separate it with like a cool looking fence or somethin' and have the other half be the kitchen, bar, and restaurant. People could come into the restaurant and then book tours of the brewery if they wanted, or just eat and drink and be merry."

"That's how I'd envisioned the space too," I admitted. "I was thinking that we put the bar in this corner where this garbage is."

"In the corner?" Greg said, his voice doubtful.

"It would be perfect," I insisted as I walked over to the trash pile. "You just can't picture it with all this stuff in the way."

I bent down to grab an old board and immediately felt a sharp pain in the palm of my hand. I shouted and jerked my hand back, and the whole board came with it, along with excruciatingly sharp agony.

"Stop, don't move!" Greg shouted as he ran over to me. I'd fallen into a crouch as I stared at the nail that was now stuck through my hand and the board attached to the other side. I went to pull on it, but Greg's hand wrapped around my wrist, stopping me.

"You can't pull it out, you don't know what kind of damage you could do," he said softly.

Tears were streaming down my face, and I felt my cheeks heating with embarrassment. I hated crying in front of people, and the very *last* person I wanted to cry in front of was happy-go-lucky Gregory.

"It's gonna be okay, Justine, I promise." His voice was so warm and kind. "We've got to go to the hospital though."

"I hate hospitals," I managed to bite out.

"Yeah, most people do," he laughed a bit. "But you're gonna need a doctor to take a look at that, and at the very least you'll need a tetanus shot. Here."

He stood up and started pulling on the hem of his shirt. He finally ripped enough off to wrap around my hand a few times, leaving him in a makeshift crop top. Through the blur of tears, I could make out a distinct V that drew my eyes to the waistband of his pants. Then he grabbed my hand, and a jolt of pain made me close my eyes tightly.

"This should help stop the bleedin' a bit until we get to the hospital," he explained as he wrapped my hand carefully. His hands were so steady, even as my heart pounded wildly in my chest. I didn't know if it was from shock, panic, or Gregory being so close to me and speaking so gently.

"You look ridiculous," I sniffled, taking in his crop top and jeans with sandals.

"You always think I look ridiculous," he laughed as he helped me stand. "You're gonna have to think of a better insult than that."

I felt a laugh leave my chest and then blinding pain raced down my arm.

"Don't make me laugh," I growled.

"You'd have to find me funny for that. Come on, we've got to get goin'." He wrapped an arm around my shoulder and led me out of the warehouse, making sure he locked it behind us.

He held me all the way to his truck. He kept a hand comfortingly on my forearm as he drove the five miles to the hospital, all the while keeping up a string of oddly comforting jokes. His arm was back around me as he helped me out of the truck and led me into the emergency room. He insisted on coming back with me and held my hand through the entire x-ray and as they brought me back to a curtained off bed.

"The doctor will be over in just a few minutes to get the nail out, and then we can give you a tetanus shot. You'll be good to go soon," the nurse said warmly. "Your boyfriend can stay with you through that, too."

"He's not my boyfriend," I said, just as Greg insisted, "I'm not her boyfriend."

The nurse looked at us knowingly before smirking a little and closing the curtain behind her.

There was an uncomfortable silence as Greg shifted from foot to foot.

"I guess I can kind of see why she'd think I was your boyfriend," he grumbled.

"I can't understand you when you mumble like that," I snapped. My wall was back up and being mean to him was the only behavior I was comfortable with in that moment.

"I said," he projected exaggeratedly, his accent thicker than ever, "that I can see why she'd think I was your boyfriend."

"Don't be ridiculous."

"I mean, who else would sit with your whiny ass through a whole damn hospital visit?"

"Look, bub," I said acidly. "You are not my first choice to be my hospital buddy, but here we are. That does not make us boyfriend and girlfriend."

"I never said it did," he huffed. "I just said I could see why she'd say that. It's a real boyfriendy thing to do."

"Not really. You'd do it for anyone you saw get a freaking nail through their hand. At least, if you were a half decent human-being you would."

"I'd've dropped them off in the ER. I definitely wouldn't have gone in with them, let alone gone through the x-ray and then waited for the doc, and then drove them home afterword."

"Then why are you still here?"

Silence dropped sudden and heavy in our little cubby. We were both heated, our breathing fast and our faces flushed. I couldn't remember the last time I'd argued with someone like this.

The pain from my hand was only fueling my anger, making me demand an answer.

"Well?"

"I don't know, okay?" he snapped. "I don't know why I volunteered to meet with you today when Bell couldn't, instead of lettin' him reschedule like he wanted. I don't know why I drove you here and stayed with you. I don't know why I can't leave now. I just don't know, alright?"

"Well, I don't know either!"

I watched him as he ran his hand over the back of his neck. He looked sad, and as much as I loathed to admit it to myself, I didn't like that look on him. I found myself wishing he'd flash that stupid smile I hated so much.

I sighed, letting go of the tension in my shoulders.

"I'm glad you're here, though," I said softly. "I would've hated to go through this alone."

81

Our eyes met and he opened his mouth before closing it again. He looked lost for a moment, and then the curtain parted, and the doctor came in.

"Ready to get that nail out of your hand, Miss Wilkson?"

Chapter Twelve

Greg

Justine was quiet in the truck on the way back to her car.

"I could've just driven you home, you know?" I said lightly, trying to break the tension. "You could've had a friend drive you back to pick up your car tomorrow, once you were feelin' a bit better."

She shifted uncomfortably in the seat before huffin' out a sigh. "I don't have any friends that I could call to do that."

"You don't have *any* friends?"

"I didn't say that," she snarled.

She was so quick tempered, and I had no idea what would set her off. It was like playin' with a snake, never knowin' when it would strike you.

"Sorry, my bad," I said quietly.

The cab was silent for another minute or so before she broke it.

"I have friends." She sounded almost like she was convincin' herself. "We just aren't close like that. I'd hate to be a burden to them by asking them for a favor."

"If they're your friends then it wouldn't be a burden."

"I'm always a burden," she said it drily, like a joke, but I could hear the very real pain underneath.

Silence filled the cab since I wasn't sure what to say to that. She was starin' out the window, and it looked like she was gonna cry again.

I remembered that from college, how easy she cried. How hard she tried not to.

"We were friends, once," I said softly. I immediately wished I hadn't because I felt her tense up beside me.

"You sure had me convinced we were, anyway," she finally muttered acidly.

"We were," I insisted.

"Look, I may not have had many friends in my life, but I know that real friends don't treat each other the way you treated me." Her words were sharp and sad.

"What are you talkin' about?"

"I can't believe you're trying to pretend like you didn't sabotage my last final. Like you didn't humiliate me in front of the entire school!"

My brain was runnin' in circles tryin' to make sense of what she was sayin'. We pulled into the parkin' lot where her car was, and I parked so I could turn and look at her fully.

Her cheeks were flushed and her eyes were fillin' with tears.

"I genuinely have no idea what you're talkin' about, Justine," I said, my voice calm and as soothin' as I could make it.

She sniffed and glared at me.

"If that's true, then you aren't the person I thought I knew. You never were."

She flung the door open and grabbed her things before slammin' it shut and hurryin' to her car.

Leavin' me slack jawed and confused.

***

First Semester, Third Year

That summer was one of the longest, loneliest, and busiest summers of my life. I got a job at the local farmer's market, helpin' people set up their stalls and signs and helpin' to direct traffic. They did the market three times a week during the summer, so it was pretty steady work.

The days I wasn't workin' there, Bell and I spent every wakin' hour creatin' a feasible business plan. It was much harder than we thought it'd be. The money we would have to sink into it was in the hundreds of thousands, not to mention the permits, findin' a space, hirin' staff. There were times that it all seemed so impossible that we just sat and stared at the walls in silence, each of us locked in our own heads.

And other days we were the most obnoxious pair of dreamers this side of the Mississippi. More than once Bell's Pops had hollered at us to keep the noise level down because we were jumpin' around, so excited about the future.

Because that was the thing about the two of us – we were never down for long. We could see the end result so clearly in our minds that it trumped any and all obstacles that we came across.

When I wasn't workin' the farmer's market or plottin' with Bell, I was starin' out at nothin', picturin' two big brown eyes and the faintest hint of a smile on full, rose red lips.

It was towards the end of summer when Bell finally brought up the elephant in the room.

We were out on his Pops' little fishin' boat and the sun was just startin' to come up over the ridge.

My line was in the water, and I was sippin' on an ale I'd been workin' on for most of the summer. I watched him bait his hook and cast out, watchin' it land and reelin' in a bit before he settled down next to me and opened his own bottle. We touched them together and fell into a comfortable silence.

After about ten minutes of me starin' into the water, thinkin' about the way Justine's hair would glimmer in this early mornin' light, Bell finally sighed.

"So, you gonna ask her out this year or what?"

I closed my eyes and took a deep breath through my nose.

"She won't say yes."

"She might."

"She won't."

"Not with that attitude."

"Bell." My tone was a warnin'.

He chuckled softly to himself and held his hands up in surrender. "I'm just saying. The answer's always no if you don't ask."

"What fortune cookie did you rip that off of?"

"My mom."

My eyes flicked over to his in sympathy.

"It was one of her favorite sayings. She said it so much that it's just stuck in my head whenever I'm scared to go for something," he sighed and leaned forward, pickin' up his pole. "I don't remember her much, but apparently, I used to parrot it back to her every time she said it. First time I said it after she left nearly gave Pops an aneurysm."

I nodded and took a swig of my beer.

Bell took a long pull from his and smacked his lips. He looked at the bottle with a smile. "I'm tellin' ya, once we get these really selling, we'll be unstoppable."

I nodded and contemplated mine. It was good. Not my best, but I'd never worked with peaches before, and they were a bit tricky.

"Everythin' good is a bit tricky, isn't it?" I said to myself.

"And everything worth fighting for is gonna put up a fight," Bell said sagely.

That startled a laugh out of me, and I reached over to punch him in his massive arm. He wasn't fazed by it in the slightest but laughed along with me.

"Look, ask her out. If she says no, then she says no. You come find me and we go out for a drink."

"What if she says yes?"

"Then you take a shower, put on something nice, and take your girl out on the town."

I leaned back as that image floated through my brain. A smile spread across my face, so big my cheeks started to hurt.

"Hey, loverboy, you've got a bite."

I laughed as I grabbed my pole and started reelin' in. Something had bit me, that was for sure.

***

I'd never seen someone soak up the sun in such a magical way.

But there she was.

Justine Wilkson.

Pretty as a peach sittin' there on that bench, her face turned up to the sun, eyes closed. Lookin' like pure bliss. It took everythin' I had in me not to stand there starin' at her like a creep.

I shook myself off and blew out a long breath.

Justine and I were friends. We were … well, we were friend*ly*, at least. There was nothing stopping me from just walkin' up to her and askin' how her summer was. But my feet were glued to the pavement.

After me standin' there far too long with my tongue hangin' out, she must've felt me because suddenly those deep, warm eyes were locked on mine.

Before she could stop herself, I watched a smile light up her face and her hand came up in a little wave.

That's all it took to melt my frozen body, and suddenly I was right in front of her.

"Hi," she said softly.

"Howdy," my voice was just as soft.

We simply watched each other for a long moment before she laughed lightly, the magical sound breakin' the tension.

"How was your summer, Gregory?"

"It was good. Nothin' excitin'. Yours?"

"It was very…educational."

"Don't you get enough educatin' during the school year?" I laughed.

I was pleasantly surprised when she laughed along with me.

Surprised enough to really look at her for a second. There was somethin' different about her. She'd matured over the summer, but I'm sure I had too. That was a part of gettin' older. But it was more than the new sharpness of her cheekbones and the delicate way her collarbone flirted with the collar of her shirt.

She seemed more settled, I finally decided. There was less manic panic in her eyes. Less doubt in the way she held herself. She was confident and calm.

It was sexy as all hell.

"Success at the business consulting firm, then?" I asked, settin' my backpack down and sittin' next to her.

She nodded, a faint blush coloring her cheeks. "He actually offered me a full-time position once I graduate."

"That's great, Justine!"

"Thanks." She smiled softly. Her gaze wandered up to the sky, and I watched the sun play with her caramel skin. "I'll take it. Work there for a year or so, get good hands-on experience and then branch out and start my own business. It'll be just me at first, but once I have enough clients, I'd love to hire a few more people."

"You'll be runnin' the world before any of us know you took over," I nudged her shoulder with mine.

She chuckled as she swayed with me. When she stopped movin', her shoulder was still barely brushin' mine, and she didn't move away. We fell into a comfortable silence.

It was now or never.

"Look," I started, "I know you've got a crazy busy year, but –"

We were interrupted by Dansby Ruthers, star quarterback and all-around meathead extraordinaire. He walked right up to Justine and swooped in, plantin' his lips on hers.

An anvil landed on my chest.

A grenade went off in my head.

Bees started buzzin' through my veins.

My soul shattered into a million little pieces.

When they broke apart, Justine was agitated, clearly embarrassed, and blushin' up a storm.

"Dansby, I've told you not to do that," she said, annoyed.

"What, I can't kiss my girlfriend when I see her?"

"Point of order," she snapped, "I'm not your girlfriend."

A little of the blood rushed out of my ears and my heart started beatin' again.

"In everything but title, baby," he smirked.

I stood up quickly and stuck my hand out. "I'm Greg, pleasure to meet ya."

He looked at my hand like it was an alien. Then he turned the same gaze on me. Like he couldn't fathom that anyone wouldn't know who he was.

"Dansby Ruthers," he said smugly.

"Right," I drawled, stickin' my hand back in my pocket. "I thought I recognized you. You're...football, right?" I flicked my eyes down to Justine, who was watchin' with a slightly horrified look on her face. "So, how do you know our Justine, here?"

His face twisted in the kind of confusion only someone with fewer brain cells than an amoeba could muster.

"Our?"

"Oh, yeah, Justine and I go way back," I lied glibly. "Known her since we were in diapers. She's basically part of the family, if you know what I mean."

"You're from Connecticut?"

"Couldn't' ya tell? I mean, I know I've managed to get rid of some of that northern accent, but I thought it was pretty obvious," I grinned. I was havin' a blast watching his face grow more and more flustered.

Finally, after an unfathomably long moment while he tried to reason me out, he huffed angrily and turned to Justine.

"Babe, who the fuck is this guy?"

She stood and glared.

At him.

My stomach did a stupid little flip in victory.

"How many times do I have to remind you that I'm *not* your girlfriend," she snapped. "I'm not your 'babe'. I'm not your anything." She grabbed her bookbag and slung it onto her shoulder. "And Greg is just who he said he was. A friend." Her voice dropped

90

to arctic levels of cold. "Now, we're leaving, and I expect you won't try to find me again, Dansby. Have a good day."

Without lookin' in my direction, she grabbed my shirt sleeve and dragged me behind her while she stormed off.

I marveled for a moment. Usually, when she was huffy and stormin' off it was because of me. This time, I was along for the ride. For two blissful minutes I was yanked along behind this beautiful, angry goddess of a woman. Until we rounded the corner of the next building. She stopped abruptly and turned to me.

Yep. My turn. I knew it was too good to last long.

Before she could finish the breath she was takin' to start her tirade at me, I held up my hands.

"I'm sorry," I said quickly. "I can't explain why I did that. I know it was rude, probably. I just..."

Her eyebrow ticked and she crossed her arms. "You just what?"

I looked at her.

I didn't want to ask her out now, not when she was all mad at me and comin' off the heels of her rejectin' another guy right in front of me. But I didn't know how to explain that I'd fucked with him because I saw him kiss her and I'd been insanely jealous. She was watchin' me with those big eyes, her cheeks pink with anger, and I knew I had to say somethin'.

I blew out a long breath and rubbed my hand over the back of my neck.

"I don't like Ruthers," I finally settled on. It was enough of the truth. "I've heard him talk about women before and he's a grade A jackass. You deserve to be with someone better'n that."

She blinked at me for a moment before her face softened.

"We spent some time together over summer," she said. She wasn't looking at me, her gaze instead focused on her feet. "For some reason, he got the impression we were dating. We weren't.

Ever. But he never seemed to get the message." She glanced back in the direction we'd come from. "I hope he gets it now."

"You were pretty clear," I chuckled.

She rolled her eyes, but her lips turned up a bit. "That doesn't seem to help some people."

I laughed and marveled when she joined in with a quiet laugh of her own.

We stood for a moment, watchin' each other. There was something goin' on in her head. I could see the wheels spinnin'.

She opened her mouth and then closed it with a small sigh. I went to reach out to touch her wrist, thinkin' this could be the right moment.

Then the bell rang out from the tower on the other side of campus. Her eyes widened and flicked to her watch.

"You've got to go," I said softly.

She focused back on me and nodded.

Neither of us made a move to leave. We were just standin' there, watchin' each other carefully.

I didn't know if she felt whatever was floatin' in the air between us, but it seemed so thick to me that I could see it.

Finally, she sighed gently and shifted her bag strap.

"I'll see you and Bell on Wednesday?"

For some reason, my heart dropped just a little. But I nodded and gave her my trademark smile.

"We're more of a sure thing than cicadas in the summer."

She laughed and shook her head.

"See you later, Gregory," she said, givin' me a little wave before walkin' away.

I couldn't make the words come out until she was too far away to hear.

"Bye, Justine."

***

Bell leaned over to me as the professor pulled up her presentation on the computer.

"Ruthers? Really?"

"Swear on all that's holy," I mumbled to him.

"Just came right up and kissed her?"

"If you could call maulin' her face like that a kiss," I growled. The image still made my blood pound in my ears.

"And then she told him off?"

"I told you the whole story already, man," I huffed. "Do you really need to play-by-play it?"

He held up his hands and laughed softly. "Sorry, bud. It just sounds so out of character for her."

"What does? Tellin' off a dumbass guy?"

"No, being with Dansby Ruthers in the first place."

I blew a hot breath out my nose. He was right. It didn't seem in character for her. Not that I didn't think she was capable of dating, but I could never have imagined her with someone like Ruthers. She was too smart to fall for any of his moves, which meant that she'd *chosen* to be with him over the summer.

And that thought made me madder than a yellow-jacket in a shirtsleeve.

"So, you didn't ask her out, then?" Bell asked.

I shook my head.

"You gonna?"

I closed my eyes and shook my head again.

"Greg."

"Look, it just ain't the right timing, Bell," I sighed. "And besides, if Ruthers isn't good enough for her then there's no way in hell I am."

"But –"

"We're still gonna see each other on Wednesdays, and she said she'd try and hang out with us more outside of studying, so I'll just take that for now."

Bell looked disgruntled, but smartly dropped the subject as the professor started her lecture.

I wish I could say that I retained any of the lesson, but I was too busy thinkin' 'bout the way Justine's eyes had flashed when she'd told Ruthers to get fucked.

But honestly… if Ruthers wasn't her type then I knew for sure I wasn't.

Maybe I'd been readin' everythin' wrong this whole time? Maybe the only relationship we could have was a begrudging friendship? Maybe the attraction was completely one-sided.

My chest ached at that thought.

Why would I think I deserved someone so incredible? If my life had taught me anythin' it was not to wish for too much. Not to dream too big about things that were out of my control.

Justine Wilkson would never be somethin' I could control. And I'd never want to.

That's what guys like Ruthers would never understand about her. She wasn't ever goin' to be someone's little wifey. She was a summer storm. You just hunkered down and got out of her way, and if you were lucky enough to have her attention for a while then you took it. But you never try to bottle lightnin'.

She was lightnin', all right. Pure, unadulterated heat. Somethin' cosmic that couldn't quite be explained by science or superstition.

I needed to stop tryin' to catch Justine. As my Ma would've said, "What's meant to be will always be. But if you have to force it then it's not for you."

Tryin' to ask Justine out was startin' to feel like pushin' molasses through a strainer. But goddammit if I didn't think about her all the time. Before I knew it, the lesson was over, and I hadn't listened to a word the professor had said.

"Bell, I'm gonna need to borrow your notes," I sighed as we packed up.

"Bold of you to assume I took more than a few notes," Bell chuckled. "Why do you think I need Justine's help all the time?"

"Damn, boy, really?" I moaned and ran a hand over the back of my neck. "I completely spaced the entire lesson, how am I supposed to catch up?"

I felt a hand tap my shoulder and when I turned around there was a mousy girl with long blonde hair and big blue eyes starin' at me. She was sweet-lookin', and in the back of my mind I felt like I should know her name, but it wasn't comin' to me.

"Hi, there," I grinned.

"Hi, Greg," she said softly, tuckin' a lock of her hair behind her ear. "Sorry, I couldn't help but overhear. If you needed to borrow my notes to copy, I'd be happy to lend them to you."

"Oh, wow, that's awful nice of you." I hesitated for just a second, tryin' like hell to pull her name out of somewhere.

"Kelly," she smiled. "We had Econ 305 together last semester."

"Kelly, right, sorry," I grinned sheepishly. "My brain's a little mush today."

"No worries!" she chirped.

"I'd love to borrow your notes, actually."

"Sure thing," she said softly. "Maybe we could meet for lunch off-campus and exchange?"

I felt Bell's curious eyes on me. Did this girl just ask me out on a date? I glanced back at Bell, wonderin' if I should accept. But then I thought about how badly I needed those notes. And gettin' lunch with Kelly didn't seem like it would be the worst thing in the world.

"Yeah, lunch sounds great," I drawled, flashin' her my trademark grin. "Let's say Ernie's at one?"

"It's a date!" her cheeks flushed, and her blue eyes danced.

She fluttered out of the classroom with Bell and I watchin' her.

"Do you get the feelin' she's been meaning to ask you out for a while?" Bell asked, hikin' his backpack over his shoulder.

"A little bit, yeah," I said slowly. "But come on, she's harmless. And it's just lunch."

"And you need those notes," Bell chuckled.

"That too."

***

Ernie's was my favorite spot off-campus. Just a little burger joint, decked out in 1950's era vinyl with neon signs on the walls and a jukebox in the corner. Nothin' fancy, but the staff were great, and it was usually quiet enough that I could at least try to study.

Kelly was waitin' at a booth when I got there. She lit up when she saw me, so I gave her an easy smile.

"Howdy, Kelly," I drawled as I slid onto the bench across from her.

She honest-to-God giggled and tucked her hair behind her ear.

"Hi Greg."

There was a small pause as the waitress came over to take our order. After she left, Kelly started diggin' around in her backpack before finally pullin' out a pink notebook with little hearts drawn in pen all over it.

"So, these are the notes from today, but this also has all my notes from the semester in it. I know we've really only just started, but if there's anything you wanted to review it should be there!" She was all smiles and sweetness, and I found myself relaxin' a bit.

"Gee, thanks Kelly, that's awful nice of you," I said, takin' the notebook and thumbin' through the pages. "You're crazy detailed in here!"

"Oh yeah," she blushed. "That's just how I am. I can be a little obsessive."

"Obsessive isn't necessarily a bad thing," I was absent-mindedly readin' through a page on supply and demand and realized I should be payin' attention to the girl sittin' across from me.

I closed the notebook and looked at Kelly, only to find she was already lookin' right at me. She chuckled a little and dropped her head, blushin'.

"People usually think I'm a little weird," she admitted.

"Hey," I said softly, reachin' out and patting her hands that were folded on the table in front of her. "The best people worth knowin' are the weirdos."

"You're so sweet," she murmured. "Everyone always told me that I'd never find a guy who was cute *and* kind, but here you are."

I huffed a laugh and ran my hand over the back of my neck. "Well, that's a very nice compliment, thanks."

"You know, I couldn't believe it when you agreed to come to lunch with me," she said, droppin' her eyes and fiddlin' with her hands.

"Oh?" Was all I managed. I hadn't thought it was that big'a deal, but she seemed real nervous all of a sudden.

"You're gonna think this is silly, I'm sure," her voice was soft. "But I've had a crush on you for a few semesters now. I just couldn't ever seem to muster up the courage to ask you out."

"Oh." Well now I felt bad. I didn't want to lead her on, but I didn't know how to let her down.

The waitress came over and interrupted the long, increasingly awkward moment to deliver our food.

"Look, Kelly," I finally said to break the silence. "You're obviously a super sweet girl, and crazy smart, and pretty. And I'm gonna be honest with you, because I feel like you deserve that."

She looked up at me with sad eyes and I blew out a breath, runnin' my hand over my neck.

"If I wasn't hung up on someone else, I'd be more than happy to take you out again," I said. "But I am, and that just wouldn't be fair to you."

She blinked at me and seemed to be thinkin' real hard. Her head tilted and her hair fell off her shoulder. Then, suddenly, her head snapped straight and a knowin' look came over her.

"Wilkson," she breathed. It was almost as if she hadn't meant to say that out loud. Her mouth snapped shut and her cheeks flooded with color.

"I'm so sorry," she said quickly. "I just…I know that you and Bell study with her, and she's the only person I've ever met who doesn't seem to give anybody the time of day. I know I'm probably way off-base."

"No, no, don't worry about it, Kelly," I tried to smile, but somethin' was twisting in my stomach. "It's not…it's not her."

She took a breath and looked at me. It felt like she was evaluating me, tryin' to catch me in a lie. But I was hopin' that my face was straight. It was bad enough that Bell knew how infatuated I was with Justine, but if Kelly could figure it out then there was no way that Justine herself didn't know. After a long moment, Kelly's face relaxed and she smiled softly at me.

"Thanks for being honest with me, Greg."

I let out a breath and smiled back. "Sure thing, Miss Kelly."

Chapter Thirteen

Justine

Business logistics and management as a class was turning out to be a colossal waste of my time. I couldn't fathom how anyone would need this much common-sense lecturing on how to run a business.

Then again, I had been raised watching my father build his from the ground up. He hadn't kept me away from it. I'd seen all aspects of building a successful empire. The struggle and the blood and the sweat and the sacrifice that it takes to create something that works.

My parents' love for each other was the first thing I remember thinking was real in this life. It was tangible. The way they looked at each other, spoke to and about each other. It was a thing of beauty. But there were some years, as my father was building his restaurant, that they were almost hostile towards each other. The stress. The long hours. The distance it created. I sat by his side some nights as he tried like hell to make the numbers make sense. To treat his workers fairly. To coordinate with vendors and order supplies. I saw the mundane. The ridiculously boring inner workings of one of the riskiest ventures a person could take on. It was stressful, and difficult.

I also saw the joy that it brought my father, to walk into the restaurant that he'd raised from the ground up. And to share that with his family. Once the restaurant was successful, thriving, the lifestyle he provided was more than comfortable. It was privileged. More privileged than he had grown up, definitely.

Watching him during those first few years, watching the pride in his success and the life it brought to him and his family, was what made me want to pursue the career I was chasing. Because I also saw that without Mr. Chestham, my father wouldn't have had the success he had. He knew that he needed to invest in a team that could make his dreams a reality, and by hiring a business management consultant he did.

I wanted to do the same thing for others.

Which meant sitting through an insufferably boring class with people who just couldn't seem to wrap their minds around the most basic of concepts.

Like labor laws and employee compensation.

Bell and Gregory weren't struggling as much in this class as they had in others, but there were still things that they didn't understand. So, our weekly study sessions continued.

If I was being honest, they were the highlight of my week. Despite what many of my classmates seemed to believe, I wasn't a robot. I needed human interaction and connection just as much as the next person, I just had a hard time finding people that were worth the energy of interacting with. Bell and Gregory, against all my initial reservations, could keep up with me. I found myself looking forward to revisiting the lessons with the two boys. It was like practice for trying to explain things to business owners in the real world.

I knew that a large part of being a consultant was going to be explaining the basics to people who would be practically clueless. And while Bell and Gregory were intelligent young men, they were still young. Brains not fully developed and all that. It took some time for them to come around on some things. But it taught me patience, and they eventually always caught on.

The moments when Gregory finally understood something we'd been working on were secretly my favorite. He would whoop and holler like he'd just won a contest at a county fair. Completely uncivilized. But his excitement was always contagious. His laugh made his eyes crinkle at the edges and sparkle just a bit more than normal. It made my traitorous heart beat just a bit faster.

Sometimes I caught Bell watching me instead of Gregory during these moments, and I worried that he could see right through me. See the pesky little crush that I was trying so hard to tamp down. But he never said anything. And now that we were over halfway through the semester, I figured if he had something to tell me he would have. Bell wasn't exactly a subtle person.

Case in point, we were just finishing up a study session and Gregory went to the restroom when Bell turned to me with a shit-eating grin.

"So, Justine," he drawled.

"Yes, Bell?" I said, my eyes focused on packing up my books.

"Greg and I are going to The Hot Toady. Wanna join us?"

"The Hot Toady?"

"It's a bar off-campus," he said, crossing his arms behind his head, and watching me carefully. "They've got a trivia night tonight, and we could use another player on the team. You in?"

I opened my mouth with a rejection on my tongue, but then I looked at Bell and he was watching me intensely. My mouth snapped shut as I held his gaze.

I couldn't say why, but as we watched each other I found myself close to tears.

If I went with them, that would be an admission that I wanted to spend time with them outside of studying. That we were not just a study group, but actual friends. If I acknowledged that Gregory was my friend, it was a stone's throw to him finding out that I had feelings for him. Feelings that I absolutely did not have the time to entertain. Feelings that I was sure weren't reciprocated.

Nor should they be. Gregory didn't deserve to be with someone as boring and un-fun as me. He deserved the world. Someone sweet and kind and open. Spontaneous and silly. Not someone who followed the rules to a T and couldn't stomach chaos, no matter how frivolous. I couldn't be what he needed. And somehow me saying yes to this invitation was what all of that hinged on.

Bell slowly reached out and rested his palm on my forearm, drawing me back to the present where tears were threatening to spill down my cheeks.

"It's not a bad thing to have a drink with your friends, Justine," he said softly.

I blinked and could feel the warm saltwater run down my face. I went to jerk my arm away from Bell's to angrily wipe the tears away, but he kept a firm grip on it. He reached out and gently wiped them with hands that were softer than the giant possessing them would have led one to believe.

"He just wants to be your friend," Bell said, his eyes more serious than I'd ever seen them. "Give him a chance. You might be surprised."

He held my gaze for another moment. Then his eyes flicked over my shoulder, and he leaned back against his chair.

Gregory arrived back at the table with a jovial grin.

"You ready for some trivia, Bell?"

"More than, buddy boy," Bell laughed. "You ready to get our asses kicked, again?"

"Every week, same ole shit," Gregory sighed.

There was a pause as they gathered their things and I fiddled with the strap of my bookbag.

Back and forth and back and forth in my head. I *wanted* to go. So desperately. But I shouldn't. But I wanted to, and when was the last time I did something fun because I wanted to?

After what felt like an eternity, but was only a few seconds, I lifted my head to look at Gregory.

"What if I joined you?" I managed to squeeze out. No going back now. "Do you think your asses might stand a better chance?"

Gregory's hands stilled and he turned to look at me with surprise.

"You wanna go to trivia with us?" he asked slowly.

I shrugged one shoulder, trying to be nonchalant. "Why not?"

"Well, it's in a bar for one thing," he said. "And it's a group activity, for another."

"You think I can't work well in a group?" My tone was sharper than I'd meant.

"Do *you* think you can work in a group?" he shot back.

"I will have you know that collaborative group work is the foundation of a successful business. And I am nothing if not successful in everything I do," I snarked.

"And? That didn't answer my question, darlin'," he said with a smirk.

"If you were actively listening, you'd know that it did, in fact, answer your question. Quite satisfactorily, I thought."

"You are such a –"

"An asset?" I grinned. "One that might keep you from any further humiliation at this trivia night? Tell me, Gregory, have you boys ever come close to winning?"

His eyes narrowed as his cheeks got pink. A feral part of me loved riling him up like this. Poking at him until that 'nice guy' façade broke and he showed me the ruthlessly intelligent person hiding underneath.

"We come in second almost every time," Bell chimed in, clearly enjoying tonight's sparring match.

I grinned and stood, slinging my bag over my shoulder.

"Well, with me on your team you'll place first."

Gregory looked at me for a long moment, and then glanced at Bell. Whatever silent exchange they had made him deflate and he looked at my slyly.

"You'd better deliver then, Miss Justine."

"Lead the way, Mr. Hudson."

Chapter Fourteen

Justine

The Hot Toady was an English style pub. Old maroon leather booths, dark mahogany wood trimmings and bar, and those 1950's green desk lamps gave the entire place an air of antiquity, even though it was filled with college kids.

There was a karaoke machine up on top of the bar and a portly, short man with an incredibly waxed mustache getting cards ready.

"That's Marty," Gregory said softly as we made our way to a booth. He was right behind me, and every hair on my body stood up as he whispered in my ear. "He is the strangest but nicest guy, and he knows a helluva lot of random trivia."

"He runs the show," Bell laughed. "Drink, Justine?"

Here was my first test. I knew what I liked to drink at home, but were the boys going to judge me for my favorite drink? *You're overthinking this, Justine. Don't make it weird.* As matter-of-factly as I could I said, "I'll have a Sex on the Beach, please."

As I knew it would, this made both boys stop in their tracks. I could feel their stares as I continued to the booth. I refused to turn to look at them, and instead slid my bookbag onto the faded leather and myself in after it. I looked up just in time to see Bell grinning at

Gregory before making his way to the bar, leaving the Alabaman trying desperately to look anywhere but at me.

Eventually, though, he had no choice but to take his place in the booth.

It was awkward. Almost painfully so, as he sat down. I felt heat beginning to creep up my neck and sucked my teeth.

Finally, Gregory broke the silence.

"Sex on the Beach, huh?"

"The drink, not the act. Yes."

"How'd that get to be your favorite drink?"

I blinked and thought about it. I wasn't exactly sure when I'd discovered that alcohol was much easier to stomach if it was mostly fruit juice.

"I believe it was my mother that led me to that particular choice of drink," I said softly.

"Your ma?" He sounded incredulous, and it made me chuckle softly.

"Alcohol was never taboo in my house," I explained, turning to face him a bit. "It was more of a lesson that was taught to me. My mother taught me everything that went into being a good hostess, and making cocktails was a part of that. For the modern woman, you know."

"How old were ya when she taught you that?" Gregory was genuinely interested. He wasn't judgmental or scornful. Just curious. It was like he couldn't take his gaze from me. I found myself being pulled in by the gold flecks that floated around the green in his eyes.

"Fourteen," I laughed. "I could make the meanest Manhattan outside the city itself by sixteen."

"So, that's somethin' we have in common then," he said quietly, almost to himself.

"Pardon?"

He blinked as if he realized that he had spoken out loud. Clearly, he hadn't meant for me to hear that comment. Then he took a deep breath and looked at me with a smile.

"That's somethin' we have in common. Makin' drinks," he said.

"Oh, right. Your brews," I smiled softly as his eyes lit up. He was excited that I'd remembered. "How did you get into that?"

"A job I took in high school." He ran a hand through his hair and leaned back against the booth. "I was workin' in a mechanic shop, fixin' up cars and tractors. Anythin' anyone brought in really. My daddy'd taught me young how to work on engines, and I picked it up quick. We needed the money. So, I worked at Andy's every day after school. One of the other guys there had a moonshine business on the side."

I raised an eyebrow, and he laughed and held his hands up.

"Cliché as all hell, I know," he smiled. His eyes were far away, and he seemed to get lost in the memory. "But he made good stuff, and I thought it was just the neatest thing to take somethin' as simple as barley or wheat and turn it into somethin' completely different. So, he taught me how it worked, and I've been makin' my own stuff ever since. Never moonshine! But beers, ales, things like that."

There was a small silence as I pictured a sixteen-year-old Gregory learning the ins and outs of making alcohol. I could picture his eyes flashing as he understood how something worked. His excitement when his first batch was ready.

"And you and Bell want to turn this into a business?" I asked after a moment.

"Yeah," he said softly, his eyes on his hands which were folded on the table in front of him.

"That's —"

"Risky, we know," he laughed. "But we've been talkin' about it since the end of freshman year, if not earlier than that. And why not, right?"

"Do you have a business plan laid out yet?"

"Nope!" Bell's booming voice interrupted us. "We're implementing rules for the night, apparently."

Gregory and I both blinked at his sudden appearance. Bell set our drinks down and slid in beside me.

"Don't look so spooked, I've only been standin' there for a minute or so," he chuckled and winked at me, which made my cheeks heat.

"What are you talkin' about with rules?" Gregory asked, taking a sip of his lager, and then raising the glass appraisingly.

"No shop talk," Bell said sternly. "We've been talkin' business all night already, and we all need a break. So, taboo words for the night. Business. Plan. Capital. Investments. Anything in that ball field, alright?"

I chuckled softly and nodded. I took a sip of my drink and saw that Bell had also managed to produce notecards and a pencil. Gregory followed my gaze and smiled blindingly at me, bouncing a little in his seat.

"You don't know the deal, so let me clue ya in," he said excitedly. "This ain't your momma's trivia, where everyone just shouts out answers willy-nilly, or buzzes in. We're civilized here at The Hot Toady." I snorted and was rewarded with a cheeky grin from the straw-haired boy next to me. "As civilized as you could ever believe me to be."

"So, hardly?" I joked.

"Two steps shy of," Gregory laughed. "Anyways, the rules. There are five answers in each round, four rounds total. Team with the most points at the end of the night wins. For each answer in the round, you'll assign a point value out of these five – obviously you'll assign more points the more confident you are in the answer. Each point value can only be used once. Make sense?"

I nodded and sipped my drink, relishing the sweetness.

"Good. Each round gets harder than the round before it, and we've only got a minute to answer each question before we have to turn in our card. And, I think it goes without sayin', no cheatin'."

"I've never cheated at anything in my life," I said, making my tone deadly serious, which earned a laugh from the boys.

"Then we're in good shape," Bell said, downing the rest of his beer before getting up to get another.

Gregory shook his head in dismay. "That boy doesn't know how to savor his beer. It's a damn shame."

"I didn't know beer was something to be savored."

"Good beer is. Trash beer, yeah, down in one. But a good beer, aged and doted on through the processin'. That deserves to have some time spent with it."

"I've never been a beer drinker," I admitted, sipping my fruity concoction.

Greg looked at me for a long moment, and something flashed behind his eyes that I couldn't quite name but that sent shivers through my heated body.

"Always a time to try somethin' new," he said, and his voice was suddenly husky.

The air rushed out of the room as we stared at each other. Just as quickly as it came, the moment passed with Bell's return. Though I didn't miss the pointed glance he gave to Gregory.

Then Marty was tapping the mic and trivia night was off.

I will admit, I had more fun than I thought I would. Our team, the Sweet Home Alabrainiacs (their longstanding name and one the boys weren't willing to budge on), was competing with five others.

The Trivvy Trivvy Bang Bangs, You Must Be This Tall to Ride Burt Reynold's Mustache, the Encyclo-maniacs, DTF (Dylan, Tommy, and Frank), and What Don't We Know?.

Shockingly enough, What Don't We Know? were the leading team, and right off the bat their arrogance annoyed me. I made it my personal mission to crush them, and Gregory and Bell seemed to share my feelings.

Round one was easy enough. Who was the first woman to win a Nobel Prize? Marie Curie. Simple questions like that. We got every single question right, including the ten-point bonus. We were tied at the end of round two with What Don't We Know?, and Marty took a break.

Bell offered to go refresh our drinks, once again leaving myself and Gregory alone in the booth.

"Tell me somethin', Justine," he said after a moment. He wasn't looking at me, which was fine because I couldn't seem to look away from him, and if he caught me, I'd probably die of embarrassment.

"Sunlight takes approximately five hundred seconds to reach Earth," I said softly.

His eyes flicked up to me, confused. "What?"

"You said to tell you something, but you weren't specific," I blinked. "So that was the first thing that came to my head. I'm not sure why."

He blinked back at me and then laughed. "No, I had somethin'. You just move too fast for me."

"I think I probably move just fast enough," I sniffed, but I wasn't truly offended. "So, what did you want me to tell you?"

Our eyes met and for the second time that night I couldn't breathe looking at him. It was the damned alcohol, I knew it. It lowered my walls, and this stupid crush was starting to leak out.

"Why do you want to graduate early so bad?"

110

My stomach rolled a bit. Of all the things he could have asked, that was the furthest thing from my mind in this moment. I sighed and ran a hand over my forehead, leaning back against the booth.

Gregory was leaning forward on the table, his eyes watching me carefully.

"I just can't seem to figure out why it's so important to you to get started before the rest of us have even finished," he said softly. "I know it is, and that's great for you. I just don't get it."

"Some things aren't for you to understand, Gregory," I sighed. He looked hurt, so I hurried on. "I'll try to explain it the best I can." I took a deep breath and leaned forward. As I did, Bell came back with our drinks for the next few rounds and Marty was tapping the mic again.

"Ladies and gents, we're going to keep on rollin' right along," Marty said in his 1950's sportscaster voice. "First category of round three: Astronomy. Ready folks?"

Round three passed quickly, and we still hadn't missed any. Between the three of us we had a wide breadth of knowledge, and some of the facts that the boys knew honestly surprised me.

Before I knew it, we were on the last question of round four, which had been far tougher than the previous rounds.

"Alright kids, the category is: Countries," Marty swayed back and forth a bit with a wicked grin. "Ready?" There was a general shout of yes, and Marty laughed. "Alright, alright. Which two countries are the only ones with 'the' in their official names?"

Bell, Gregory, and I looked at each other perplexed.

"We have to get this right, guys," Bell whispered. "We're tied with those arrogant dicks, and I'm pretty sure they cheat, even though I can't prove it. So, they're probably gonna get this right, and I just can't lose to them again."

"Okay, so let's think," I said softly, leaning in. "The only one that I know for sure, well ninety percent certainty, is Gambia."

"Gambia?" Bell asked, incredulously. "Where the hell is Gambia?"

"Africa," Gregory chimed in, his brow furrowed.

I blinked at him for a moment. "Yes, Africa. It's officially titled The Gambia. My father imports peanuts from there sometimes, that's the only reason I know that."

"Okay, so there's one, write it down." Bell waved at me as I had the pencil.

"The Bahamas," Gregory suddenly whispered, his voice so low that Bell and I had to lean even closer to hear him.

"You're sure, bud?" Bell sounded skeptical.

Gregory looked at him, and then looked at me, and smiled widely. I found myself smiling back and quickly wrote it down.

"And that's time, kids!" Marty called. "Bring your slips up to me."

Gregory grinned and grabbed the paper from me, scooting out of the booth to take it up to Marty.

In the brief moment he was gone, Bell nudged me with his shoulder and gave me a sly grin.

"Not so bad, being our friends, is it?"

"Oh hush," I said, blushing. "I never said it would be bad."

"Just 'cause you don't say somethin' doesn't mean it hasn't been said."

I started to laugh, but then panic started to bubble from somewhere in my chest. It felt like seltzer was sitting in my esophagus. I looked sharply at Bell, but he just gave me a warm smile and a pat on the arm, and then Gregory was back.

"Okay teams, just as a reminder, What Don't We Know? and the Sweet Home Alabrainiacs are tied for first place. If they both get this right, we go to a tie – breaker," Marty announced. "The two countries that officially recognize 'the' as a part of their names are…"

We were all looking towards Marty with bated breath. My hand somehow made its way to Greg's forearm, gripping it tightly in anticipation.

"The Bahamas and The Gambia!"

My hand gripped Greg's arm even tighter.

"There you have it, folks! Sweet Home Alabrainiacs officially beat out What Don't We Know? for first place tonight! Congratulations, boys!"

Cheers went up around the place. Bell shouted in victory and immediately jumped up to get drinks. Gregory started whooping and hollering, almost flying out of the booth to take a lap around the bar before rounding back and sliding in next to me. His hands cupped my face, and he looked like he was about to kiss me when he stopped, just staring into my eyes.

I found myself swaying towards him, eyes half-lidded. I wanted him to kiss me. To break this strange tension that had been building between us all night. I could feel the soft calluses of his hands, fading since they were formed during summer. The pulse of his palm tickled my cheek, and his eyes flared as they bounced between my own eyes and my lips. His thumb gently traced my cheekbone. It was a moment that lasted millennia and milliseconds. And then it was gone. He dropped his hands down to his lap, staring at them like they'd betrayed him.

I sucked in a breath and leaned back a bit.

"Congratulations," I managed.

He looked up at me like I was a stranger, and then smiled softly. He stuck out his hand to shake mine, and if he didn't seem to linger, I certainly didn't notice.

"We couldn't have done it without your dad and his peanut imports," he joked.

I laughed shakily as Bell returned with celebratory drinks.

"On the house," he announced proudly, holding his beer in the center of the table. "Cheers to the best trivia team this bar has ever seen."

"Bold claim, considering this is the first time you've placed first," I laughed and raised my glass to his.

"The first of many with you on the team," Gregory said, his voice tender and meant only for me, though he also raised his glass.

The clinking rang in my ears as I took a deep gulp of my drink and resolved to focus on enjoying the rest of my night.

We only had a few more drinks before heading out. Gregory walked me back to my apartment where I was living off-campus. It was closer to the bar than I'd realized, though in a college town like this most places weren't far. As we got to my door, he let out a sigh and ran his hand through his hair.

I turned with my keys in my hand, not prepared to find him so close behind me. I stumbled a bit, and he caught me with a surprisingly strong arm behind my back. The move pulled me close to him, and I could smell his soap. Fresh and light. It reminded me of him. And summer as a child. Light and happiness. Gregory deserved someone with that same light and happiness. He deserved to be doted on and cherished. He deserved someone who would never put him second to a business meeting or late office hours. Someone better than me.

"You never told me," he said softly, his lips dangerously close to mine.

He still hadn't let me go, and I wasn't fighting to get away. It felt good in his embrace. Safe.

My mind took a moment to catch up, but then it did, and I felt tears stinging my eyes.

"Don't cry, Justine," he whispered, his other hand coming up and tracing my jaw. "I just...I really think you're amazin'. And obviously you're gonna do incredible things. But I can't for my life understand why it all has to happen so quick."

I searched his face and saw nothing but the truth. He believed in me. He didn't want me to leave. He deserved an explanation.

I placed a hand on his chest, giving me some distance when he dropped his arm.

"I have a plan for my life," I started, slowly. "I have since I was twelve years old. High school valedictorian, graduate undergrad in three years, apprenticeship at a business consulting firm while I get my Masters, and then start my own firm. Help people whose businesses would otherwise fail. Make them succeed. Make peoples' dreams come true." Make my father proud to have me as his daughter. I didn't say that part out loud.

"I have to stick to the plan. That's just who I am. I need to start making my way. Earning my life."

Gregory was quiet for a long moment, his eyes on the ground. When he finally looked at me, I was surprised to see pity in them.

"You don't have to earn a life, Justine. You've got one. It's been given to you free of charge. I love that you wanna help people. Hell, if my daddy'd had someone like you to help him maybe he wouldn't have lost the farm. But sacrificing your own happiness for unnamed strangers you haven't even met yet? Seems a trifle silly to me."

It was my turn to be quiet. No one had ever understood what drove me so hard. Hell, I didn't understand it most days. I couldn't bring myself to tell him about my father's judgement or my intense upbringing. I couldn't say that never having truly related to other people was another driving factor behind why I needed to get started

115

as soon as possible. Because truly, it came down to the fact that I had never understood people and they'd never understood me. But building a career. Becoming a success in my field. Earning the respect of my peers and being able to help people who needed it. I understood that. That was my life's ambition. And I wasn't going to let anything stop me. No matter how badly I wanted him to.

I gave Gregory a small smile. "Thanks for walking me home, Gregory."

"Greg."

I bit my lip and felt every nerve ending in my body screaming. I leaned forward and kissed his cheek lightly. When I pulled back, he looked dazed, but happy. I smiled at him again before turning and unlocking my door.

"Good night, Gregory," I said as I walked inside, leaving him on the porch.

Chapter Fifteen

Greg

"You didn't kiss her?" Bell was incredulous as he leaned back in his chair.

I ran a hand through my hair. It was gettin' long. Ma'd say it was time for a cut.

"She was standing right in front of you, looking at you with those eyes you won't shut up about, and you couldn't muster up the balls to kiss the girl?"

"It wasn't that simple," I protested.

"Sure about that?"

"Nothin' about this girl is simple, man," I moaned, fallin' back onto the twin bed in Bell's bedroom.

"What's so complicated?"

"She's just," I sighed. "I don't know how to put it to words. She's just so focused on her future. She knows exactly what she wants it to look like. And it doesn't look like me, man. She's way too good for me."

"I think you're underestimating your own value, buddy," Bell's voice was light, but his eyes were serious.

"No, I know I'm not good enough for her. She's amazin', and she's gonna graduate early and she's gonna forget all about me."

Silence filtered through the room, punctuated only by the soft thud of Bell's chair legs findin' the ground again. I could feel him lookin' at me, but I couldn't force myself to meet his gaze.

After a long moment, Bell came over to where I sat with my head in my hands. He didn't say anythin', just rested a giant hand on my shoulder.

"She's gonna forget all about me, I know it," I whispered.

Bell squeezed my shoulder. I choked back the fear that suddenly gripped me.

I didn't want to lose her, but it wasn't my choice.

***

"Wilkson!" I called, joggin' to catch up to her as she walked purposefully across the quad.

"Oh, hello Gregory," she smiled warmly at me without breakin' stride. "How are you today?"

"Finer than the prize winnin' hog at the Putnam County Fair," I grinned. "Yourself?"

"Well, I'm not sure I could compare myself to a prize winning porcus, but I'm not terrible," she laughed.

It nearly stopped my heart, hearin' that laugh come from her. For me. It almost distracted me from what I had stopped her for.

"I had a question for you, a query if you will," I said, strugglin' a bit to keep pace with her.

"I'm in agony with anticipation," she said drily, but her eyes sparkled.

"Has anyone ever told you you're a bit impatient?"

"People are too afraid to tell me things like that."

"Afraid?"

"That I'll bite their heads off. Literally," she chuckled.

118

"Well, I'm not afraid of you."

She paused a moment and looked at me. She actually stopped walkin' to look me up and down.

"You never have been," she said softly, and after a beat she kept goin', but she had slowed down a touch. "Your query?"

I blinked and took a double step to meet her.

"I'd wanted to see if you were available for a quick bite to help me with a section of this chapter for micro?"

"When would you want to meet?"

"Can we go to Freddy's tonight, and you can coach me over burgers?"

"Burgers?"

"And fries, if you wanted."

"Do I strike you as a burger type of girl?"

"I'd honestly be surprised if you ate anythin' other than raw spinach," I joked, bumpin' her with my shoulder a bit.

"Kale."

"My mistake."

We shared a warm look and then walked on in a beat of comfortable silence that, the longer it stretched on, began to veer into uncomfortable.

Finally, she took a deep breath.

"We should invite Bell."

That stuttered my step a bit. "Why?"

Lookin' at the ground she muttered, "I just think we should."

"Why?" That seemed to be the only thing I was capable of sayin'.

She huffed in frustration. "Because if you're struggling with a concept then it's a fairly safe bet he is too," she snapped.

That pulled me out of my confusion as my defenses rose. "Hey, Bell and I are not the same, and I'm not strugglin' with anything. It's just a lil' confusin' and I thought you'd be able to explain it better'n the professor or the textbook."

"You can't rely on me for every little section of the curriculum that you don't understand, Gregory."

"Wait, wait, wait," I took a breath and stopped walkin'. "What in the hell are we fightin' about?"

"We're not fighting," her words were clipped, but she'd stopped a few steps ahead of me.

"We're not *not* fightin'," I sighed. "Seems like we're always close to fightin'."

She shuffled her feet nervously and was lookin' at the ground. "I know."

"Can't we just…be friends?"

The question sounded so pathetic, but it was the most important thing I could think to ask. The question that'd been on my lips from the moment I saw her in my doorway freshman year. I just wanted to be her friend at the very least. I'd be okay if that's all we ever were. Eventually the stronger feelin's would shift, I knew it. But not if we couldn't get past this weird spot we were in of dancin' around the truth.

"I don't know how to do that," she said softly, "with you."

"You really don't like me that much that we can't even be friends?"

"It's not – that's not the…" she sighed and managed to look at me with wide, scared eyes. Her lips parted and she looked like she was lookin' at a ghost.

Time stopped and I could feel what she was thinkin'. I could see the thoughts racin' around that beautiful brain of hers and I don't know how, but I knew that it wasn't just me in this. Her eyes filled with tears and her cheeks flushed. I could feel my own face heatin' and my thoughts spinnin'.

120

We were so close. She was so close to lettin' me in, I could almost taste her lips. Feel her heart beatin' through the space between us.

Then she dropped her eyes. Time started again. The connection broke.

"You should ask Kelly Dimas," she finally said, her voice low and husky.

All my blood had rushed somewhere else, so it took me a minute to hear her. And when I did it didn't make a lick of sense.

"Kelly?" The girl who'd been nice enough to lend me her notes at the beginning of the semester. We'd been friendly, but there hadn't been any more than a few words passed in class.

"She likes you," Justine's voice broke. "And she's smart. She can help with the micro stuff that's tripping you up."

"But –"

"I've got to go, Greg," she said.

Greg. Finally. But why did it sound so much like goodbye?

"Don't." I reached out and took her hand. It was warm and delicate, just like she was. I never wanted to let it go.

"I'm going to be late for class," she sighed. "This professor has it out for me, for some reason, and docks me points for the most inconsequential things. Being late would likely drop me an entire letter."

"That's not right."

"It's not," her voice was hard. "But it is the situation. So, I really... I have to go."

She turned, but my grip on her hand stayed. She closed her eyes and took a deep breath before lookin' at me. Her mouth was softly smilin', but her eyes still welled with tears.

"Kelly will help. She's sweet." She squeezed my hand once and then pulled away.

I watched her until she'd turned around the side of the language buildings. I could still feel her hand in mine, the way it'd felt when she'd squeezed it. I couldn't quite put my finger on it, but somethin' inside of me was sayin' that she'd been tellin' me goodbye. For good.

***

Kelly Dimas was in fact a sweet, smart girl who seemed eager to help just about anyone. She was helpful during class, especially with lending me her notes. I was a notoriously bad note-taker, and she'd taken it upon herself at some point to help me with that. It was probably when I'd needed to borrow her notebook for a full three days at the beginning of the year that she'd realized I might need some lookin' after. And she was more that willin' to volunteer, even though I'd never asked her to, other than that once.

Somehow, just a few classes after Justine had said goodbye, Kelly had plopped herself down in the seat next to me and started chattin' away. I hadn't asked her if she'd help me study.

I knew that if I asked, she'd help me with the econ stuff with a smile on her face. For some reason, I just couldn't bring myself to ask her. It felt like…cheatin' almost. Logically, I knew it wasn', but my heart was sayin' somethin' different than my head. So, I never asked her. But there she was in class, helpin' me with notes and whisperin' to me under her breath as the professor talked.

That's as much as I let her do, though. I could tell she might still have a lil' crush on me, and I just didn't see her the same way. I was hung up on the Connecticut girl who'd been freezin' me out since our last talk.

I had foolishly hoped that, come the next Wednesday after that conversation, I'd show up in the library and Justine would be sittin'

122

there with Bell, ready to review with us. When I made it to the table she wasn't there. It was just Bell, lookin' confused and concerned. I'd waved him off, not wantin' to get into just how final that last conversation with Justine had felt.

Instead, I buckled down and tried to use some of the study techniques that Justine'd taught me and Bell during our study sessions. Lo and behold, she hadn't just been teachin' us the material, she'd been teachin' us how to learn. How we learned, as individuals. And after a few hours, Bell and I were mighty surprised at how much we actually understood.

Wednesdays continued just like that throughout the rest of the semester. Just me and Bell, workin' through things. We learned how we worked together, which was good considerin' we were gonna own a business together. It just worked with us. Whatever he didn't understand, I usually did. And reverse. And if there was somethin' neither of us could get, we figured out how to help each other so that eventually we did.

Finally, we were three weeks away from the end of the semester. That meant all the frats were fixin' to throw their biggest parties of the year. In between studyin' and goin' to classes, I'd been workin' on a special brew for the last month or so, a cinnamon and apple one that was finally about ready. It was the largest batch I'd ever made, and I was itchin' to get some feedback.

Bell was friendly with some of the guys at Zeta Sigma Gamma, and they heard free beer and were in. Their Holiday Bash was the biggest on campus. Everyone who had a pulse knew to go to that party. The boys were smart about it, too. They set up designated drivers to shuttle people to and from the party – all anyone had to do was text. And they hired honest-to-God bartenders to make sure nobody got overserved.

The night of the party, I'd shown up a few hours early to help set up and to drop off my beer. I wasn't plannin' on getting too wasted that night – that was never really my thing. But I knew how to loosen up and have a good time, and I was lookin' forward to lettin' go and blowin' off some steam.

I set up the bottles in the kitchen as the brothers got the sound system and other drinks organized. Bell came in and when everythin' was ready, we took a shot with the rest of the boya. Then, before I knew it, the house was filled with what seemed like everyone who went to the school. Music pounded through the walls, people were laughin' and dancin' and talkin', and it seemed like nobody cared about anythin'. Like, just for that night, everyone had decided to forget about school, about tests, about homework. The only thing that mattered that night was having a good time.

"Greg!" Someone called my name from across the room.

I looked up and saw Kelly wavin' at me from the doorway to the kitchen. I smiled as she came up and gave me a hug.

"How are ya, darlin'?" I asked.

"I'm so happy to see you!" she gushed. "I wasn't sure you'd be here tonight."

"I helped supply some of the beer," I said. "Are you a beer girl?"

"Not usually," she hedged.

"Well, this brew is my own design. Nothin' too strong. Wanna take a sip of mine to see if you like it?"

Her blue eyes went big, and a smile stretched her face as she nodded. I offered her my bottle and she took a small sip. Her nose scrunched as the beer hit her tongue and she handed me the bottle back as I laughed.

"Still not a beer girl, then," I said.

"No, it's good," she insisted.

"I know it's good," I laughed. "But if you don't like beer, you don't like beer. No offense taken on my part."

She giggled and spun a lock of her hair around her finger.

"So, what can I get you to drink?" I asked, pointedly movin' away from her to put some space between us.

"Whatever you think I'll like."

I gave her a small smile and ordered her a quick fruity vodka drink from the nearest bartender. She thanked me by running a hand down my arm.

Now, I wasn't an idiot. I knew she liked me, and I knew she was flirting. But I had a lil' buzz goin', and I was feeling pretty lonely. So, I didn't deter her. I let her flirt and even flirted back a little. There was nothin' wrong with flirtin', I told myself.

Right when I was starting to have a good time talkin' with Kelly, I looked up and saw Justine comin' through the living room. She was talkin' with Bell and had a small smile on her face. She looked up at me and our eyes met.

Call it cliché, but as I locked onto her all the air left my lungs. It was the first time she'd looked at me for weeks, and with one glance everythin' I'd convinced myself I didn't feel for her rushed through me.

"Do you have any plans for the summer, Greg?"

I slowly brought my attention back to Kelly, who was lettin' her fingers drift over my forearm.

Without thinkin', I jerked my arm away and stepped back a bit. Hurt flashed across Kelly's face as she followed my gaze to where Justine was now talkin' with Bell and two of the Zeta boys who looked like they were two sips away from fallin' in love.

"Sorry, Kelly," I mumbled, shaking my head. "Had a weird twitch in my arm. You ever get those?"

She bit her lip and studied me for a moment before laughing softly. "Oh, yeah. Usually when I'm falling asleep my leg twitches like that."

"I think I'm gonna go run some water over my face. I'll be right back," I smiled at her and left her in the kitchen starin' after me.

I could feel Bell's eyes on me as I skirted around their little group, purposefully not stoppin' to talk. I made my way up the stairs and into the bathroom, lockin' the door behind me. It was quieter up there, givin' me some space to gather my thoughts.

Was seein' Justine ever gonna not knock me on my ass? What was she even doin' here in the first place? She hated things like this. And it was the end of the semester, there was no way she was gonna skip studying for her finals. Unless she was already done, I knew a few other students who had all early finals. There were only a couple of classes that had finals the next week and then break started.

I splashed another handful of water over my face and smoothed my hair back. I needed to get a fuckin' grip.

I looked in the mirror and saw that I was flushed, and my eyes were a little crazy.

Maybe if I talked to her. Cleared the air. Then my nervous system would calm down and I'd be able to enjoy the night.

I took a few deep breaths and felt my heart stop racin'. With one last look in the mirror, I steeled myself and walked out the door to find Justine.

Chapter Sixteen

Justine

Parties were clearly not my natural environment. If I hadn't been done with all my finals, I would never have come.

When Bell had approached me and told me about the Zeta Sigma Gamma party he and Gregory were "catering", for lack of a better word, he knew that I was done with tests for the semester. He also knew how hellish my semester had been.

After I'd suggested that Gregory study with Kelly, I'd stopped meeting the boys for study sessions. In part because my own courseload was quickly becoming overwhelming. The other part was that I couldn't keep spending time with Gregory without my feelings for him growing. And knowing that he couldn't possibly care about me the same way, and even if he did he deserved better than what I could give him, which was nothing, kept me away from the library.

I'd been locked in my apartment, leaving only to go to classes, for about two weeks when someone had knocked on my door. I had warily answered, but when I saw that it was Bell and that he was holding two humongous salads and a pitcher of lemonade my fears had quickly dissipated.

"You stopped coming to study with us," he'd said as we sat on the floor of my living room with the food on the coffee table in front of us.

I couldn't meet his eyes, so I just nodded.

"Why?"

"I've just been a bit overrun with schoolwork this semester," I said.

"Is that really it? Or does it have anything to do with the moon eyes I see you makin' at Greg every time you're together? When you're not biting each other's heads off, of course."

I glared at him, but my body betrayed me by letting my eyes tear up. He just watched me, his eyes soft. There was no judgement on his face. There never was. He was just there. I sighed and a tear managed to escape and trace down my cheek. Frustrated, I wiped at it, mentally logging that this was the second time I'd cried in front of him.

"I'm not someone who has friends, Bell," I said quietly. "I don't know how to do it. Everyone that I ever thought was my friend ended up talking about me behind my back. Calling me strange and cold. You and Gregory are the closest I've had to friends probably ever. And Gregory..."

"Is more than just a friend," Bell said knowingly.

I sighed and nodded. "To me. I'm sure he doesn't feel the same way."

Bell was silent as he chewed his bite of lettuce, his eyes not meeting mine. He looked deep in thought, so I didn't interrupt him.

"Greg doesn't have a lot of friends, either," Bell finally said.

I gave him a look and he laughed softly and then sighed.

"I know it seems like he does, but he's not close with ninety percent of the people he talks to or hangs out with. It's really just me that he's actually friends with. And, up until a few weeks ago, you."

My fork dropped into my bowl as I processed this. If he was right, then Gregory and I were more similar than I'd thought.

"We're throwing a party with Zeta house in a week to celebrate the end of the semester," Bell said, slowly putting his salad away. "Well, Greg's supplying the beer, anyway. You should come. It's their Holiday Bash, pretty much the whole school comes. But I know Greg'd love to see you."

Which was how I'd ended up trying to weave my way through a throng of bodies with Bell leading the way and a drink in my hand. We were making our way to the kitchen when we got stopped by some of the frat brothers. I glanced up and my eyes locked with mossy green ones.

The music faded, and I couldn't hear what anyone else was saying. I felt like I was being pulled across the room, but as soon as I took a step, he broke the hold, looking down at his arm. I followed his gaze and saw petite, delicate fingers playing with the cuff of his sleeve.

Kelly.

Cold water would have been a better shock than that.

My body seemed to go numb. I was blinking, but the image wasn't going away. Before I could get too lost, I felt a warm hand on my elbow. Bell. My only friend in the world, it seemed.

"Justine, Kevin was just wondering where you're from," Bell's voice was low in my ear.

I blinked at him and then took a long drink from my cup. The alcohol, one of Gregory's brews apparently, was crisp and tangy and light. It warmed my chest and loosened the knot of panic that had settled there.

"Connecticut," I answered, throwing a small smile at the tall redhead that I was hoping was Kevin.

"Oh really?" a brown-haired boy to my left responded. Shit. "My grandparents are from there."

"Kev, can we move on from the genealogy report? Are you gonna ask the girl to dance or what?" the redhead said loudly.

Kevin laughed and brushed his hair back from his eyes.

I saw his lips start to move again, but someone brushed my shoulder on their way up the stairs. I didn't have to look to know it was Gregory. Every hair on my arms stood up, and Bell's eyes tracked his back as he disappeared.

"I'm sorry, I think I need some air," I mumbled, making my way toward the door I saw in the kitchen.

As I sped across the room, I felt Bell's worried eyes on me. Why was this so hard? To just be *normal*?

I made it through the kitchen and out onto a small porch. The air was frigid. I knew that if we got any rain it would quickly turn to snow.

I took several deep breaths, letting the icy air into my lungs. It woke me up. Shook me out of the strange place my body had been.

I had never wanted to be normal. Maybe a few times growing up I'd wished I wasn't so different, but I'd always known that I was special. Driven. Smart. I'd known there was nothing that was out of my reach, a combination of my privilege and my personality. I had never before wanted so badly to just…be someone who knew how to form relationships. Who was able to divide her focus. But that wasn't me.

If I were to pursue Gregory, it would consume me. Right now, I needed my career to consume me. I needed that to be my focus. To start my life. To run to the place I could see so clearly in my mind. Comfortable. Successful. Taking my parents on trips around the world. Being able to provide for them so that my father could retire. I knew that he'd built up a sizeable nest egg, but he could live for

130

another twenty years. He had given everything to provide for us, it was my responsibility to give that back to him.

Thinking of my father helped to settle my nerves. I needed to make him proud. To earn the life he'd given to me.

Gregory was wonderful. Kind. Intelligent. Often infuriating. But he had not given me anything. My father had given me everything. My duty was to him. To finish school, start my career. As quickly and efficiently as possible.

A soft cough behind me broke through my thoughts.

"Sorry, Justine," Kelly Dimas' voice was just as soft as her cough. She stepped up beside me and rested her arms on the railing. "I didn't mean to interrupt your thoughts. You just looked..."

I knew how I'd looked, racing through the house. Panicked. Scared. Overwhelmed.

"I'm fine." My voice was steady, thank God.

"Okay." She bit her lip and looked out over the lawn.

An uncomfortable silence stretched between us. Finally, I heard her sharp intake of breath and knew what was next.

"Are you and Greg...?" she trailed off.

God, how I loathed people who couldn't finish a thought.

"Are we what? Study partners? Not anymore. Friends? Sometimes. Lovers? Absolutely not." My voice was sharper than it needed to be, but she irritated me.

"Oh, okay."

More silence.

"It's just, I've been trying to get him to notice me all year. I thought, maybe, at the beginning of the semester. But he told me he was hung up on someone else."

My heart pounded in my ears. I didn't care. I couldn't care.

"Well, Kelly, it sounds like you should move on then," I sighed. I took a long drink and let the alcohol warm me against the brisk chill that wasn't all due to the weather.

"I was trying," she said sadly. "But then tonight, he was flirting with me. I thought it was going well. Until you walked in."

"I don't control his behavior, Kelly," I deadpanned. I really did not want to have this conversation with her. I wanted, more than anything, to leave.

"No." Her voice was firmer. Interesting. "He was fine, and then he saw you and he got weird. So did you. Well, more weird than normal."

The last bit was said so quietly that I knew it wasn't for me to hear. But I did. Suddenly, I was so tired of trying. Of being around people who couldn't possibly understand me. Who wouldn't even try.

I turned and looked at Kelly with my back to the door, assessing her. She was fine. Pretty, petite. I knew she was smart. People liked her. She could carry a conversation without blowing up. Enjoy a night out without wanting to leave immediately. She was everything that Gregory deserved. And I hated it.

"There's nothing between Gregory and myself," I said resolutely. "I've been tutoring him and Bell, that's all. We're not friends. And I'm graduating next semester anyway. So, if you want him, tell him. It won't be my fault if he rejects you again."

I turned to go back inside and found Gregory lingering in the doorway, his eyes wide and hurt.

Almost instantly, my own eyes began to sting. I hated that he'd heard that. I hated that I'd hurt him. But nothing I'd said had been untrue, and it was better that he realized that. If, and that was a strong *if*, I was the girl he was "hung up" on, he needed to know that we couldn't be together.

I blinked once to get rid of the tears and pushed past him. I needed to say goodbye to Bell, as decorum dictated, before fleeing to my apartment.

"Justine!"

Gregory was calling my name. I didn't look back.

I spotted Bell on the dance floor with a brunette who looked like she would fall in love with him if she could. She couldn't. Bell wouldn't let that happen. I caught his eye and waved goodbye as I grabbed my jacket from the couch by the door. I upended two intertwined coeds to get it, and in the moment it took me to yank it from underneath them Gregory caught up with me.

"Justine, can we talk?"

I swallowed and shook my head. I couldn't look at him. I needed to leave.

I barreled out the front door and away from the house.

A hand lightly grabbed my arm, stopping me and spinning me around. As soon as I was facing him, Gregory's hand dropped to his side. His breath was coming fast, and his cheeks were pink. He had no coat, just jeans and a T-shirt. He must've been freezing, but he was standing there solidly. Just staring at me.

"I don't wanna be with Kelly Dimas," he finally said.

I sniffed. "Then you should tell her that. She's holding a massive torch for you. It's better to let her down now."

"I will." His voice was soft.

Heavy silence hung between us. My chest ached. My feet were starting to numb. I should have walked away, but my legs wouldn't move.

"Don't graduate early," he finally said.

I blinked.

Of all the things he could have said, that wasn't what I was expecting.

"What?"

"Don't graduate early. Don't leave early. Spend another year with me."

"I can't," I said softly.

"You can," he insisted. He took a step toward me. "You can just take a few less classes next semester, and then you can space them over next year. Just...don't go."

"I'm not..." My words failed. My words never failed.

But Gregory was standing in front of me, practically begging me to delay my plans solely for him. Exactly what I said I would never do.

"If you graduate early, you're gonna forget all about me," his voice cracked. "I can't...I couldn't live in a world that you didn't remember me."

"Gregory," I said his name slowly, hating the way it burned in my throat. "This, us, it would never work."

"You don't know that," he insisted.

"I do."

"You don't know everythin', Justine."

"I know," I said defensively. "But I do know that it's unfair of you to ask me to set my goals aside because of your own insecurities."

"I'm tryin' to tell you that I care about you," he said heatedly. He ran a hand over the back of his neck. "I have for a while. I just didn't know how to say it."

"And I'm saying that it doesn't matter." My voice was hard. My heart was breaking.

He cared for me. In the same way that I cared for him. But it would never work. Especially since he was asking me to compromise on my life plan. My goals and ambitions. My dreams.

"Doesn't matter?" he breathed. He blinked hard, as if he couldn't comprehend that.

"Correct."

"Someone likin' you doesn't matter?"

"No," I tried to soften the blow, but I could tell it didn't help.

"You –" he huffed and turned sharply, his hands in his hair as he took a few deep breaths. He turned back to me, and I saw his eyes glittering with rage.

"Everyone thinks you're this cold, uncarin' robot," he spit. "I've defended you for years, sayin' that they just needed to get to know ya. But, truly, all you care about is your own feelin's. Your own plans. Your own whatevers. You just care about yourself. You don't care who you hurt in the process."

"I never wanted to hurt you, Greg." Tears bit at my cheeks. I wasn't sure when I'd started crying but hearing him say those words hurt more than anyone else who had ever said them to me. And I'd heard them all my life.

"Oh, it's not me you're hurtin' Justine," he snapped. "It's yourself. You're gonna end up alone, unhappy, with just your money to keep you company. And that's no life."

"Greg, I –"

"Gregory."

I reeled as though he'd slapped me. He glared at me for another moment before a violent shiver racked his body.

"I really liked you," he said sadly. "I really thought you weren't what everyone said. I saw this light in you. But you only care about yourself, and that's not the kind of person I want in my life. Have a good one, Justine."

He turned and jogged back into the house. My eyes followed him. I knew tears were streaming down my face. I could feel them starting to freeze.

Icy tears to match my icy heart.

Chapter Seventeen

Justine

Six Years Later

When we broke ground on the warehouse, Bell had insisted I be there for the photo. It was the first time I'd seen Gregory since the unfortunate visit to the hospital. I couldn't believe that even after all these years he refused to admit what he'd done to me. He'd acted like he had no idea what I was talking about, as if the entire campus hadn't seen what had happened.

Bell had planted himself between us, trying yet again to break the icy wall that we'd managed to build.

"Alright, smile kids," Bell had joked, giving us each a poke as he draped an arm around us and the camera had flashed.

Construction began slowly at first as they worked with an architect to finalize the drawings. The place was cleaned out, floor to rafters. The concrete floors were repaved, the brick freshened, and then the brewery equipment was brought in.

Neither of the boys were able to be there when the equipment was delivered, so the task fell to me. I knew the general vicinity that it needed to go, but other than that was completely ill-prepared for the questions the installers began asking.

"Can you just call the brewmaster?" One of the men asked.

"I'd really rather not," I grumbled, but my phone was out, and Gregory's name was on the screen.

"Hello?"

"It's Justine."

"I didn't know you had my number," he said warily.

"I'm your business manager, of course I have your number," I snapped. The man beside me chuckled, but it died in his throat when I glared at him. "Where is this damned equipment supposed to be connected?"

"Bell wasn't able to be there?" Panic entered his voice.

"No, and conveniently neither were you," I bit. "Can you just talk to the installer? I don't know anything about this."

"Justine Wilkson admittin' there's somethin' she doesn't know?" he whistled. "Hell must be mighty chilly at the moment."

"Shut up, Hudson," I snarled. "Talk to the man."

I shoved the phone at the installer, who was watching me with curious eyes. He took the phone, and he and Gregory fell into an easy rapport. It took five minutes for Gregory to explain what needed to go where, and where all of the hook ups were, and then the phone was back in my hand.

"Problem solved," Gregory chirped. "I'll be there in about five just to make sure everythin' goes smoothly. Can you stay until then?"

"We've got another delivery of kitchen equipment coming in half an hour," I sighed. "*That* I actually do know about, so I'll stay."

"You sure you can handle bein' in the same room with me?"

"Just get your ass down here, Hudson."

***

After all the kitchen and brewing equipment had been installed, it was eerily quiet in the warehouse. It was just Gregory and I, sitting in silence as we took a moment to survey everything.

"It's gonna be amazin'," Gregory breathed as he looked at the shiny copper that took up half of the space.

I looked at him and saw what I'd seen in so many of my clients' eyes. It was the moment they saw their dream coming true. I knew it was a powerful moment, and I felt intrusive, so I ducked my head and began to walk away.

"Justine," Gregory's voice was soft.

I turned back, but he wasn't looking at me. He was still looking at the stills. I took a deep breath and walked to stand next to him.

"I get it now," he said softly.

"What are you talking about?"

"Why you wouldn't…couldn't even entertain not graduatin' early."

I stiffened.

"You needed to follow your dreams," he said. His voice was warm, and he still wasn't looking at me. I was grateful for that. "And you needed to do it on your own timeline. It wasn't fair of me to ask you to do it on mine just because I had a crush."

I gulped around the lump that was suddenly in my throat.

"And you did it," he turned, finally, and his eyes met mine. They were sparkling and a smile played on the edges of his lips. "You are exactly where you said you'd be. Successful. Respected." His eyes traced my face. "Beautiful."

I stopped breathing.

"I thought that the years would, I dunno," he laughed softly, taking another step closer to me. "Harden you? But it's just the opposite. You're exactly where you're supposed to be. Doin' exactly what you're supposed to be doin'. It suits you. You're effervescent."

His eyes dropped to my lips. He was so close I could smell the mint on his breath. I couldn't seem to move. I couldn't remember why I didn't like him. Nothing about our past seemed to matter anymore. The warmth of his skin invaded my senses, and I found myself wishing just one thing.

That he would kiss me.

Instead, he traced his thumb lightly down my cheek before turning back to look at the shining equipment that caught the afternoon light.

"This is my dream," he breathed. "And it's finally happenin'. If it wasn't for you, we wouldn't be here."

He laughed loudly and it filled the space. Filled my ears, my chest, my entire body. He turned to me one more time and his smile was blinding.

"Thank you, Justine." He reached out and squeezed my shoulder before making his way to the door and disappearing.

I stood in the middle of the warehouse, my heart pounding in my chest and my breath trying to catch up with what had just happened.

I felt like I was in college again, pining over the Alabama boy with emerald eyes and knowing that we couldn't be together.

But we weren't in college anymore. I'd built my business. I was exactly where I wanted to be, just like he'd said. There was no reason we couldn't be together.

A giddy feeling washed over me as I pictured the look on Gregory's face if I were to ask him on a date. I wasn't even sure I knew how to do that, but everything in me wanted to try. I bit my lip as I thought about it a moment more. If I ran after him now, I could catch him before he made it to his car. I could ask if we could put the past aside, move forward. Be together.

My hand was on the door when a recollection hit me like a brick in the face.

The stares and whispers of my classmates as I'd made my way out of my last final. The posters that had been hung all over campus. The humiliation as tears had run down my face. The despair as I'd realized that Gregory was the only person who could have done something like that.

Six years was a long time. Clearly Gregory had grown, matured, changed. But he had never apologized to me. Hell, he still refused to admit to any wrongdoing at all.

A few sweet glances and a trip to the ER didn't change that. He was still the man that had torn me down when I should have been flying. I couldn't let myself forget that.

Chapter Eighteen

Justine

Second Semester, Third Year

I was fucked. Well, and truly. One month into my last semester of college, and things were going horribly.

Just in one class. I was taking four, and the other three were going wonderfully. The professors and I got along, the coursework wasn't anything too difficult, and I was always on time for lectures. But my last class, Investment Strategy, was kicking my ass and for no fault of my own. This class was at eight A.M. on Mondays and Thursdays. Inevitably, something made me late every Monday and Thursday.

First, my apartment door wouldn't open. Something had been jammed underneath it and it wouldn't open more than a few inches. My landlord had to come and unwedge it. It ended up being a handful of pamphlets for a Thai place that I frequently bought from.

Then my bike chain had frozen through, forcing me to walk in the cold to class.

Little things like that, each week on the day I was supposed to go to this class, resulted in my being late consistently. Unfortunately, Professor Sparks was not only my advisor, but he was a stickler for punctuality. I'd barely managed to convince him to be my advisor after showing up late to my final two years ago, and he'd told me that he didn't stand for tardiness in any form. He'd pulled me aside after three weeks of consistently coming in a few minutes after the lecture had started.

"Miss Wilkson, you're not usually a problem student," he'd jumped right in.

I sighed and closed my eyes tightly. "I know, sir, and I do apologize. It's been one thing after another this month on my way to your class."

"Well, I suggest you find a way around that. I don't want to see you late again."

The unspoken threat of a failing grade hung between us as I nodded, resolved to be twenty minutes early from now on. And I was. I left my house an hour early each day, just to ensure that if anything did go wrong, I'd have time to work around it. I wasn't late anymore.

When tardiness stopped being a problem, other issues started cropping up. Assignments that I knew I'd handed in were not graded or marked incomplete. Lecture note emails not being delivered to me. Once, the lecture hall was changed and I wasn't made aware of that until I showed up and the door was locked with a note on it. The new room was all the way across campus.

The result of all these little things was that I was in danger of failing the class. I understood the concepts, was doing well on exams, but Professor Sparks docked points for every single one of these infractions. He was very clear in his syllabus that he didn't tolerate anything less than one hundred percent effort in his class, and it seemed to him that I was slacking off.

I wasn't. I had absolutely no idea what was happening.

And then, one month in, my notebook disappeared.

That made absolutely no sense to me, because I always had my bag with me. Usually on my person. But this week it had vanished. I was rooting through my bag before class, panic building in me as I took everything apart. My desk was a mess of other books, notebooks, papers, pens, my laptop. It wasn't there.

"Is everything okay, Justine?" Kelly Dimas' voice said from over my shoulder.

I jumped.

I'd known she was in this class, but she usually sat a few rows behind me, so we didn't ever need to talk. But, I supposed, with the scene I was creating it was only normal for her to be concerned.

"I'm fine, Kelly," I huffed. "I just can't find my notebook, that's all."

"Oh gosh," she said. "Well, you can always borrow my notes if you want?"

I closed my eyes and rubbed my temple, trying to fend off the headache that I knew was coming.

I turned to her with a small smile.

"That would be great, thank you," I said softly.

"Sure thing!" she chirped. "I'll lend it to you after class."

"Thank you. I'll have it back to you first thing tomorrow."

Her smile brightened and her eyes glinted. "Great."

I hated that I had to borrow her notes, which I was sure were going to be much less comprehensive than mine. But I needed at least an outline to follow for the end of semester test.

More stressful than losing my classroom notes, however, was the fact that I couldn't seem to stop thinking about Gregory.

I felt horrible about the way I'd treated him at the party at the end of last semester. He'd been vulnerable and open with me, and I'd not only shut him down but slammed the door on any kind of relationship moving forward.

And I missed him.

Loathe as I was to admit it.

I missed studying with him and Bell. I missed hearing his jubilation when he understood a concept, and the warmth I felt whenever he looked at me.

I still knew that dating him was out of the realm of possibilities, but I missed being his friend. Because I knew now that we had been friends. He and Bell were the only friends I'd ever had that I knew liked me for exactly who I was.

And I'd ruined it. Bell hadn't even talked to me since that night. I had a feeling they were both actively avoiding anywhere I might be. Which shouldn't have been hard, considering I was only ever two places. In class or at home.

I'd wanted to find them. To apologize. To make an effort. But with everything else that had been happening, I just didn't have the bandwidth. I needed to make it through this semester. Graduate. Then move on.

***

I was late. Again.

For my last final. Of course, it was for Professor Sparks' class. The class that had haunted me all semester.

The air was thick with heat as I *ran* from my apartment. Someone had stolen my bike last week, so I was on foot.

At some point during the night, all of the power in our building had gone out. It had knocked out my alarm clock. Thank God for circadian rhythm. My body had woken only ten minutes later than my alarm usually went off. So, as long as I sprinted, I would be able to make the final.

As I raced across campus, I felt people staring at me, but I knew I was running like a bat out of Hell, so I didn't think much of it. My mind was focused on the conversation I'd had with Professor Sparks two weeks ago.

"If you can't turn in your assignments on time, Miss Wilkson, I'll have no issues with failing you this semester."

"Professor, please, I promise you I *am* turning them in," I'd pleaded. "I don't know why they're not coming across your desk, but I pass them forward every day. And I'm doing well on my exams. I understand the material, there's just something that's been making my work not come through this semester."

"A lack of work ethic, possibly?" he'd mused, his icy eyes glaring at me. "Which, granted, is out of character for you. Case of Senioritis, perhaps?"

"I assure you, Professor, it's not been from a lack of effort on my part."

"Well, you need to sit the final and get a stellar grade to keep me from failing you this semester."

That had sounded easy enough. I hadn't been lying. I knew the material. I understood it. I'd do well on the final. I had set myself up for success. Had a good night's sleep, set my alarm, laid out my clothes. I'd been ready to go.

And yet, here I was, flying across campus, my lungs burning. I was in comfortable clothing, at least, but I was not a runner. It was nothing but sheer panic that was keeping my body moving.

I made it with thirty seconds to spare, throwing myself into a seat as Professor Sparks entered the room and locked the door behind him.

As he made his way down the stairs, I saw him take in my disheveled appearance and heaving breaths. His eyes were narrowed, but his face was soft with something akin to pity.

I didn't care. I'd made it. I was here. I was going to sit my final, pass this godforsaken class, and graduate. I'd done it.

***

It was done. The test had been simple, as I'd thought it would be. I knew I'd passed with flying colors. And Professor Sparks would hold to his word. He'd pass me, and in a week, I'd have my diploma in hand.

Everything was going according to plan.

I stepped out of the building and into the warm May sun.

Summers in the South were something that I hadn't acclimatized to yet. The air was sticky, oppressive, and sweet. It made the heat worse, somehow.

I closed my eyes and let a deep sigh leave me. This horrible semester was over. Strangely, my first thought was that I wanted to find Gregory. To apologize, rekindle our friendship, and let him know that I wouldn't forget about him once I graduated.

I opened my eyes and started to make my way across the square when I felt eyes on me. I looked around and saw that nearly every other student was snickering and staring at me. Not kindly. I wasn't running, I wasn't doing anything to draw attention to myself, so I couldn't fathom why everyone was staring at me.

Until I reached the bulletin board in the middle of the square. Plastered on every spare inch of space were posters.

Of me.

It was a picture I hadn't even known had been taken. I was standing with my books in my arms, and there was a group of students behind me socializing. I was alone. Someone had photoshopped metal plates all over my body and had made my eyes glow orange.

The text on the poster read: "Good riddance, Yankee Robot."

All the blood left my body. I froze. I looked around and saw that these posters were plastered on every wall, every board, all around the square. I was sure they were all over campus.

No wonder everyone was staring at me. No wonder they were all laughing.

Heat flooded my cheeks, and I knew I was already crying. There was no use trying to pretend I wasn't.

But it wasn't the poster itself that hurt the most. I'd been bullied before; people had pulled pranks at my expense in high school. Never on this scale, but it wasn't foreign to me.

No, it was what the posters said.

Good riddance, Yankee Robot.

Only one person in my life had ever called me a Yankee.

Suddenly, my skin felt cold. I remembered standing in the frigid air and Gregory's words came back to me.

Everyone thinks you're this cold, uncaring robot.

My breath shattered and started coming in gasps.

He had done this. I could hardly believe it, but all the evidence pointed to him. Had he been sabotaging me all semester as well? Trying to keep me from graduating? For what? Out of spite?

A thousand questions raced through my mind, but my body was frozen. A sob wracked my body, and my knees hit the ground.

I don't know how long I was down before a strong arm wrapped around my shoulders.

"Justine, come on." Bell's voice was soft in my ears. "Time to get up."

With no conscious thought, I let him get me standing. I heard more than saw him grab my bag from the ground and start walking me away from the square.

He walked me all the way to my apartment. I let us in. I wasn't crying anymore. Just numb.

"Are you okay?" he said gently. "I don't know who did that, but it was a shitty thing to do."

I stared at him. I knew he wasn't an idiot, but I also knew that Gregory was his best friend. Maybe that's why he couldn't see the obvious answer that was staring at us.

Gregory had made those posters. Put them up all over campus to humiliate me. He'd tried all semester to force me to fail my class.

I didn't know how he'd done it, but he was charismatic enough that I knew he was perfectly capable of charming a TA to steal my assignments. He knew where I lived, so he was able to sabotage my ability to get to campus on time.

His revenge for my rejection was to make me fail a class, and when that hadn't worked, he'd made sure that everyone on campus knew exactly how he felt about me.

Bell stood in my kitchen awkwardly. I realized I was just staring at him, but I was trying to assess if he'd been a part of it.

No. I didn't believe that. Bell had nothing against me. And I truly believed that if Gregory had asked him to help with this, he would have stopped it. He'd rescued me. Brought me home. He'd been my friend.

Gregory had been my friend too, I'd thought. It turned out that he was just like every other "friend" I'd had in life. Saying one thing to my face and another behind my back.

"You should go, Bell," I finally managed. My voice was cold, and my body was stiff as I stood and opened the door for him.

"You gonna be okay?"

"I'll be fine," I nodded. "I always am."

His eyes were sad, but he didn't seem to know how to comfort me. And, in truth, I didn't want to be comforted. I wanted to sit with this pain.

It was a sharp reminder of why I pursued my career over a relationship. My career was never going to let me down. Humiliate me. Torment me. I was making the right decision.

"Call me if you need anything," he said as he made his way out.

"I won't, but I appreciate the offer," I said. He nodded once and turned. "Bell." He turned back. "Tell Gregory that I hope he had his revenge. And that I never want to see him again."

Bell's face was all confusion as I shut the door and locked it before crumpling into a ball on the ground.

Chapter Nineteen

Greg

Six Years Later

"Do you think it's inappropriate to ask your business manager out on a date?" I asked Bell as we strolled through a home improvement store. My question stopped him in his tracks, and I ended up rear-ending him with the cart.

"For my clarification, you wanna ask Justine out on a date?"

"We're twenty-eight years old, I think whatever happened in college we can put behind us."

He was quiet for a moment before lookin' at me seriously. "What did happen in college?"

I blinked at him. "What are you talkin' about? I've told you. The night of the Zeta party we had a whole ass fight in the front yard. I told her I liked her, and she shot me down."

"Nothing happened after that?"

"Not that I'm aware of, why?"

He blew out a deep breath and leveled me with his steadiest gaze.

"Last day of school that year, Justine..."

"Justine what? Spit it out, man."

"Someone put up posters of Justine all over school. They made her look like a robot, metal all over her body. They were everywhere. I happened to be walkin' through the square and I saw her cryin' on the ground in front of the bulletin board. She was devastated. I took her home and she said something strange when I left her."

I blinked at him. I'd finished all my finals early that year and had gone home. I'd gotten a cheap plane ticket that had left early. Nobody had said anythin' to me about it when I'd gone back the next year. Then again, I hadn't really brought up Justine much.

"What did she say?"

"She said to tell you that she was glad you'd gotten your revenge, and that she never wanted to speak to you again," Bell's voice was low and there were questions in his eyes.

"What in the Hell does that mean?" I asked. I was gettin' worked up, but I was mostly confused. "What was she talkin' about, revenge? Revenge for what?"

"Look, that's all I know," Bell held his hands up. "You wanna know more, you'll have to talk to her."

"Oh, I'll be talkin' to her," I mumbled.

I nearly sprinted through the store, itchin' to get this whole mess sorted out once and for all.

***

I was beyond nervous when I pulled up in front of Justine's house. I hadn't realized she lived near town, but she was less than an hour from Hartworth.

The house was nice. Smaller than I'd thought it would be. It looked like a stone cottage out of a fairy tale. There were lavender bushes linin' the walkway, vines climbin' the walls. Hell, a pair of butterflies were flitterin' across the lawn.

I could see Justine through the kitchen window. She was sittin' at her table with her laptop open. As creepy as I knew it probably looked, I just stood there starin' at her. I was mesmerized. She was so naturally beautiful. The graceful line of her neck, the glow of the light on her skin, the way she brought her cup up to her lips and sipped from it. She was so focused.

It hit me that none of my feelin's for her had changed. It was like I was in college again, starin' at her from across the square. I had a stupid, massive crush on the woman. And she hated me for a reason I didn't know.

No time like the present to find out.

I took a deep breath and walked up to the door, givin' it a small knock. When she opened the door, her face was shocked. She quickly cooled her expression into one of professional interest.

"How can I help you, Gregory?"

I hesitated. How do I even start this conversation?

"I didn't make those posters of you," came tumblin' out of my mouth.

Her eyes went wide, and her cheeks flushed. "What?"

"I just found out about them," I rushed on. "Bell literally just told me about it this mornin'. I had no idea that you thought I did that."

"Of course, you did it," she hissed, her arms crossing.

"Why would I?" I demanded.

"To get revenge on me for not wanting to be with you," she said, her voice was small.

"That's not the kinda person I am, Justine," I huffed. "I thought you knew that."

"I thought I did, too, but…"

"But, what?"

She took a breath and looked around. "Get inside. The neighbors will talk."

She stood aside and ushered me into the house. The inside is what I would have expected from her. Minimalist. Modern. All clean lines and sharp edges. Nothin' like the idyllic outside, the décor was stark. Nowhere to hide.

"That semester was Hell for me," she snapped as she led me into the kitchen. She turned and propped her hand on her hip. "I was late almost every lesson for Professor Sparks. Had assignments go missing. On the last day of school, I had my final for that class, and I was almost late. I made it. Sat my final. I was so happy to be done, to have achieved my goal, only to go out to find those posters all over the school. Everyone saw them. And you're saying you didn't even know about them until today?"

"I wasn't there," I insisted. "I was home, visitin' my parents. I left the day before."

She was quiet, her eyes flickin' across my face for any sign that I was lyin'. I huffed and grabbed her hand, puttin' it on my chest.

"See? Steady. I'm not lyin' to you, Justine. I had no idea that had happened."

Silence stretched thick between us. Her gaze searched mine, and then I watched her deflate a bit.

"The posters said Yankee Robot. You're the only one who's ever called me yankee." Her voice was small, and her eyes didn't leave my face. She wanted to believe me, but I knew that after believin' somethin' for so long it'd be hard to reevaluate everythin' you thought you knew.

"It wasn't me," I whispered. Her hand was small and cold under mine, but I didn't let it go. Instead, I took a step closer to her. "You broke my heart the night of the party. I didn't understand you then, but I do now, and I get it. I'm not mad anymore. But it kills me to think that all these years you thought I was…what? Sabotagin' you?"

She nodded and her eyes got misty. "You were the only person that made sense. You were mad at me for rejecting you. Everyone liked you, so I knew it'd be easy for you to get Sparks' TA to help you steal my assignments. You knew where I lived. It all just made sense."

"But I'm tellin' ya, it wasn't me." My voice was steady, and I took another step toward her. "I was pinin' for you the entire rest of the semester. If I wasn't in class, I was in my room. Holed up. I didn't make any brews that semester, but I passed all my classes with flyin' colors I was doin' so much studying."

Her eyes were trained on mine. She was a logical person. She was tryin' to make sense of all of this. I could see seven years of hurt makin' their way up.

"I would never hurt you, Justine," I whispered. "I cared about you. I-"

Her brows furrowed.

"I still do."

I felt her sharp gasp. So small. Her fingers trembled and mine tightened reflexively.

"Gregory, I don't know what to think," she said softly.

"God, Justine," I groaned. "For once in your life, stop thinkin'.."

She blinked at me, and then before I could process anythin' else her lips were on mine. Her fingers curled into my shirt and pulled me to her while her other hand gripped my forearm. I was stunned and then she pulled back, her eyes glistenin' with questions.

My hands moved on their own, one grabbin' her hip and the other her neck, pullin' her back to me and locking my lips on hers.

She tasted like honey and lavender, and something a little sharp, like bourbon. And she melted for me. She fit in my arms like she was made to live there. Her arms wrapped around my neck and her body

154

molded to mine. The kiss seemed to last forever, and yet it was over too quickly.

She pulled back, her breath comin' in pants and her cheeks flushed. God, I wanted to look at those flushed cheeks for the rest of my life. I wanted to see how she'd look after more than just a kiss. See how rosy she'd be with my lips explorin' every inch of her body, pullin' the sweetest sounds out of her sour candy mouth.

"Greg," she murmured, her eyes flutterin'.

"Say that again."

A shiver ran through her at the command and all my blood rushed away from my brain.

"Greg."

"Justine."

"Go out to dinner with me?"

I blinked and tried to focus. "You're askin' me out?"

She nodded and ducked her head. "I wanted to the other day, but the poster incident was something I couldn't get past." Her eyes met mine again. "I want to believe that it wasn't you. I don't know who it was, but I want to believe you. Go to dinner with me?"

"I've been waitin' years to take you out to dinner, Miss Justine," I said, kissin' her again because I could. Because she was still in my arms. And it wasn't a dream.

So, I kissed her again.

And again.

We stood in her kitchen, kissin' like horny teenagers until her phone started buzzin' on the table.

She pulled back and looked at it angrily.

"I have to work."

"It's Saturday," I teased, lettin' my fingers trace her collarbone. Her skin was so soft, just how I'd always imagined it'd be.

She leveled me with a gaze that I couldn't quite understand. "That's the business, Greg. Always on call."

I soothed a hand down her arm. "I know. I'm not begrudgin' you that." I kissed her and then nuzzled her where her neck and ear met. "I like you callin' me Greg."

She shivered and giggled, a sound neither of us were expectin' because we both pulled back to look at each other in surprise.

She rolled her eyes and shook her head, wavin' her hand like it didn't matter. I caught it and planted a kiss on her palm.

"Greg," she said softly, her eyes warm.

I flipped her hand and kissed the back of it before lettin' her go.

"I'll call you with dinner plans," I said as I made my way to the door. "Keep your phone on."

"My phone's always on," she laughed.

I sent a playful glare her way and she stuck her tongue out at me. Man, she got my blood pumpin'.

"Watch yourself, Miss Justine," I drawled, lovin' the way her eyes sparkled when I said her name. "That mouth of yours'll get you in trouble one day."

"Promises, promises," she muttered, but a smile played on her lips as she followed me.

I ducked in for one last kiss before I waved goodbye and walked to my truck. She watched me the entire time I loaded up and backed out. She watched me as I drove away.

I had to pinch myself to make sure I really wasn't dreamin'. I hadn't expected this when I'd gone, but I was happier than a Collie on a sheep farm with the way things had turned out.

Now I just had to figure out where to take her.

Chapter Twenty

Justine

I hadn't expected the Ritz for our first date, but when Greg pulled up outside a faded wood building with nothing but a buzzing neon sign out front that looked to be of a horse's rear, I'll admit I had my misgivings.

"You've taken me here to kill me, is that it?" I asked drily as he opened my door and helped me out of his truck.

"Please, I know at least ten better spots to kill you, if I really wanted to," he joked.

"Then, what are we doing here? It's the middle of nowhere."

I wasn't lying. We'd driven about forty minutes out of Hartworth to get here, and there was nothing around but rolling fields of grass. The driveway was entirely dirt, and I understood now why Greg had said to wear jeans and shoes I didn't mind getting dirty.

"We're goin' dancin'," he said with delight. His eyes were sparkling.

I appraised him with narrowed eyes, and it was only then I really looked at what he was wearing. A tight-fitting flannel tucked into a pair of dark jeans and boots. He looked good. Delicious, in fact. But they were very country clothes.

I hadn't been able to stop thinking about our kiss in my kitchen. The taste of hops and mint had lived on my tongue far longer than I'd cared to admit, even after brushing my teeth. He was a good kisser. Firm, but gentle. Decisive. It was like we were made to kiss each other. And the thought of spending the night dancing with him wasn't abhorrent. The thought of dancing, in and of itself, however, was terrifying.

"What kind of dancing?" I asked warily as he led me through the honest-to-God saloon doors.

"Country line dancin', obviously," he rolled his eyes and swept his arm at the room.

It was a one-room bar with a large wooden dance floor. The band was just starting to set up, testing strings and speakers. But there was a decent crowd of people gathered already.

"Hungry?" he asked, leading me to a booth on the side wall, directly across from the stage.

"Actually, yes," I said. I was dubious they provided food, so I was curious what he was going to offer me.

"I thought you might be." He winked and made his way over to the bar. He greeted everyone as if they were long-lost friends. Maybe they were. He said something to the bartender, whose eyes found mine and winked at me. Then he produced two plates and a candle, which he handed to Greg.

Greg, who practically skipped his way back to the table. I was struck again by just how different we were. He was exuberant, wore his heart on his sleeve. I kept my emotions masked, hiding them for my own protection. But he made me want to be more open.

He set the plates down, produced a matchbook and lit the candle, leaving it in the middle of the table.

I looked at the plate in front of me and saw a rib-eye steak, mashed potatoes, and collard greens.

"How did you know I wasn't vegan?"

He quirked and eyebrow at me. "You? Please. I had to convince the chef to put a little color on that meat because after I told him about you, he was convinced you'd want it practically mooin'."

"So, the steak wasn't your idea?"

"Oh no," he laughed. "I let Redd plan the menu. Jus' told him a bit about ya and let him figure out the rest. How'd he do?"

I studied the plate and then cut into the steak. A perfect medium rare. I cut a small piece and, eyes locked on Greg, popped it in my mouth. It melted and I barely suppressed a groan. My eyes slid shut, and when I opened them again Greg was watching me like I was what he wanted to eat. Pure, unadulterated heat poured from his gaze.

"Redd did well," I said softly, biting my lip.

The way Greg was looking at me sent shivers all over my body, and I couldn't stop one. His eyes focused even more, somehow, and he made a small noise in his throat.

"You're so…" he whispered. He couldn't seem to find the word he was looking for, so instead he picked up my hand and kissed my fingers gently.

There was something so carnal about Greg, but then he was so soft with me that I almost wondered if I imagined the heat.

The bartender came up to the table and set down two drinks in front of us.

"Nice to meet you, Miss Justine," he said. He was a kindly older gentleman with the thickest mustache I'd ever seen. "Our boy Greg doesn't shut up about you these days."

I had the decency to blush as I accepted the drink. "Well, we've known each other awhile."

"Little bit of a break in the middle there, but on solid footin' now," Greg joked. "Thanks for the meal, Redd."

"Thanks for the bestseller of the month," Redd laughed.

"This is one of yours?" I asked, lifting the glass to my mouth. It was smooth, almost caramely with hints of peach.

"What do you think?" Greg looked worried.

"It's amazing, Greg," I said softly, my hand finding his. "Are you going to sell this one?"

He shook his head, but his cheeks flushed with pride. "Nah, that one's a Redd's Special. I'll do something similar in fall. The caramel is touchy to work with, but it makes a nice autumn brew."

Redd smiled, clapped Greg on the shoulder, and then made his way back to the bar.

Greg lifted his glass, and we touched them gently before taking another sip. It really was amazing. It warmed me from the inside and managed to take the edge off my anxiety about dancing.

"Eat up. Dancin' starts in a bit and I want you to be able to learn a few first so you don't embarrass me," he joked.

"I'm more worried about embarrassing myself," I sighed. "I'm not a particularly talented dancer, Gregory."

"You don't have to be," he said warmly. "I've got you. Let's just have fun tonight, alright?"

Looking at him, I knew that I could trust him. A voice in the back of my mind was still railing against that concept, but I'd seen the look in his eyes when he'd told me he had nothing to do with those posters. I'd felt his heartbeat. I believed him fully. Or wanted to, at least.

So, I cut another piece of steak and offered it to him from my fork. He smiled widely at me and took it, not holding back his own moan. It sent a jolt straight to my core, and I resolved to have fun being with him.

I wanted to let go of the past, and tonight was the first step towards that.

We ate and the conversation flowed surprisingly naturally. We had a good rapport. He was clever, and he could give back exactly what I gave him. He laughed off my sharp tone and made me smile with stupid jokes. I couldn't remember the last time I had felt so comfortable with someone. Actually, I could. Studying with the boys in college.

Greg had launched into a story involving Bell, a trip to Cabo, and too many margaritas. I couldn't take my eyes off of him. He was captivating. His eyes sparkled, and he talked with his hands. His lips were pulled up slightly at the corners, like he was on the verge of a smile at all times. He was beautiful. How had I never noticed how handsome he was?

Maybe because I'd spent the majority of college refusing to acknowledge my feelings for him. I'd never looked because I didn't want to give myself away.

But now…now I could look all I wanted.

And he seemed to feel the same way. His eyes never left my face. He kept blinking like he couldn't believe was still there, sitting across from him. He would reach out and his fingers would skim the back of my hand before disappearing, like he was checking that I was real.

"I have a question," I interjected when he took a pause to drink.

He raised an eyebrow and rested his chin on his hand. "The floor is yours, darlin'."

My stomach flipped at the endearment, and I bit my lip to try to curb my smile.

"Don't hide from me, Justine," his voice was soft. It was more a request than a command, but the lack of a question mark nearly made me shiver. I hadn't realized I was someone who would melt for a decisive man, and I certainly had never expected that man to be

Gregory Hudson. But he had this way of demanding things without expecting me to comply that made me immediately want to.

So, I smiled. For him. At him. Fully. And the smile I got in return was blinding.

"Your question?"

I took a breath. "Were you ever... afraid to be alone with me? In college?"

He cocked his head and thought for a moment. "Afraid isn't the right word. You made me nervous as all Hell," he admitted. "You were so smart and clever. We fought like banshees. I was always nervous I was gonna do somethin' to muck it up. And I seemed to every single time."

"I was terrified of you," I said.

"Of me?" he looked truly confused. "You weren't scared of anything back then."

I laughed and shook my head. "I was scared of everything back then."

"Well, you could've fooled me," he laughed. "But me? Really?"

I bit my lip and decided to be honest. "I liked you so much." He blinked in surprise and his mouth fell open a bit before he managed to school his expression into one of polite interest. "You were one of the only people that ever made me feel normal. Like I wasn't some...robot. You made me ridiculously angry, of course, but you also made me contemplate my entire plan."

"I did?"

I nodded. "That's why it was so heartbreaking for me when I thought you'd been the one to put up those posters. I'd never really had friends that hadn't secretly hated me, and I thought I'd finally found some in you and Bell. And then the poster incident happened, and it just seemed to confirm that I didn't deserve to have friends. That I'd been silly for feeling as strongly for you as I did.

"I thought that the years would help to erase the way I felt about you, but as soon as I saw you again, it all came flooding back," I took a deep breath and forced myself to look into those shimmering green pools. "I'm trying to tell you that I like you. And I want to see where this goes with you. I'm in this."

He was silent for a moment, giving me nothing but a calm stare. Then, he slowly reached across the table to take my hands in his.

"I never hated you," he said gently. "I never saw anythin' in you but the fierce, intelligent, beautiful goddess that you are. And, if you let me, I'll spend every wakin' moment tryin' to show you what I see."

***

Dancing had been more fun than I'd thought it would be. After I'd stumbled through a few line dances, the band switched to what Greg called, "two step music". I had no idea what that meant, but the result was spending the evening being twirled and dipped and sashayed around by Greg, who was a surprisingly skilled dancer. He led me around the hardwood floor like we'd been moving together our whole lives.

The last half hour the band had slowed down, letting us hold each other. Greg was the perfect height for me to rest my head on his shoulder as his strong hands guided me in a languid waltz. I'd laughed picturing my mother watching me dance like this. Very little structure, covered in dust, and happier than I'd ever been before.

I'd felt Greg's heartbeat in my chest and it matched mine. Our bodies were literally in sync with each other. He never let me more than an inch from his side, taking every opportunity to plant sweet kisses on my cheeks, my nose, my lips.

Then, the band had called it a night. We'd stayed close, his arms around my waist.

"I have one more surprise," he'd whispered, taking my lips again. There was something else in the kiss this time. A promise. Heat. It was a bit more demanding, and I melted beneath him.

We'd said goodnight to Redd, climbed in Greg's truck, and he'd begun driving. He didn't say anything as he drove, just held my hand, randomly bringing it up for a kiss every so often.

We pulled off onto a dirt road and drove another minute before he turned the truck off. He cut the headlights and we plunged into darkness. My heart rate kicked up. I'd never been the biggest fan of the dark, and this was an all-consuming darkness that settled around us. Greg's hand in mine was the only anchor I had as he opened his door and tugged me out with him. My eyes quickly adjusted to the dark as he led me to the bed of the truck and lowered the tailgate. Inside were blankets and pillows, piled up into a nest.

"What have you done?" I asked, my tone wonderous.

"Climb up," he laughed, offering me his help.

We both climbed in, and I sat, waiting to see what this was all about. He stretched out on one side and smiled at me. Even in the dim light of the night I could tell his smile was beautiful.

"Look up," he said, rolling onto his back with one arm tucked beneath his head.

I huffed out a laugh, not quite sure what we were doing. But I'd promised myself to go along with the night and have fun, so I laid beside him and turned my face up to the sky.

The sight of the swathe of stars stole my breath.

The midnight blue sky was broken by hundreds of thousands of glittering lights. Purples and blacks were painted in streaks across the inky blue. It seemed like the sky was lit up just for us.

I looked back at Greg and saw the stars reflected in his eyes. I had to pinch myself. Literally.

"What was that for?" he laughed. His voice was quiet and yet still seemed too loud.

"I just had to make sure I wasn't dreaming," I muttered.

His hand came up and traced my cheek. "I know I must be. Nothin' I've done in this life deserves a reward like this, so it must be a dream."

"Gregory, that was surprisingly romantic." I'd been going for teasing, but the breathlessness of my voice undercut the tone.

"I'm a hopeless romantic, Justine. You'll see."

I swallowed and took a deep breath.

"This is beautiful."

"Yeah," he sighed and turned his gaze back to the stars. "Nothin' makes you feel quite as insignificant as lookin' at a sky full of stars."

"I've never seen this many stars at once."

I could feel his gaze on my face. "Come here," he said, patting his chest.

I chuckled as I scooted closer and laid my head down. His arm wrapped around me and pulled me into his warmth. I could hear his heart beating through his shirt. His touch felt electric on my skin as his fingers traced shapeless patterns on my shoulder.

"I can't lie, I've had this dream quite a few times," he said lightly.

"Oh?" I my hand rested on his chest, letting my fingers drift along the collar of his shirt. "Do you want to tell me about this recurring dream of yours?"

He stilled beneath me, and I heard his heart start beating faster. I could tell that the particulars of this dream were probably not appropriate first date conversation, but I was having so much fun with him. I was so comfortable with him. And, after all these years, I was still insanely attracted to him.

I'd never been great at seduction. It was never a skill that I'd felt the need to cultivate. I wasn't sheltered or a prude, by any means. But men were simple creatures. When I wanted sex, I asked for it.

There was something in me that knew that Gregory deserved more than that. He deserved effort, concentrated and deliberate. And, for him, I was willing to try.

"Well," his tone was low. "It's not always stargazin' in the back of my truck, but the gist is the same. You in my arms. Lookin' more perfect than a hazy fall mornin'. Feelin' the heat of your skin on mine."

I hummed softly and let my fingers drift down his chest, playing with the buttons on his flannel. I wanted him closer. I wanted to feel him.

"Greg, I'm a bit cold," I said, propping myself up on my elbow so that I could look at him.

His eyes were wide as he processed what I'd said, and then a sly smile flickered across his face.

"Well, darlin', we can't have that," he said, slowly sitting up and undoing his buttons.

He slid his flannel off and wrapped it around my shoulders. As he did, he scooped me onto his lap and let his hands rest on my hips.

"This okay?" he asked. His voice was soft, and my heart stuttered.

I nodded and wrapped my arms around his neck, pulling him in for a kiss.

This was different than any kiss we'd shared so far. It was slow, molten, with an edge running through it. His hands tightened and he pulled my hips closer. My fingers grabbed at his undershirt. I could feel the blood pounding through my body, and I was starting to feel frantic.

I had never wanted someone like this. I had never felt like there was too much space when we were touching everywhere. Like I was drowning in his presence, and the only thing that could save me was his kiss.

His knuckles ran up my back, underneath my shirt, and I arched into his touch.

He pulled back and his eyes were full of wonder.

"Justine," he panted.

"Greg," I breathed.

"We've gotta slow down, darlin'," he laughed softly.

"Why?" I was pouting. I never pouted.

"Because you're too special for the first time I take you to be in the back of my truck." He brought his hand up and traced my cheek with his thumb.

"You don't want me?"

"That's not what I said," his voice darkened. He gripped my hips and ground them against his.

I gasped at the hardness I felt there and at the electricity that buzzed through my body at the friction.

"I've wanted you for longer than I care to admit," he said. "But you deserve more than this. I want to take my time with you." He placed a kiss on my neck. "I want to make you make more of those delicious noises. I want you to fall apart on my tongue." A kiss to my collarbone. "I want you beggin' for more that I couldn't possibly give because I'm givin' you everythin' I have." He dragged his nose up the line of my neck, inhaling and letting out a low moan.

I couldn't breathe. My voice was stuck in my throat and the only thing I could do was close my eyes.

"Look at me, Justine." It was somehow both a demand and a request.

So I did. The man in front of me was wrecked. He looked how I felt. Completely gone.

"God, you're so perfect," he nearly growled. His lips crashed into mine and his fingers curled around the base of my neck, pulling me somehow closer.

My body responded without my conscious permission, going limp in his arms and letting him flip us around so that I was on my back with him hovering over me. He broke the kiss and trailed his lips down my neck, my chest, my stomach. Even through my shirt, I could feel the heat of his breath and I trembled.

No one had ever made me feel like this. This on fire. This electric. This wanted.

He stopped at the button of my jeans and rested his head there. I could feel him evening out his own breathing, and I tried to do the same but instead I found myself wanting to cry.

It surprised me. Crying and sex weren't things that happened at the same time with me. But this wasn't just sex, or even lust. This was…worship.

I don't know how, but he must've heard a hitch in my breath, because I was suddenly being pulled up and into a hug.

"You're okay," he whispered into my neck, his arms tightening around me.

"I know I am," I huffed. I tried to push away, not wanting him to see me emotional, but he simply hugged me tighter.

"You deserve to be treated like a goddess, Justine."

I paused. Was that what was so different? Gregory cared about me. He wanted me and respected me. There was an emotional investment with him that nobody had ever made before.

I pulled away again, and this time he let me. I didn't go far, resting my forehead against his.

"You're right," I sniffled. "We should go slow."

He laughed and kissed my cheek. "Never think that I don't want you. I want you all the time. I have since the first moment I saw you. Even if I didn't fully know it. Through every argument, all the time and distance. It's always been you, Justine."

I met his gaze and saw the truth shining there.

"I..." my throat constricted and I could get out the words.

"It's okay, I know."

I bit my lip and his thumb came up to pull it out.

"Only I get to bite those lips of yours," he joked, landing it with a soft kiss that ended in a nibble.

"You're ridiculous," I laughed.

"Yet here you are."

I shook my head, looking up at the stars and taking a deep breath.

I'd never wanted anything like this before. I could see a future with Gregory. I saw it in college. It was why I'd pushed him away so hard. But now...life had brought us together again, and I wasn't going to make the same mistake twice.

I looked back to the man holding me, his green eyes sparkling.

"Here I am."

Chapter Twenty-One

Greg

The warehouse was quiet when I got there. I hated silence. Always had. I pulled out my phone and flicked through my playlists, finally settlin' on an early eighties rock mix. Steel guitar echoed off the rafters, and I took a deep breath.

Things were finally falling into place.

Bell and I were startin' our business, makin' strides forward every day. Justine had been invaluable, negotiatin' contracts, hiring a marketing manager, buildin' community awareness. Hell, she'd managed to expedite quite a few of our building permits because of her connections at City Hall.

And she was more than just our business manager. She was mine.

I still couldn't believe it. If someone'd told me at the end of college that six years later I'd be datin' Justine Wilkson, I'd've laughed them out the room.

But here I was.

After our date at Redd's, we'd agreed to take it slow. We could both feel that this was somethin' real, and neither of us wanted to mess it up this time. And, if I was honest, I was terrified she was gonna just up and leave. Realize she was way too good for me and pack it all up after the business launched and just go.

Good things didn't tend to last for me, and I needed Justine to last. I didn't know what I'd do if I lost her again. My chest got tight just thinkin' about it, so I decided not to.

I looked around the warehouse. We were gettin' the wrought iron fence installed in the space today. The way the architect had concepted it was to divide the space with a wall, but Bell and I liked the idea of a tall fence that people could still see through. We were gonna cover it with some fake plants to provide a sound barrier, but people'd still be able to catch a glimpse of the copper stills on the other side from the restaurant area.

Wrought iron was a feature throughout the space. We'd decided on single light bulbs to hang over each table and they'd be hung with wrought iron. The bar had a beautiful filigree design made by a local blacksmith. I hadn't even known those still existed, but Justine had found one when we'd told her what the plan was.

"You're thinkin' about her again," Bell's voice boomed through the space.

I turned to see him comin' through the kitchen carryin' a big box. He must've come in the back, because I hadn't heard him. Which was no small feat bein' as big as he was.

"Maybe you didn't hear me because you were fantasizin' about someone a helluva lot prettier than me," he laughed.

"Get outta my head, man," I laughed back, but I was only partly jokin'. He had this habit of readin' my thoughts straight from my face. It was nice sometimes to not have to try to put my thoughts into words. Other times it was downright creepy.

"I don't have to be in your head to know where it's at," he said, settin' the box down on the bar.

"What's in there?"

"Glasses," he deadpanned.

"No, seriously, what's in there?"

"I am bein' serious. It's the stout glasses."

I went over and peeked in, and sure enough there were about two hundred stout glasses in there.

"Why in the hell did we order glasses before we installed the cabinetry to store them?"

Bell shrugged. "We ordered everything all at once and scheduled them to be delivered in a few months once everything was installed, but I guess these slipped through and got here early."

"What're we supposed to do with them?"

"That depends," Justine's voice appeared from behind me.

I turned to see her saunterin' in the front doors, her eyes flashin' behind her glasses. God Almighty, that woman could stop my heart with a flick of her fingers. She was gorgeous. Her pantsuit was huggin' her hips and her short hair was curlin' around her ears.

"Depends on what?" I asked, leanin' against the bar even though every atom in my being was tellin' me to walk up and kiss her breathless.

"Well, you've had those stills installed for weeks now," she smirked, and my mouth went dry. "Do you have anything to share with the group yet?"

I laughed. "It's gonna take another month at least before those are ready."

"Hmmm, pity." She put on a pouty face as she joined us at the bar. "I guess we'll just have to make do with these then."

She pulled out three bottles that had a beige label on them. Hudson's Hops, with a rabbit sittin' on a pile of wheat.

"What are these?" I asked, takin' one from her and inspectin' it.

They were amazin'. I'd never seen my name written on any of my drinks, and it was a bit surreal.

"I hope you don't mind, and you don't have to use them," she said, her voice uncharacteristically small. "I thought it'd be a good

172

idea to brand your brews. So that people know what they're drinking, and so that if you wanted to market them and sell them on a larger scale you could."

I looked at her and couldn't help myself. I grabbed her and gave her a big ole kiss, dippin' her back as she squealed and threw her arms around me.

I brought her back up and gave her a quick hug before lettin' her go.

"They're amazing, Justine!"

She laughed, lookin' a bit self-conscious, and smoothed her top.

"I'm glad you think so," she said. Then she turned to Bell. "We also need to brand the restaurant. Have you boys picked a name for the place yet?"

We looked at each other and grinned. I'd waited to tell Justine because I wanted the three of us to be together when she learned what we'd decided on.

Bell looked at me with an eyebrow raised.

"All you, brother," I said.

He took a breath and looked back at Justine. I knew how much he valued her opinion, and names were a tricky thing. Try as we might to not get attached, once you found one you liked it tended to stick. And I knew he wanted her to like it as much as we did. Because she was a part of this team. She always had been. She got us through school, she'd gotten us our loan, she was our miracle.

"The Bell Tower."

She was silent for a moment while she thought about it, and then her face split in a grin.

"I love it," she said simply.

"Yeah?" Bell said.

She nodded excitedly. "It works on several levels, actually." She reached into her purse and pulled out a bottle opener and opened the three beers, handin' one to each of us. "There's the connection to your nickname, obviously, which will be a fun little 'in' joke for the people who know you and that story. But a bell tower is what calls people to gather. It sounds across the town and brings everyone together. And I believe that's what this place will become for Hartworth. A gathering place."

We were quiet as she finished speaking.

I didn't know if she was like this with all of her clients, but Justine just *got* us. She understood our vision and did everythin' in her power to make it come true. She believed in us, in our dreams, and in our ability to make them come true. More than that, she knew exactly what we were about and made sure that we reflected that in everythin' we did. She held us accountable, and she was able to articulate what we couldn't.

I never would've been able to specify exactly why The Bell Tower was the perfect name for our place, but I knew it was. And then she came in with exactly the reason.

She was incredible.

"That's right," Bell said softly.

"You should definitely write the story for the menus," I joked.

She rolled her eyes and blushed a pretty rose.

"To The Bell Tower,." She raised her bottle. Bell and I were all smiles as we clicked the glasses and we each took a long drink.

I wanted to kiss her again, but instead I settled for reachin' over and squeezin' her hand.

We drank in silence for a bit, but it was comfortable. Everythin' felt right, havin' the three of us together.

Chapter Twenty-Two

Justine

Those boys were something else. Their drive and their passion were outmatched only by their ambition and kindness. It was a rare combination to find in the business world, and one that I was realizing I loved being around.

After the fence was installed in the warehouse, I could have easily gone home, finished up some paperwork, sent off a few emails before getting ready for bed and calling it a night. But I didn't want to leave.

"What would you boys say to some dinner to celebrate?" I suggested as we made our way out the front doors and onto the sidewalk.

It was the start of summer, and the weather was lovely. The night air was warm but not humid yet, and there was the slightest hint of a breeze that carried waves of magnolia blossom perfume.

Greg's hand was steady in mine as Bell locked the doors behind us, and, on an impulse, I turned and kissed him on the cheek.

He looked as shocked as I felt. I wasn't big on offering PDA. I had no problems with it, I just wasn't usually so demonstrative. And I definitely wasn't impulsive. But then he grinned, and my heart did a little flip.

I didn't understand who I was becoming when I was with him. It was like this romantic person had been locked inside me my whole life but was only just now getting to stretch her muscles. Everything he did made me feel gooey inside, and I thought about him all the time.

I was logical. Pragmatic. Decidedly not *gooey*.

But, the more I came to know Greg, the more I realized how intelligent and dependable he was. I didn't have to worry about half the things I usually did because I knew I could trust him to pick up any slack that I left behind. For the first time in my life, I didn't have to be in charge of everything. It was strange, and if I thought about it too much, I'll admit it made me uncomfortable. I felt out of control, but I was trying to lean into it instead of running away like I had in the past.

As if he sensed where my thoughts had gone, he tugged me closer and placed a gentle kiss on my temple and I thought that might have been the happiest I could ever remember being.

"Alright, you two," Bell laughed and barreled between us, wrapping an arm around each of our shoulders. "That's enough of that. Dinner sounds great. There's a neat little Mexican place around the corner. Sound good?"

"Sounds great, man," Greg laughed.

Bell led the way and soon we were three bowls deep in endless chips and queso with plates of some of the most aromatic, mouth-watering food I'd ever had. The conversation flowed easily from food to travel to bucket lists. No topic was off limits with them. I knew that they would never push me for more than I was willing to share. It was so easy to be around them both. Greg looked at me like the sun shone from my skin, and he used any excuse to touch me. Soft and gentle, a poke on the side or a tender squeeze of my hand, he simply enjoyed showing me that he cared.

Bell was a terrific sport about being the third wheel. It honestly never really felt like he was, because I knew the boys were a package deal. While I loved having Greg all to myself sometimes, there were always going to be nights like tonight when it was the three of us. It was hard to picture Bell settling down. I wasn't sure what woman could ever make him, but she'd have to be something truly special.

As much as I was loathe to admit it, Greg and Bell were becoming more than just my friends. We were starting to feel like a family. I was struggling a bit with that, considering I'd never counted on anyone other than myself for anything in my life. But I wanted to trust these new relationships. I wanted to let them both in, especially Greg.

And I was trying.

***

"You know, Justine, we never asked," Greg said towards the end of the meal, "what did you do to celebrate graduatin' early?"

I froze and tried to take a deep breath. From my peripheral I could see Bell tense as well. Was Greg being serious?

"Nothing," I said slowly, my eyes watching Greg's face closely.

He sensed the change in mood. He wasn't that big of an idiot. But he was clearly confused.

"Why not?"

Bell let out an audible sigh, and I couldn't help the tears that sprang to my eyes.

"Wait, wait, why are you cryin'?" Greg cried, his hands coming up to my face.

I jerked my head away from him, feeling shame and anger rising in my chest. I knew I was probably overreacting, but it was such an insensitive question. How could he not see that?

"I can't believe you," I whispered. "Things were going so well, and I was finally – *finally* – starting to move through the past. Our past. All the nastiness and anger and resentment. But you're just –"

"Justine, don't say anything you don't mean," Bell interrupted with a hard look.

"Justine, I'm so sorry," Greg began, taking my hand in his. His eyes were wide and his voice full of panic. "I forgot about what happened. It just slipped my mind. That was a stupid thing to ask."

"It was," I sniffed. My vision was swimming, and I could feel the lump in my throat solidifying in the way that it did before a meltdown. "I have to go."

I grabbed my purse and rushed out of the restaurant. I took some deep breaths. Four counts in, hold for four, four counts out. It was a trick my therapist had taught me to help me work through my "big emotions".

I'd started therapy a few weeks after the poster incident on the suggestion of my mother, of all people. That had thrown me for a loop, considering my mother was probably the world's most uptight woman. But I'd been a wreck after that day, refusing to go to the graduation ceremony, barely leaving my room. So, my mother had recommended a therapist that she would see about twice a year for a "tune up", as she put it. I'd gone through a few before finding Dr. Laura in Hartworth. She was kind, but no nonsense, and was helping me through getting to the root of a lot of issues I wasn't even aware I'd had.

Four counts in. Hold for four. Four counts out.

It took three rounds before my heart slowed down and my eyes stopped stinging. I took one more big, deep breath and let it hiss through my teeth.

I needed to go home. I felt like an idiot, standing there just *breathing* in front of the restaurant.

178

I'd thought that Gregory would have followed me out, but he clearly had other priorities. I'd parked at the other end of downtown, so I started to walk to my car, trying to let my anger out through my footsteps.

"It's not Gregory's fault," I muttered to myself. "About the posters, anyway. He says he wasn't there, and I believe him. But I cannot believe that he didn't come out to comfort me."

I shoved my purse further up my shoulder and huffed.

"Typical. I start to fall for a guy, and he doesn't even have the emotional intelligence to apologize properly."

"Anybody that pisses you off should be on his knees begging for forgiveness," a voice said from my right.

I jumped and whipped around to see who had spoken.

I'd made it to the parking garage, and a man stepped out from behind a support column. He was filthy, his hair long and oily. As he stepped into the light, I saw that his eyes were sunken. Clearly homeless, probably on drugs.

I did not have the patience for this tonight.

"Have a good night." I flashed a passive smile and continued on my way.

His vice-like grip on my arm spun me around and into his chest.

My heart rate kicked up and the knot in my throat was back, but this time it was fear that swam through my body.

"Let go of me," I hissed, shoving at him violently. His grip only got tighter.

"Apologies," he laughed.

He backed me up roughly. I kicked my legs out trying to gain some purchase, any purchase, on the concrete ground, but all that happened was my heel breaking and my breath getting knocked out of me as my back hit the pillar.

He lowered his nose to my neck and sniffed. Bile rose in my throat. I wasn't sure I'd be able to get out of this. He didn't look strong, but his grip never loosened. It didn't matter how hard I twisted.

His other hand was in my hair, pulling so hard I thought chunks might be coming out.

"Hey, let go of her!"

Greg's voice boomed loudly, echoing in the space.

Everything froze.

The man's eyes grew wide, and his lips snarled.

He squeezed my arm one last time and then vanished.

I looked around, trying to see where he'd gone, but he was smoke. There and then gone.

I crumpled to the ground, my knees giving out as the panic fully set in.

I was hyperventilating. My vision narrowed to the crack in the paint on the ground in front of me.

"Justine?" Greg's voice was far away.

I felt him come up and kneel beside me, but he didn't try to touch me.

"Justine, darlin', you've gotta breathe for me."

I felt a soft touch on my wrist and my eyes whipped up to his. There was comfort in the warm green pools that met me. They were panicked but made me feel strangely calm.

My gaze dropped to his lips, which were moving.

I tried to focus.

"Justine, can you feel the ground?"

Greg's question didn't make any sense.

Of course I could feel the ground.

"Touch the ground for me. Put your full hand on it and feel how solid it is," his voice was calm, mesmerizing.

I didn't know what he was aiming for, but I followed his instruction.

I spread my palms over the concrete. It was cool beneath my touch. I could feel my heartbeat in my hands. I started breathing in time with it.

"There's my girl," Greg's voice sounded calmer, somehow, and he wrapped an arm around my shoulders. "Is this okay?"

I looked up at him and nodded, feeling myself lean into him and he seemed to absorb all my fear and stress.

He held me for a long time, running his hand gently over my arm where the man had grabbed me, soothing it.

He didn't speak, just held me. Soothed me. Calmed me. When I finally broke down in tears, he let me cry into his shirt. It was an ugly cry. Heaving sobs. Coughing. Snot. But he stayed, and he cradled my head against his shoulder. When the last tears finally left, I sat up and wiped my face. God, how embarrassing. That's why I'd run from the restaurant, to avoid the public hysterics.

"None of that now," he said with a soft smile as he gently brushed the last tears from my cheeks.

"I feel so stupid," I sniffled.

"Justine," his voice carried an edge. "You were attacked. You are havin' an entirely appropriate response to that. That's on top of the fact that you were already upset from my stupid ass. It's been a long day, darlin'."

I nodded and blew out a heavy breath.

"I need to file a police report," I said.

Greg's jaw tightened and darkness passed over his face. There was something in his eyes, and it took me a moment to recognize it as guilt.

I reached over and cradled his cheek in my hand.

"It wasn't your fault either, Greg," I said softly.

His eyes met mine and melted. "If I hadn't been so thoughtless —"

"Then you wouldn't have been here to save me," I whispered. "You saved me, Gregory. And not just from this guy. You've saved me in every sense of the word. Even if I overreact sometimes to the things you do, it's important to me that you know that."

For a long moment we simply looked at each other. There was so much unspoken, and the longer I looked at him the more I realized I didn't want it to be.

Life was too short to leave things unsaid. I could, apparently, get attacked in a parking garage. If this had ended differently, and I hadn't told Greg how I felt about him, I would have been filled with regret.

Adrenaline flooded my system, and I was suddenly gripping Greg's hands in mine, staring into his eyes with purpose. I saw surprise flit across his face and then it quickly turned to concern.

"Justine, are you okay?"

"I love you."

"You –"

"I love you." It was softer this time.

He stared at me like I was his next breath while I held mine.

He wrapped his arms around my waist and somehow brought us both to standing so that he could sink his fingers in the hair at the base of my skull and kiss me.

I'd never been kissed like that before. Like I was giving him life directly from my lips. He was claiming me, owning me. Loving me.

When we finally broke apart, we were both panting, and his cheeks were flushed.

His eyes sparkled, but his face was solemn when he said, "Justine Wilkson, I've loved you since the first time I laid eyes on you. I promise you I will do everythin' in my power to be the man that you deserve."

A fresh set of tears pricked my eyes and all I could do was kiss him again.

And again.

And again.

Chapter Twenty-Three

Justine

Greg held my hand as he drove me to the police station so I could file my report.

He held my hand as an officer took my statement and photographed the bruise already forming on my arm.

He held my hand while I sat with a sketch artist who brought to life the haunting emptiness that had been in the man's eyes.

He held my hand as we made our way back to my house. Up the front steps.

At the door, he let his hand slide up my arm and cup my cheek, pulling me in for a sweet, chaste kiss.

When we pulled away, a thread of tension bound us. My chest ached to be closer to him. I looked in his eyes and saw that they were fierce. Fiery. One might even say smoldering. And I knew.

"Gregory," I whispered. My voice was husky and low, and I swear I heard him growl in response.

That was all it took.

We crashed together.

His hands gripped my hips and pulled me flush to his body, where I could already feel his arousal.

The kiss was hot. Sloppy. Gnashing teeth and ragged breaths.

He backed me up against the door and a low moan escaped me. He kissed down my throat, nipping now and then, his hands roaming my body until I was writhing against him. Fully clothed. In full view of my neighbors.

With a gasp, I managed to turn and fumble with the keys. His lips were on my neck and then at my ear.

"C'mon darlin', open the door," his voice was rough, commanding.

I'd never wanted to follow someone's direction so badly. My fingers shook as I found the right key and somehow managed to get it in the lock.

He reached around and turned the knob, his other arm wrapped around my stomach. As the door opened, his free arm swept my knees up and he carried me inside.

I heard the door slam behind us, but my feet still hadn't hit the ground. We hadn't stopped moving.

"Bedroom?"

"Um –" my mind went blank, and my hesitation earned me a growl and a nip to my ear.

"Justine, focus."

With a shaky exhale, I managed, "Last door on the left."

Greg's eyes shone in the darkness of my hallway. I kept waiting for my brain to catch up with the situation, but she seemed to have clocked out for the night.

Greg captured my lips in another heated kiss as we moved. Then, my back hit the down duvet and I bounced, gasping.

Greg stood at the end of my bed, his chest heaving and his cheeks pink. His hair was tousled (had I been grabbing it?) and I could see his erection straining through his jeans.

When he slowly walked toward me, he was in total control. His movements were slow. Deliberate. Careful.

He lifted my leg and slid my heel off. The other heel had disappeared somewhere in the hallway.

His fingers caressed my calf, and then gripped it tightly and dragged me forward so my ass was at the end of the bed. My legs fell open, and he stepped between them, reaching down and lifting me by my neck for another searing kiss.

My toes curled into this one, and my hands scrambled to lift his shirt.

He chuckled at my impatience and leaned back.

"What do you want, darlin'?" I'd never heard his voice like this before. Deep and commanding, his accent thicker than molasses and just as sweet.

"You. Naked. Now."

"Are you sure?"

I blinked up at him.

"Of course, I'm sure," I whispered. His gaze blistered as it met mine, and his face was serious.

"We do this, and you're mine. That's it. Forever. Do you want that?"

I gulped and my heart exploded just a bit.

"I want all of you," I breathed.

"You wanna be mine?"

I nodded and his gaze darkened.

"Words, darlin'. Lemme hear the words."

"I want to be yours, Greg."

His answering smile was blindingly beautiful. He kissed me softly, full of promise, as he laid me back.

"Well, it's about goddamn time, Wilkson ," he teased.

My eyes flew to his, but before I could sass back he ripped my blouse open. Buttons flew to all corners of the room, and I had a brief thought of sympathy for my tailor before all coherent thought went away. He dragged my bra off my shoulders and down my breasts. I was so exposed and he was fully clothed. There was something so intoxicating about that.

He was tracing his way down my chest with his tongue, stopping every so often to bite softly. Then he took a nipple between his teeth and electricity ran through my entire body. My back arched off the bed and my eyes closed.

"So responsive," he moaned.

His lips closed around the other breast, and he repeated the process, switching back and forth. Each nibble sent a wave of pleasure straight to my core, and before long I was a writhing, mewling mess.

"Do you think you could come just from this?" he asked, bringing his face up to kiss me again. "Or do you need more, darlin'?"

"More, please."

I don't know where this beggar came from. Normally in bed, I was the one in total control. Greg didn't give me a chance to take it. He barely gave me a chance to breathe, let alone tell him what to do. But I didn't seem to need to tell him.

He listened to my body, to the sounds I made. It seemed to be his sole mission to make me moan as loudly and as frequently as possible.

As evidenced by him sliding my pants down, stopping halfway to place his nose between my legs and take a deep breath, moaning to himself.

"You smell so good, darlin'."

"Greg." My tone was sharp. Impatient.

"I'm movin' sweetheart, I promise," he chuckled, sliding my pants fully off my legs, and letting them drop to the floor.

He stood up and looked down at me.

I was spread out for him, my blouse pooled behind me. My lace bra had settled around my ribs, and the matching panties had been a good choice, clearly, as he drank in the sight of me, and I watched spots of pink appear on his cheeks.

I'd never felt so sexy. So desired. He looked at me like I was his entire world. Like he couldn't believe how lucky he was to be here with me.

Our eyes met and a small cry escaped me at the intensity of the connection.

"Greg," I moaned.

His eyes flashed and before I could blink his shirt was gone, his pants were on the ground, and his hands were back on me.

He lifted me and his deft fingers unhooked my bra. I let it slide off and fall to the floor as he moved down my body and grabbed my panties with his teeth, pulling them down my legs.

My shirt found its way off the bed, and his underwear joined it.

"Scoot up, darlin'," he commanded.

He cut a powerful figure, standing naked and erect at the end of my bed. I took a moment to drink him in.

He was lean, muscled. Surprisingly tan. And, my god. Mouthwatering was not a word that I was prone to using, especially in regard to a penis, but his stood glistening and pink, thick and hard, begging to be touched.

But Greg had given me a command, and as my eyes focused back on his face, he had one eyebrow raised. Waiting. I scrambled to obey. Who was this girl? This obedient person?

His gaze followed me as I moved and laid my head on the pillows.

I reached my arms up, desperate to feel him, and was rewarded with him covering my body with his. Sparks lit up my skin everywhere we touched. Instinctively my legs wrapped around his waist as he kissed me, and I started to rock against him.

Like lightning, he gripped my waist and grinned at me.

"Patience is a virtue, Justine."

"Patience can kiss my ass," I whined.

His hand drifted from my hip and his fingers ran through my center. He moaned at the slick heat he found there.

"God, you really are ready for me, aren't you?" His eyes were dark, and it was all I could do not to cry out as his fingers found my clit and pinched it.

"How do you want to come first, baby?"

All I managed was a deep moan in response to his teasing.

"Fingers or tongue, those are your options."

"Cock."

He laughed, drawing slow circles through my folds. He dropped his head to my chest and sucked a nipple before biting it softly.

I couldn't stop myself from arching off the bed.

"Fingers or tongue, Justine?"

"Fingers, please god."

"Never claimed to be God, darlin'," he growled.

I was rewarded for answering. Two fingers sank into my heat swiftly, curling. I felt myself floating as his fingers played me like a fiddle. Expertly. His other hand started rubbing my clit as he added a third finger. I was so keyed up and it took me less than a minute to feel my orgasm building.

He let his forearm rest across my hips, keeping steady pressure as his fingers pumped in and out of me, his thumb playing concertos.

Then he bit my thigh, and it sent me over the edge. Every muscle in my body tensed as I bowed off the bed. He never stopped, finger fucking me through the most intense orgasm of my life.

Before it was over, I heard a condom being unwrapped and then he was hovering over me.

188

"Tell me what you want, Justine," his voice was rough. I couldn't imagine the self-control it was taking him not to just sink into me.

"You, please, Greg," I moaned brokenly. "All of you. Now."

"Goddess," he whispered. It was so low I wasn't sure I was meant to have heard.

Before I could ponder it, he was thrusting.

I'd never been so filled before. My eyes flew open and got caught in his gaze. He sank into me, inch by inch, our eyes never leaving each other as we fully connected.

Something hot and strange welled in my chest, and I felt tears pricking the corners of my eyes.

"It's okay, darlin'," he whispered, tracing my cheek with a finger as he slid out and back in. "I've got you. It's okay."

He thrust into me again and again until we had a rhythm. A push and a pull. Inevitable. The tides and the moon.

He filled every part of my soul.

Our eyes couldn't seem to leave each other.

Nothing had ever felt like this. This intense. This close.

As my body built up to another orgasm, I tried to close my eyes, but Greg took my chin in his hand.

"No, no, darlin'," he murmured, kissing my lips gently without ever breaking his stroke. "Look at me when you come. Let me see all of you."

My eyes opened and he was right there. He was everywhere.

His paced picked up and my breath was coming in gasps.

My fingers gripped his arms, trying to ground myself, but I couldn't. I was floating above us, watching myself come undone for him. I was right there, he was too. I reached up and touched his face reverently.

"I love you."

He moaned and lost control. Pounding into me, flooding my senses. And that's all it took.

As my second orgasm ripped through me, I heard myself babbling. I had no idea what I was saying, but when I finally came back to myself, it was a litany of "I love you".

And he was saying it back. He pumped a few more times and then his entire body spasmed. His voice was deeper than I'd ever heard it, saying my name over and over like a prayer.

When he finally stopped trembling, he rolled onto his back, taking me with him without ever pulling out of me.

He settled me on top of him and found my lips.

I broke the kiss to rest my forehead on his chest.

"Justine, look at me," his voice was soft.

I lifted my head, and he kissed me gently. "You're mine now, darlin'."

I chuckled and shook my head.

"I always have been."

***

The clock next to my bed said it was two in the morning, but I wasn't tired. I was wrapped in Greg's arms, and we were talking.

About everything.

He told me about his family, growing up in the country, losing the farm. He told me how he'd never had any really close friends before Bell. How he'd been convinced for a long time that if people knew the real him then they wouldn't want to be his friend. But Bell had changed that. He'd seen all of Greg's quirks and stuck by his side through everything. He told me how it gave him the courage to believe that I could love all of him, as well. If one person could, so could another. He told me that his happy-go-lucky attitude had started out of self-preservation. A "fake it 'til you make it" sort of thing when he was depressed in high school. How eventually, and he wasn't even sure when, it had stuck. He loved seeing the good in things. Cracking jokes. Lightening the mood. It made him feel good.

He was so vulnerable. So honest with me.

So, I was finally honest with him.

I told him about my father. How he wanted me to be the very best, and how I felt that nothing I did was ever good enough for him. How I still loved him, despite the resentment I had towards him. How I had strived my entire life to make him proud of me. I told him about my mother, and how even though I knew she loved me, I knew she loved my father more. I told him about growing up on the outside of the social groups, always feeling alone and unlovable. How that made me so determined to build my own life where I didn't need anybody else to provide for me.

"Justine," Greg whispered into my hair. His fingers were intertwined with mine, and my head was resting on his shoulder.

"Greg," I said with a soft laugh.

"You never have to be alone again, Justine. I see you, I want you, and I love you. You're mine, forever."

A lump formed in my throat, and I felt something light and airy rising in my chest.

"I know you don't need me," he continued with a small laugh. "I love that you don't need me."

"Really?"

"Yes," he kissed my head gently. "It means that you chose me. And that means more to me than someone declarin' their undyin' need to be with me."

"I do choose you," I muttered, realizing how true the words were.

"I choose you, too, darlin'," he said sweetly.

I felt a wide smile crack my face, and then my eyes were drifting shut.

"I will always choose you."

Chapter Twenty-Four

Greg

Waking up next to Justine was the most magical moment of my good-for-nothin' life. She was breathtakin'ly gorgeous like this. Relaxed, no worries marring her features. Just…bliss.

We'd spent all night talkin'. Makin' love. I was never gonna get enough of her kisses. Of the way her eyes half closed whenever I told her what to do. Of watchin' that big brain of hers shut off, if only for a few moments. The thrill of her trustin' me enough to let herself fall apart was stronger than any Tennessee whiskey. It buzzed through my veins all night long, only makin' me love her more.

And I was. In love with her. I'd realized that I always had been. From the moment she'd pounded on my door freshman year. Those eyes and that blush that'd colored her cheeks. I was a goner.

And finally, *finally*, she was mine.

Nothin' was gonna take her from me now. Until my last breath, she was mine.

***

What I hadn't been countin' on was how sound a sleeper the girl was. I'm sure a tornado could've torn through and she wouldn't'a woken up.

There was only so long a guy could lay awake starin' at his girl before it bordered less on sweet and more toward creepy stalker. So, I finally roused myself and found my way to the kitchen.

Lookin' in the fridge, it was clear that Justine took care of herself. Fresh veggies, lean proteins, complex carbs. Hardly any junk food in sight, save a pint of Moose Tracks in the freezer.

I found some farm fresh eggs on the counter, some Canadian bacon in the fridge, and some strawberries, so I set about makin' breakfast.

Momma had always said that breakfast was the most important meal of the day. It set the tone for the rest of your choices, and she was a firm believer that, if you had a good breakfast, you'd make good choices.

I wanted Justine to be in a good choice makin' mood today. Really, I just wanted her to be in a good mood every damn day for the rest of her life. And, now that she was mine, that was my responsibility to make happen.

As the ham sizzled in the pan, I figured I had a few minutes and I should make myself useful and get the mail.

It was a beautiful morning out. The air still cool with just a hint of the humidity that was sure to set in once summer fully hit. There was a mist that had settled low on the ground, wettin' the grass. My feet hit the wet blades and I scrunched my nose.

Luckily, it was a short walk to the mailbox. She didn't have much mail, and I found myself whistlin' as I turned around.

My tune dropped out as soon as it started.

Scratched across Justine's front door was the word "homewrecker". Scratched doesn't quite do it justice. Gauged. That's better. Carved would also work. Sloppily. Angrily.

My heart rate picked up, adrenaline pumpin' through my veins as I quickly scanned the area. But I didn't see anythin' out of place. No random cars on the street, nobody lingerin' on the corner. As I searched, my eyes caught on a piece of paper stuck underneath my windshield. I carefully made my way to my truck and removed the scrap.

How could you?

Big, loopy handwritin'.

A shiver raced down my spine. I recognized the handwritin'; I just couldn't remember where from. It itched the back of my brain, like a locked memory that I desperately wanted to set free but couldn't for some reason.

I numbly made my way back inside.

"Greg!" Justine's sharp voice admonished me from the kitchen.

I went in and saw that she was standin' at the stove. She looked at me disapprovin'ly as I came in.

"You just left something cooking on the stove?" Her voice was incredulous. "Basic common-sense dictates not to do that. What's wrong with you?"

I blinked and took a deep breath before lookin' at her.

"Justine, somethin' weird is going on."

She took a moment to assess me. Her eyes roamin' up and down my body should have set my blood on fire. Instead, I was doused in ice.

Immediately, concern flitted across that beautiful face, and she came to me. Her hands came up to trace my cheekbones and, when I focused on her eyes, I saw worry there.

"What's going on, Gregory?"

Gregory. She called me that when she was tryin' to put some distance between us. I wasn't even sure she knew she did it, but I'd noticed. I tried not to flinch at what she would have thought if she'd been the one to see the note. Seen the vandalism to her front door.

"Justine, someone carved up your door and left a note on my car," I said softly.

Her brow furrowed in confusion and then her expression cleared.

"What did they say?" She was all business.

I swallowed, my nerves flarin', and led her to the front.

Her hands flew to her mouth and fear crossed her face. Then anger. Then resolve.

"And your note?" Her tone was firm, givin nothin' away.

I handed it to her and watched the myriad of emotions that made their way through her eyes.

Confusion. Recognition. Hurt. Betrayal. Finally, they landed on nothin'. Numbness.

"You know how this looks." Statement, not a question.

I nodded and waited for her to say somethin'.

"So, am I?"

"Are you?"

"A homewrecker." Her tone was icy.

My defenses rose, even though I knew it was the logical question.

Men were trash. Cheatin' on their women left and right all the while tellin' them they were the only ones for them. There was no good reason for Justine to think that I wasn't like every other man on the planet. I knew I wasn't, but she was still learnin' that. I shouldn't be defensive. She was completely in the right here. It still hurt that she could even entertain the thought.

I took her hands in mine, crushin' the note between our palms.

"There is no one else but you, Justine," I told her fervently, hopin' the truth of the statement came through every pore of my skin.

"I have no idea who did this, but we're gonna find out," I promised her.

Her eyes dropped to our hands, and she took a shaky breath. It took a few seconds, but I felt a hot tear drop onto my skin and knew she was more hurt than she'd been lettin' on. A soft, strangled cry left my lips and I pulled her into me.

"Justine, tell me what's goin' through that head of yours," I whispered into her hair. "We have to be honest with each other. No secrets."

She sniffled and pulled her head back, lookin' right into my soul, it seemed.

"It's giving me college flashbacks," she said in a voice so small I wouldn't have believed it came from her if I hadn't heard it myself.

"What do you mean?"

She huffed angrily and wiped her eyes.

"The entire last semester of school was shit like this," she growled. "Someone was sabotaging me, marking up my property. Generally making my life miserable. It was horrible, and it all culminated in me almost being late to my final and then those fucking posters. It was humiliating. Degrading. Horrible."

I still couldn't believe I'd missed all of that. But Justine and I weren't speakin' that last semester, and I'd finished my finals early and had headed home. I hadn't even seen the posters. The entire next year of school, no one had so much as mentioned them to me. Strange, in hindsight, considerin' everyone knew Justine and I used to be friendly. Even Bell hadn't said anything, though he'd since explained that he hadn't wanted to betray more than Justine had wanted me to know. Apparently, he'd helped her back to her apartment after she'd first seen them, and she was distraught. Bell had never seen her so out of control. And she'd blamed me for all of it. Thinkin' it was some stupid revenge plot.

"The entire semester?" I asked, somethin' spinnin' in my brain that I couldn't quite place my finger on.

She nodded.

"It started after our fight at that stupid party," she huffed. "I didn't connect the events at first, they were so random. But when I finally did, after everything, I figured it must be you. You were so mad at me that night." Her voice broke, and I suddenly felt like I was twenty-two years old again.

"I broke your heart, didn't I?" My whisper was rough, apologetic.

"I didn't put that together at the time either, but yes, you did. I knew I liked you then, but I didn't realize I loved you," she said softly.

My heart clenched and I had to close my eyes to keep myself from cryin'.

"I loved you then, too," I admitted. "And I love you now, Justine. There is no one else. It was always you."

She offered me a small smile and then hugged me tightly. When she pulled back, her expression was clearer, though her cheeks were still wet.

"So, what are we going to do about our stalker?" she said it half jokin', half terrified.

"We're gonna figure out who she is, and we're gonna make her stay so far away from us that it'll be like she never existed," I promised.

"She?"

I held up the crumpled note. "It's a girl's handwriting, darlin'. And I feel like I recognize it, I just don't know from where."

She nodded thoughtfully for a moment and then looked at me with fire in her eyes.

"We'll figure it out. Together."

Together. There was no better word in the English language. I laughed softly to myself and then pulled her in for a devouring kiss.

Thank God it was Saturday, because we got nothin' done after that.

***

I wanted Justine to be my wife.

I'd wanted that since college, but after comin' back together and fallin' in love with her all over again? Havin' her fall in love with me. It just felt right. I didn't want to waste any more time.

I wanted her to be my wife. My beautiful, intelligent, sexy, badass wife.

I'd talked to Bell about it, and he didn't think it would affect the business. He was happy for us. He was rootin' for us more than he'd let on. I think he had been since day one.

I wasn't sure when the right time would be to ask, and it definitely wasn't that weekend. While we were able to salvage the rest of the day, the vandalism hung like a cloud over everything we did.

I dropped Justine back at her car Monday mornin', much to her chagrin. She'd wanted to leave Sunday to go and get it, but I hadn't let her out of her bed for most of the day. If we were being honest, she hadn't fought that hard. But the bliss of Sunday disappeared when we reached the parkin' garage Monday and found all four of her tires slashed.

"Fuck," she growled as she stalked around her car one more time.

"Stupid bitch must've believed that myth that insurance won't cover four slashed tires," Justine mumbled, takin' pictures and gettin' her insurance card out.

"They will?"

"I have comprehensive insurance coverage," she sighed. "I have a two-hundred-dollar deductible, and these tires go for about one-fifty each. So yes, they will be covering the replacement of my tires."

"Well, that's good."

"Is it?" Her voice was acid.

"Better'n you havin' to pay outta pocket for them," I shrugged.

"She still *slashed* my *tires*, Gregory," she said angrily. "Clearly, whoever this psycho is, she's very attached to you. And she knows who I am, where I live, and what I drive."

I took a moment to take her in. She was vibratin', and her eyes were flashin'.

"You're scared," I said, a hint of wonder in my voice.

"Don't sound so surprised," she huffed.

I laughed softly and took her into my arms. She immediately melted into my chest, which made me feel like the most powerful man alive.

"I'm just not used to you bein' scared, that all. But I've got you, darlin'. Insurance will cover the tires," I said softly. "And I have a proposition for you, if you're up for it."

"Even sex with you couldn't help me out of the rabbit hole I'm falling down right now."

"Not what I meant, but good to know where your mind's at," I laughed.

She shook her head, and I couldn't help but kiss her. She arched into the kiss, drivin' my senses wild.

She always smelled like jasmine. Soft and floral. In complete contrast to the hard and cuttin' persona she put on.

"Come stay with me for a while," I proposed.

Not exactly the proposal I'd been hoping to drop on her, but it would move us towards that end regardless. Her body stilled in my arms, and I could feel her mind racin' through all the pros and cons of the request. I held her out so that I could look into her eyes.

"It's not too fast," was my first counter. "We've known each other for years; we've loved each other for years. Just because it took us a while to come together doesn't mean that the time before doesn't count."

"But –"

"I love you, Justine." That always shut her up. "You love me. Forgive me if I'm wrong, but modern couples in love tend to spend extended amounts of time at each other's residences." I was pullin' out my big boy vocabulary, tryin' to connect to her intellectual side. Because emotionally, I knew I had her. "And, as you've pointed out, someone potentially dangerous knows where you live and what you drive. Odds are she knows where you work. I won't take any chances with your safety."

Her response was slower this time. "But –"

"But nothin', darlin'," I laughed. "I'm not sayin' forever. Yet." I caught her eye and watched a blush light up her face. The caveman part of my brain beat his chest in victory as I filed that away for later. "Just tryin' it out for a week or so. Get you safe and see what happens."

She was quiet for a long moment, her eyes never leavin' mine.

Finally, she took a deep breath and let it out slowly.

"Fine," she said softly. "I'll stay with you."

My soul felt like it was soarin' as I leaned in and kissed her deeply. I dipped her back and tangled my fingers in the short hair at the nape of her neck, lettin' her feel all of the love that was pourin' out of me.

She said yes, and that was good enough for me.

I was gonna make sure it was the first yes of many to come.

Chapter Twenty-Five

Justine

Living with Greg felt like the most natural thing in the world. I had brought enough clothes for a few days at first. I didn't want him to get the wrong impression. I really wasn't planning on staying much longer than that.

I'd stay long enough for him to get tired of me and my neurosis, and then go back to the comfort of my own home. Long enough for him to see that this stalker, scary as she seemed to be, wasn't an actual threat. Just someone who fancied themselves in love with Gregory, and soon she'd grow tired of seeing him with me and give up.

But three days turned into a week. And a week turned into two.

We just…fit together.

I slept in while he cooked breakfast. He insisted on a hearty, protein-filled breakfast. He packed me the cutest little lunches, complete with a love note in each. We showered together, and I put on my makeup while he bombarded me with compliments. Every day I expected him to tire of waiting for me to apply exactly three layers of mascara. Instead, he found new ways to call me the most beautiful woman in the world. Every morning.

Then we went our separate ways with a sweet, sometimes not so chaste kiss. I'd reapply my lipstick, and pretend to be annoyed, but secretly I wouldn't have traded those goodbye kisses for anything. I spent all day waiting to come back together in the evenings.

I was usually home first, and each night when he came back Greg would drop his bag at the door, rush to wherever I was in the house, and sweep me up in a hug that was so full of love it felt like it could crush me.

I would cook dinner, something different every night, and he always looked amazed at the plate I put in front of him.

He thanked me. Really thanked me, from the bottom of his soul, for making him food. And I believed that he meant it. That he never expected me to cook for him and was grateful for each meal I prepared.

Gregory was, in a word, a gentleman.

The biggest change I noticed living together, though, was that he did *not* fuck like a gentleman.

He fucked me, made love to me, whatever phrase I chose to use that day, like he wanted to command my very soul.

And I loved it.

Greg was the only person in my entire life that could make me lose my mind. Quite literally. He made all thoughts disappear, and my body took over all decisions.

This wasn't something that had ever happened to me. I was usually so in my head with sex that I was unable to come. I'd resigned myself to the fact that my orgasms would be brought about by myself and myself alone. I hadn't ever imagined that I'd find a man that knew how to play my body like a finely tuned piano.

Greg gave me something that no other man in my life had ever been able to. Safety. I didn't have to be in control with him because he knew what he was doing. Always. He promised that he was going to make me feel good. That he was going to take care of me. And he always kept his promises.

Yet, his control never felt domineering. It was never suffocating, only comforting.

I knew that I loved him before we lived together, but sharing space and time and affection only proved to me that the love I felt for him was deep. Real. Raw.

It was exhilarating. And terrifying.

That fear was coupled with the fact that every few days another note appeared, and at least twice a week something happened to make my life harder.

After the slashed tires it was a broken mailbox. And when our stalker learned that I wasn't staying in my own home, the vandalism escalated. A smashed window at the brewery, dog poop smeared on Greg's front stoop.

A few weeks after I first started staying with him, Gregory came home and was seething with rage from every pore of his body. I'd worked from the house that day to try to focus on invoicing, so I was lounging comfortably at the kitchen table when I heard the front door slam.

Greg stalked into the room and my initial excitement quickly turned to adrenaline as I read his body language.

Shoulders stiff, eyes flashing, nostrils flared. His hands clenched and unclenched as he headed straight to the liquor cabinet without so much as looking at me.

No hug today then.

He poured himself a shot of something and downed it. Then another. Not good.

"Greg?" my voice was soft.

I'd never seen him truly angry before. When I was attacked, he made a huge effort to be calm for me, so I hadn't seen it then.

But this was anger. Unfiltered.

He turned sharply, his gaze finding my face. I blinked at the blind fury I saw in his normally jovial green eyes. They were clouded and dark. It reminded me of hiking in a forest and the trees getting thicker, until you weren't sure if you were lost or not.

I must have let out a small sound when he turned his eyes on me, because recognition flashed across his face, and he immediately froze.

"Justine, I'm so sorry, darlin'," he mumbled, squeezing his eyes shut and running his hand across the back of his neck.

He didn't make a move toward me, and his body was still tense. So, I walked to him, my footsteps soft so that I didn't startle him.

He didn't raise his head as I approached. He didn't move as I tucked my arms under his, wrapping them around his chest and leaning my head on his shoulder. Then, I simply held him. I tried to let him know through my touch that he could give it to me. Give all his anger and frustration to me and I would happily take it for him.

He was still for a long time, but slowly he relaxed in my arms just like I knew he would. One hand came up and nestled itself in my hair while the other gripped my waist tightly, pulling me somehow closer to him.

He turned his head and inhaled along my hairline, sending shivers through my body.

I pulled back to look at him.

"Take what you need from me, Gregory," I whispered.

I saw the moment the last of his control snapped. His eyes flashed and pink colored his cheeks.

The hand in my hair tightened, pulling my head back as he lowered his mouth to the spot where my neck met my shoulder and placed a gentle kiss there. That was all the warning I had before he bit down, causing me to arch against him and moan, my eyes falling shut.

He pulled away from me, keeping his hand in my hair and tugging just a bit harder.

"Don't you make another sound, Justine." His voice was dark.

"Greg –"

"I come undone with your pretty noises, darlin'," he muttered, letting his tongue trace across my collarbone. I had never been more grateful for the summer heat giving me an excuse to wear a thin-strapped cami and shorts all day.

"I want to take my time with you today, and if you keep makin' noise then this will all be over far too quickly for my likin'," he said. "So, no sounds. Understood?"

I nodded but didn't say a word. Which earned me an excited growl from the man holding me.

"That's my girl," he whispered.

Then, his lips were on mine. Devouring me.

It wasn't a gentle kiss. It was rough, needy. His anger flowed between us like a current, charging every touch of our bodies.

He flipped us around so that my back was against the counter. Then, he was sinking to his knees, ripping my shorts down as he went. He helped me step out of them, and then he was right there. He shoved his face in between my thighs, spreading my legs as his hands steadied my hips.

He didn't even give me a chance to take a breath before his tongue was on me. Lapping and licking me roughly, each pass coiling in my stomach. His teeth found my clit and bit down, ever so softly. I gasped and bucked into him, but he disappeared.

I looked down and saw him watching me disapprovingly.

My eyes widened and I mouthed sorry, then mimed zipping my lips.

"One more sound and you won't get to come, darlin'," he promised.

His mouth was back, making my eyes that had widened in disbelief at his threat snap shut.

While his lips were nipping and pulling at the sensitive bud, a hand disappeared from my hip and then two fingers plunged into me as he kept rolling his tongue over me.

He found the perfect pace that set my skin on fire and locked my lungs. I needed to breathe. But the way his fingers were sliding in and out of me and his tongue never relented its pressure stole the air from my body. My blood was on fire, and I wanted so badly to whimper and moan.

But I was being good for him. The logical part of my brain tried raising her hand to point out that if I came like this, I would most likely collapse on top of him and that we should probably move. But she was quickly shut down when his teeth scraped over my clit as his fingers crooked against that spot inside of me.

I slapped my hands over my mouth to keep the sound from coming out and he hummed his approval.

The slight vibration and knowing that I'd pleased him were all it took, and I fell over the edge. Heat unfurled from my stomach, racing through my body until I was shaking, and my legs trembled.

While I was still coming down, I felt him stand and scoop me into his arms, carrying me to the bedroom.

He threw me onto the bed and when I opened my eyes, he was staring at me with pure adoration.

He quickly stripped himself of his clothes and rolled on a condom while I managed to get my top off and then he was pressing himself against me.

The skin-on-skin contact was intoxicating. I loved the way that Greg smelled. Somehow earthy and tangy and sweet all at once. He traced my face as I wrapped my legs around his waist and rolled my hips, earning me a small, breathless laugh from the man above me.

"You can make noise now, baby," he crooned.

He kissed me softly as he lined himself up and sank into me fully in one stroke. He filled me so perfectly that I couldn't help the cry that worked its way out of my throat.

"I want you screamin' my name, Justine." He emphasized his point with a sharp snap of his hips.

"Yes, Gregory."

"No, not Gregory," he grunted. "Greg. To you, I am always Greg from now on, you hear me?"

I looked at him and saw that he was deadly serious.

"Yes, Greg," I whispered, his name ending on a moan as he set a vicious pace.

He kissed me swiftly and then brought himself up to his knees, taking me with him as he pounded into me.

His thumb found my clit and he circled it purposefully, watching me the entire time.

"I want you to fall apart on my cock, baby," he moaned. "Fall apart for me, Justine."

"Yes, Greg!"

"That's it, darlin'," he praised, the affirmation like champagne bubbles in my veins.

In no time at all, it felt like, I was bucking against him, the most wanton noises coming from me as he talked me through my second orgasm.

Then his lips were crashing into mine and I swallowed his moans as he pumped once, twice and then stilled. His entire body tensed, and he dropped his head to my neck, his teeth biting down hard but not enough to draw blood.

In my head I knew that I'd have matching bruises on either side of my neck the next day, but as I wrapped myself around Greg fully, I found I didn't care.

He'd come home angry and had found release in my arms.

That's what we needed to be for each other. A safe space where we knew we could get exactly what we needed from each other. And that it would all come from a place of love.

Sighing, Greg rolled onto his back, taking me with him so that I was straddled on top of him with him still inside me.

I laughed softly and went to remove myself, but he gripped me against him roughly.

"Stay," he whispered. "Just for a minute."

My brow furrowed in concern, and I traced his face lightly with one hand, marveling at the way my touch relaxed his features.

"I'll stay for however long you want me to," I promised, settling into his arms.

"Careful darlin', or I might just say forever."

I didn't say anything, but my silly heart thought maybe forever didn't sound so bad.

***

"She emptied all of my tanks," Greg admitted finally.

After a while of just holding each other, we'd gotten up and showered and I'd come out to make dinner.

Greg hadn't followed me, and I'd wanted to give him his space. As I was plating, he'd wandered out and stood behind me. He'd wrapped his arms around me and let me continue working, only letting go once everything was ready and we went to sit at the table to eat.

Now, we were watching each other, salmon going untouched. He was finally telling me why he had come home so angry.

"Your tanks?" I asked.

He looked at me pointedly until it clicked.

"She *emptied* all of your tanks?" I asked incredulously. "How is that even possible? How did she get into the warehouse?"

"We don't know," he sighed. "We have a security system installed, and when we filed the police report they looked through the security footage and said that there was nothin' weird on the cameras."

"And you're sure it was her? Our stalker?"

"Yes. I found a pint glass with a bit of beer in the bottom, a lipstick stain on the rim, and a note. The tanks were all open and leakin' onto the floor. It looked like they'd been open since yesterday afternoon, at least."

"What did she write this time?"

"*I have some notes.*"

I'd never heard Greg sound so acidic, and I watched him for a moment. My brain was firing at a thousand miles a minute because something about this note was tickling my memory.

The mocking was bad enough, but to have all of his hard work over the last few months literally down the drain was heartbreaking.

Greg took his brewing very seriously. Sometimes, more seriously than anything else. So, of course, I understood why he'd been so upset when he'd gotten home. I'd tried to guess what had made him so angry, but I never would have guessed that our stalker would go to this level of sabotage simply because we were dating.

It, again, felt just like college. The stalker was targeting things she knew were important to us. Trying to break us up. And the attacks weren't just at me anymore. She had gone after Greg's livelihood. His pride and joy. It would take months to brew a new batch, pushing the opening out further than we would have liked.

This was calculated. Diabolical.

In complete contrast with the bubbly, loopy script on the notes. We'd turned each one in to the police, but they hadn't been able to match it with anything in their system. That didn't surprise me.

If this woman had been stalking Greg for years, she would know how to be an invisible presence in his life. Someone unassuming. Who could blend into the background, not draw attention to herself.

Stalkers could be literally anyone, but I had a feeling this was someone Greg knew. Who knew how important brewing was to him. Someone who felt like they had a deep, personal connection to him somehow.

He wasn't a celebrity; his information and life weren't public knowledge. So, it had to be someone he knew. Someone he'd met years ago.

My eyes grew wide as the pieces suddenly fell into place.

"Justine, you okay?"

"Kelly Dimas," my voice was hushed, like it was afraid to speak the name any louder in case she heard us.

"Did you just say Kelly Dimas?" Greg was skeptical until he thought about it for a moment and dropped his fork.

"Holy shit, Justine, you're right," he exclaimed. "That's why I recognized the handwritin'! I borrowed her notes a ton in the last year of college, and it was the same handwritin'."

"She was completely enamored with you in school," I remembered.

"We never dated or anythin', we were just friends," Greg sounded defensive.

"With stalkers it doesn't matter what type of actual relationship you had with them," I said softly. "To them, the only relationship that exists is the one inside their head."

We were silent for a moment and then Greg's eyes shot to mine.

"How much do you wanna bet that it was Kelly who sabotaged you durin' your last semester at school?"

My mouth fell open and then clicked shut as I realized he was probably right.

"Think about it," he went on, "Your sabotage started after we had our fight at the frat party, right?"

When I nodded, Greg stood up and began pacing.

"I'd been flirtin' with Kelly a bit that night, but then I left to follow you out and we got into it on the front lawn. Anyone could've been watchin' us. Then all the next semester someone tried to make your life a livin' hell. Probably because they thought you broke my heart that night. And now, years later, when we're finally together, the sabotage starts back up again."

"I just can't believe that Kelly would hold onto this obsession with you for this long," I said incredulously.

He sighed and closed his eyes tightly, as if trying to remember something.

"Oh god," he moaned.

"What?"

"She told me," he muttered, his eyes opening and finding mine again. "Like, our second year? The day you told off Ruthers. I had been complainin' to Bell in class about it and not takin' any notes, and that was the first time Kelly offered me hers."

"I knew you not paying attention in class would get us killed someday," I sighed.

"Don't be dramatic," he waved a hand. "Anyway, we got lunch, and she told me that she could get a little obsessive."

Silence settled between us as we just stared at each other.

Then, out of nowhere, I started to laugh. It was just a giggle at first, but then ballooned into side clenching, full-blown laughter.

I couldn't stop it.

There was something just so absolutely ridiculous about the concept of waifish wallflower Kelly Dimas being responsible for some of the most horrible moments of my adult life.

Greg looked at me with concern for a moment before he too was doubled over with laughter.

God, I loved his laugh. Even through my own fit I could hear the smooth, rich tone of his laugh and it soothed me.

It also spurred me on, more giggles pealing out of me without my control until I collapsed on the floor, crying and sucking in oxygen like it might save my brain. When, clearly, that was a lost cause.

Greg and I ended up on our backs on the dining room floor, our heads next to each other, staring up at the ceiling as the laughter died down.

It was eerily quiet in the wake of it.

Without looking at me, Greg said, "It's gonna be a hard sell to the police."

"I know."

"So, how to we prove it?"

"That, I don't know."

More silence.

Then, his hand was reaching into my field of vision and turning my chin to face him. Our eyes met and I knew.

We'd figure it out.

Together.

Chapter Twenty-Six

Greg

"Kelly Dimas?" Bell sounded skeptical.

It wasn't surprisin'. The more I thought about it, the more ridiculous it sounded.

From what I remembered, Kelly Dimas was just a sweet, unassumin' girl with a big heart and kind eyes.

I knew she'd had a crush on me in college. Justine had even pointed it out at one point. But, other than one night of a little harmless flirtin', I'd thought I'd made it clear that I wasn't into her that way.

Clearly, I was wronger than wrong on that count.

"Kelly Dimas," Bell sighed, taking a long swig of his beer.

We were sittin' in our favorite bar waitin' for trivia to start. It was Justine's first time joinin' us, and my eyes kept flashin' to the door waitin' to see her walk in.

Watchin' her enter a room was one of my favorite things to do. I could picture it. Her eyes would scan the space, takin' everyone in. Her shoulders would square, like she was gettin' ready for battle. Her jaw would tense, just a bit. If you didn't know to look for it, you'd never know because she'd paint a picture of perfect relaxation. But she'd be on edge. And then her eyes would find me, and (this was my favorite part) all of that tension would melt. I wasn't sure if she was like that with other people, but I loved that she was able to be at ease with me. To let her guard down and just be herself. Enjoy her time. I couldn't wait to see that moment tonight.

As my eyes were trained on the door, I saw it all happen. It was like time slowed down.

Headlights flashin' past the window.

A horn blarin'.

Tires screechin'.

Metal tearin' and twistin'.

Deafenin' silence.

Everyone in the bar was tryin' to process what we'd just seen.

My stomach dropped out of my body, and I just knew.

Justine.

My feet were out the door and down the sidewalk, even as Bell grabbed at my shirt to try to slow me down.

The fabric tore as I saw her car wrapped around a light post.

Mangled.

My brain went numb, but my body was still movin'. I ran full speed to the driver's side door.

As I came near the street corner, I saw a flash of yellow hair disappearin'.

Kelly. I was sure.

But gettin' to Justine was top priority.

The window was blown out, the airbag had deployed.

Justine wasn't movin'.

A strangled cry crawled its way out of my throat, and I wrenched the door open. The bent metal was nothin' for the adrenaline that was coursin' through me.

"Justine." My voice didn't sound like my own. "Justine, you've gotta wake up."

My hands fluttered around her face, searchin' for injuries. She was bleedin' from a cut on her forehead, but otherwise seemed okay. I knew that she could have internal injuries. I didn't want to move her without paramedics here. My hands flapped uselessly over her body, not sure what to do with the electricity snappin' through them.

A strong hand gripped my shoulder, and I twisted towards whoever it was with a snarl. I wasn't leavin' her.

Bell's alarmed face was starin' at me.

"Just me, bud." I was grateful for how calm he sounded. "We've gotta get her out, there's gas leaking."

Ice raced down my spine and somehow all the panic that was threatenin' to overwhelm me was set aside. It raged against the walls that had just come down around it, but the need to make sure Justine was safe was foot thick steel. Nothin' else mattered.

"Gimme your knife," I said, holdin' out my hand.

As I knew he would, Bell drew a Swiss Army knife from his back pocket.

I flipped it open and turned to begin sawin' at the seatbelt.

It looked like the passenger side of the car was where most of the damage was, so once the seatbelt was off, I was able to grab Justine's legs and swing them out.

Bell took them gently as I lifted her beneath her arms. We moved her a safe distance away from the car and were layin' her on the ground just as the paramedics pulled up.

"What happened?" one of them asked as he pulled his equipment out to start takin' her vitals.

"She crashed into the light." My voice was tight. "I bet if you check her brake line, it'll be cut."

The paramedic gave me a sharp look but then focused right back on Justine.

"Ma'am, can you hear me?" He tapped her cheek lightly, but she didn't move.

"I think she hit her head pretty hard." The lump in my throat was hard to talk around.

The street was fillin' with lights and sirens and uniforms, but I couldn't take my eyes off my girl.

She looked so fragile. I'd never seen her like this. The panic reared back up, but Bell's hand on my shoulder grounded me.

Steel.

"I can give you her information," I said thickly.

"Great," the paramedic nodded. His hands moved deftly over her body, and then he placed a neck brace on her as he and his partner loaded her onto a gurney.

"Come with us so we can get her info on the drive," he said.

They wheeled her quickly to the ambulance and loaded her. I had barely jumped in the back before they were movin'.

Right before the doors closed, I caught Bell's eye and the look on his face told me everythin' I needed to know. He'd make sure the police knew this was no accident and that they launched an investigation. My job was to focus on Justine. I swallowed around the knives in my stomach and held her hand gently as we raced away.

***

I hated hospitals.

We were in the same one I'd taken Justine to when she'd gotten the nail in her hand. But everythin' was different this time.

I wasn't at ease. There was no flirty banter. Nothin' to distract me from the fact that they'd taken the love of my life back over two hours ago and still hadn't come out to give me an update.

I was pacin' the waitin' room, probably drivin' the nurses crazy. The panic that I'd been successfully shovin' away was chippin' at the walls and starting to pour out. It was a wild animal clawin' at my insides, growlin' and roaring. It wanted blood. It wanted revenge.

I couldn't even contemplate what would happen if Justine wasn't okay.

The police had come to take my statement, and I'd told them about the stalkin'. How we thought we knew who it was. How I'd seen someone blonde runnin' from the crash. I gave them the latest note that I'd been keepin' in my wallet. I told them we'd filed reports, but no one had been able to do anythin'. And now Justine was hurt.

I was livid. There was no trace of jovial, buddy-buddy Greg in that hospital. Instead, a ragin' bull seein' red was tearin' into the cops until they assured me they would launch a full investigation into what happened, and they'd bring in Kelly for questionin'.

Even that hadn't felt like enough.

My mind kept racin' in circles. I couldn't figure out why Kelly had decided to become obsessed with *me*.

It's not like we were close friends in college. I'd talked to her over social media maybe a handful of times since then. I hadn't even known she was in the state, let alone Hartworth. I started to think back over the years since I'd graduated, and little things that had never made sense before started to fall into place. I'd always received an anonymous card on my birthday. None of my relationships had lasted longer than six months. I'd thought that was because I was still hung up on Justine, but now I couldn't help but wonder if Kelly had scared them off. If she'd started to sabotage them, or if she'd insinuated that I was a cheater like she had to Justine. If I hadn't been with her, Justine probably would've believed that I was, and we wouldn't be here right now. But the few other

218

women that I'd dated over the years had all, at some point or another, said it wasn't workin' anymore and broken up with me. Was that Kelly?

And why hadn't she just come forward and told me how she felt? I would've let her down easy, and then maybe we could have avoided all of this.

None of it made sense in my head. I paced the waitin' room, trying to make sense of somethin' that I might never logic out. But what I really couldn't wrap my mind around, the thing that kept fresh waves of agony and rage washing over me, was that now, because of me, Justine was hurt. Possibly beyond repair.

She didn't deserve that.

I'd thought I could protect her, keep her safe from this stalker. They were just notes. Some vandalism. Though, after she'd trashed the brewery and emptied all my stills, I could tell she was gettin' more serious. But I never would have thought that she would try to kill Justine.

Because that's what this was. Attempted murder.

There was no way to sugarcoat it. No way to spin it. Kelly Dimas had cut the brake lines and tried to kill my girl. And there was no way I could let that stand.

"Mr. Hudson." A man in a white coat was walkin' towards me, interruptin' my tailspin.

"How is she?" The words tumbled out in a rush.

The doc placed a firm hand gently on my arm and held my gaze. It steadied me and I took a breath.

"It was touch and go for a bit there," he admitted. "She had some small lacerations in her abdominal cavity that we had to go in and fix. And she has a serious concussion from the air bag deployment. Luckily, no broken bones or punctured organs. We have her sedated, and you'll be able to come back to see her in a little bit."

"I want to see her now."

"I understand, sir," the doctor said patiently. "But really the best thing for her now is rest."

"Then she can rest," I growled. "But I'm gonna see her. Now."

The doc took a moment to observe me, and I watched his shoulders droop in defeat.

"We're moving her into a recovery room," he finally sighed. "I'll have a nurse come get you in about ten minutes once we've settled her in. And I'll let them know at the nurse's station that you are allowed to be with her at all times, regardless of visiting hours."

A bit of the tension drained from my back, and I nodded solemnly.

"Thank you, doc," I muttered. "I'll behave myself, I promise. I just need to be with her when she wakes up."

His eyes were kind when he patted my shoulder. "I understand, son. Ten minutes, okay?"

"Yes, sir."

***

The room was dim when they led me back to see her. Just the lamp in the corner was on.

It cast awful shadows across Justine's face, deepenin' the bruisin' and makin' her skin look sickly yellow.

When I stopped in the doorway from the sheer shock of seeing her like that, the nurse turned and squeezed my hand.

"She'll be okay," she said softly, her voice a whisper. As if she could wake Justine with all the drugs they'd given her.

"She looks…"

"She looks like she was in a car accident." Came the firm yet kind reply. "Because she was. Don't shy away from the reality of the situation, Mr. Hudson. She's very lucky to be alive."

I nodded but couldn't speak. My throat was closed.

I made my way over to the visitor's chair while Nurse Heather checked on Justine's vitals.

I couldn't take my eyes off her.

Her face was swollen and wrapped where she'd been cut on her head. There were bandages up and down her arms from where the windshield glass had nicked her. Her cheeks looked sunken, and her breathin' was so shallow. Up close, her skin wasn't yellow but pale. Drained of color and vibrance. Her delicate hands were covered in bruises and tubes. I wanted to reach out and hold her, but was afraid that if I did, she'd disintegrate and blow away.

"Press this button right here if you need anything or if she wakes up, alright?"

I nodded once, still not lookin' away from Justine's face.

I felt Nurse Heather watchin' me for a long moment before she left the room, shutting' the door softly behind her.

This was all my fault.

Justine was lucky to be alive, but she wouldn't have had to be lucky if she wasn't with me. If we weren't so stupidly, happily in love that some psychopath who'd been obsessed with me since college had gone into a jealous rage and tried to kill her.

If I was a better man, I would do the right thing.

So, what's the right thing? The voice in my head whispered savagely.

I shook my head as hot tears streaked down my face. When had I started cryin'? Probably the minute the door had shut, and it was just us in the room.

What's the right thing here, Greg?

I couldn't say it. I couldn't even think it.

It would kill me. I genuinely wouldn't be able to survive.

But she would survive.

I stilled and blinked slowly as I watched one of my tears land on Justine's hand.

If I did the right thing, she would survive. She was strong. She didn't need me. Her life would go on if I wasn't in it.

The right thing.

It doesn't have to be forever.

That was true, too.

I could do the right thing, keep Justine safe. Just until I had resolved the Kelly Dimas problem.

I would break Justine's heart and then come crawlin' back like the vermin I was and hope she'd still want me.

But she'd be safe.

She would be safe.

Chapter Twenty-Seven

Justine

For a moment I was sure I'd died.

The world was too still. Too dark. I was floating.

Then, I fell. Pain came crashing through my body.

This couldn't be death. Death was supposed to be peaceful, if it was anything. If we didn't just disintegrate back into dirt, then it was at least supposed to be free of pain and suffering. Wasn't that what people said?

But this. This was soul tearing. Reality-shattering.

Every single part of my body was simultaneously on fire and caged in ice.

I registered light in front of my closed eyes, and it took a monumental effort to open them.

I blinked a few times against the harsh fluorescents that flickered above my prone body. My limbs were heavy. There was beeping coming somewhere from my left and it was piercing my ears.

My eyes couldn't seem to focus. Everything was blurry.

When the room finally became clear, it was Bell who was sitting in the chair next to my bed. His head was in his hands, and he looked in pain. But that couldn't be right.

I was in pain.

I needed Greg.

"Greg," I managed to mumble.

Bell's head shot up and his eyes were tinged red. Like he'd been crying. Bell didn't cry.

"Justine." His voice was hoarse, like he hadn't used it in a while. "You're awake, thank God."

"Greg." My throat burned as my eyes strained to see if he was somewhere else in the room.

"He's…"

My eyes cut back to Bell, staring at him with a burning intensity. Adrenaline flooded my system. Was he hurt? Had that deranged woman decided that taking me out wasn't enough? That she needed to get rid of Greg too?

"Bell, where's Greg?" My voice was stronger. Demanding. Panicked.

The giant man next to my bed seemed so small when he sighed and took my hand gently.

"He's not here, Justine," Bell said softly.

"Why?"

"He's…he left."

I blinked, my drug addled brain struggling to process the words. Left?

"What does that mean?"

Bell took a deep breath and looked like he was regretting every single choice that led him to be in that room at that moment.

"He left Hartworth. Just for a bit, to draw Kelly away from you. You've gotta understand, Justine. He wants you to be safe, and for some reason, in his head, you're safer away from him."

No.

A different kind of pain was swelling in my chest. It was throbbing. Every beat of my heart sent pulses of cement through my blood.

He'd left?

Good intentions or not, Gregory had left me alone in the hospital. Well, with Bell, but still. He knew I didn't have anybody else. He knew he was everything to me. I loved him.

And he'd left.

He'd run away.

Ironic, since it was Greg who had first accused me of always running away from my problems.

"Justine, you need to breathe." Bell's voice was urgent.

I looked at him and saw concern etched onto his face. I registered the accelerated beating of the heart rate monitor attached to me. I was panicking. My heart was racing.

"Breathe, please," Bell pleaded, resting a giant hand on my arm.

I tried to follow his instructions but found that I could only manage short and shallow gulps of air.

I was alone.

I was always going to be alone.

This pain was worse than anything my body was physically feeling.

My vision was going dark around the edges, and every breath sent knives through my lungs and stomach. An ice pick was jamming into my skull, over and over.

He'd left.

I was alone.

Bell must have called the nurse, because suddenly a warm hand was resting on my back and a woman's voice was floating through the air.

She must've given me something, because my veins burned for a moment before my limbs went heavy.

She lowered me back against the pillows. I hadn't even realized I was sitting up.

My eyes searched frantically for Bell.

"I don't want to be alone," I cried.

I saw a single tear streaking down his cheek before my eyelids were too heavy to hold open anymore.

"I won't leave you, I promise." Bell's voice echoed in my head. "And Greg will come back. He'll come back when you're safe. He's gonna keep you safe, Justine."

How could he keep me safe if he wasn't with me?

An image of Greg's smiling face floated behind my eyes as the darkness took over.

***

I was in the hospital for three days while the doctors monitored my internal sutures. They wanted to make sure nothing was going to split open and send me into septic shock. Apparently, it was a horrible way to die. Didn't they know that with Greg gone I was already dead?

The police came to take my statement. They'd done a thorough investigation of my car and had found that the brake line had been cut clean through. Intent for bodily harm and death. I was lucky to be alive. I was lucky I didn't hit anybody. I was lucky that the passenger side took the brunt of the damage. I was lucky Greg and Bell were there to pull me out.

Everyone kept telling me how goddamned lucky I was.

I wanted to strangle them all. I wanted them to stop saying that, because how could I be lucky when the love of my life had left me.

226

Once the morphine had started to wear off, reality had settled in. I was alone.

He had promised. He had told me, point blank.

"You never have to be alone again, Justine. I see you, I want you, and I love you. You're mine, forever."

Icicles grew in my heart the longer I went without hearing from him. Every day I asked Bell where he'd gone, and every day he told me he couldn't say. That he'd promised Greg he wouldn't tell me. For my own safety.

To his credit, Bell visited as much as he could. And when they released me, he insisted on staying at my house to help me. I tried not to make it difficult for him, but his presence was wrong. He was too big. He took up too much space. He didn't feel like lazy Sunday mornings full of warmth and comfort.

In my anger and my hurt, I'm afraid I was unbearably mean to Bell. Snappish and barb tongued. Ungrateful. But he stayed. He made sure I took my meds and sat with me in the evenings after he got off work. We read together. He didn't speak much, but I wasn't exactly a great conversationalist at that time.

And I was happy, however begrudgingly, to have someone there, because recovering from internal injuries was no laughing matter.

The first week home I could barely move. Sitting up was excruciating, and I couldn't really shower because of the stitches. I had to go to the hospital every other day so they could check on my wounds and make sure nothing ruptured. I wasn't allowed to eat solid foods, so I was sipping bone broth and protein shakes all day.

I couldn't sleep more than a few hours because of the pain, and no matter how many pills I took there was always a dull throb in my stomach.

The second week, I started to get some of my strength back as the concussion began to fade and my wounds healed.

That's when the anger and resentment really started to build. I couldn't believe that Greg had just left. And he did it without a note. Without waiting for me to wake up. Was it really so easy for him to remove me from his life? To cut all contact?

We were in love. We were supposed to face our challenges together. Didn't he care that I could be in just as much danger with him gone? What if Kelly decided that she wanted to remove me from the equation for good this time? That she was done sending warnings? That she wanted Greg all to herself, and would stop at nothing to make sure I wasn't standing in the way anymore?

It was foolish of him to believe that running away from me would remove me from danger. It was putting himself in danger, too.

Kelly had been a part of the periphery of Greg's life for years. He'd never noticed her. What made him think that he'd recognize her if she showed up wherever he was? He wouldn't. Until it was too late.

Maybe she would decide that if she couldn't have him, then nobody could, and she would kill him.

At this point, nothing was beyond consideration.

So, I started planning.

I knew that we would have to catch Kelly ourselves. Lure her out, somehow. It would have to be something big. Something that would destroy her and push her to take drastic action.

I knew the perfect scenario, but it wouldn't work without Greg. And the police. But we couldn't let Kelly see us collaborating with the police. Everything would have to be completely covert.

In fact, Kelly couldn't know that we were planning anything at all. She needed to believe that she'd driven Greg away from me, so that when we finally came back together to enact the plan it would force her hand.

I had the card for the detective who was investigating the stalking and the accident, and I called her, letting her know what I was thinking and that I wanted to coordinate with the department to bring Kelly to justice without anybody else getting hurt.

Detective Harold was kind, but no nonsense, which I appreciated. She was completely on board, offering advice and recommendations. She didn't want to put anyone in danger, but she agreed that the escalation of events was concerning. Eventually, innocent bystanders were going to be hurt by Kelly's actions. Neither of us wanted that to happen.

So, we planned. By the middle of the third week, everything was set. I just needed to find Greg.

"Bell," I said, calling his attention up from the book he was reading.

"Yeah?"

"I need you to tell me where Greg is."

He sighed and put his book down. "I promised him I wouldn't."

"And he promised me he would never leave me alone," I said acidly. "Promises are easily broken."

A heavy silence hung between us. That was the thing about Bell. He never spoke just to fill a silence. He'd let it sit until the truth of the matter came out.

"We need to end this, Bell," I said softly. "Don't you want him home?"

"Of course, I do."

"He's being ridiculous, you know that. You've known that since he left. He's putting himself and us in danger. But I've got a plan to end this whole thing, and he has to come home for it. I need to bring him home."

Bell was quiet as he looked at me. He seemed to be weighing options in his head.

Finally, he let out a long-suffering sigh and rolled his eyes.

"The boy is being an idiot," he mumbled, pulling out his phone. He tapped on the keys, and a moment later my phone dinged. "He's at his parents' in Alabama. There's the address. Let's figure out how to get you out there without rousin' Kelly's suspicion."

He was home. He'd run away from me and gone home to his parents. Maybe leaving wasn't as easy for him as he'd made it seem.

Chapter Twenty-Eight

Greg

Momma's cookin' never failed to wake me up. There was somethin' so nostalgic about the smell of pan-fried bacon and blueberry waffles, that for a second, I thought I was sixteen again.

I opened my eyes and took in my childhood bedroom.

Crimson flags everywhere, posters of cars and tractors. My prized collection of baseball caps hung on the wall, the most cared for part of the room.

I sighed and ran my hand over my face as the guilt settled back in for the day.

I'd left her.

I told myself it was for her safety. I was who Kelly was obsessed with. She'd follow me and leave Justine alone.

Bell had been callin' with updates. He was stayin' with her, helpin' her recover. He said she was stubborn as all hell and didn't take well to being taken care of. That didn't surprise me. But it made me wonder if she would've let me take care of her. Nurse her back to health. If she would've been able to let her guard down with me enough to be that vulnerable. I think she would have.

I'd been investigatin' Kelly on my own the last few weeks. Tryin' to figure out how she'd been stalkin' me and, more importantly, why.

I'd called ex-girlfriends and finally been able to pry out of each of them that they'd received similar letters to the first one Justine had gotten. Callin' them homewreckers and claimin' I was in a serious relationship, and they were the "other woman". They all said they'd been pissed, and found it hard to believe, but they'd been more than a bit scared that my supposed girlfriend knew where they lived and worked. So, they'd just called it off, decided I wasn't worth the trouble.

But then there was Justine. Who had stuck it out. Who had stayed with me. Fallen in love with me.

That must have made Kelly royally mad, so she'd escalated. And when that still didn't drive Justine off, she must've realized that nothin' was gonna break us apart. So, she'd decided to take out her competition.

All of this was theory, of course, but I was gettin' close to findin' her. Hartworth PD had called me and taken another statement over the phone. I'd told them everythin' that had been goin' on, and they'd promised me they would do drive-bys of Justine's home and try to locate Kelly.

Fat chance of findin' her, given she'd done a swell job of hidin' in plain sight all these years.

I had to draw her out. I had to find her. And then this would all be over.

"Greggy," my ma's voice called up the stairs. "Break your fast while it's still hot."

"Yes, ma'am," I called back.

I was gonna figure this out.

Then I could go back and beg Justine for forgiveness.

***

I was cleanin' up the breakfast dishes when there was a knock on the front door.

"I've got it," I heard Pop call from the livin' room.

I was starin' out the kitchen window as I scrubbed a pot, so I wasn't really payin' attention to who was at the door. I heard Pop sound a bit surprised, and then ask someone to come in.

As soon as the person stepped in the house, I felt electricity buzzin' on my skin. The hair stood up on the back of my neck and my hands stilled.

It couldn't be.

I turned to the kitchen entrance and my breath was knocked out of me.

Justine.

She looked amazin', considerin'. Her skin was still a bit pale but was gettin' its glow back. She was holding herself delicately, as if standin' was difficult. My eyes raked over her body, finally landin' on her face. Her eyes were blazin'.

She was pissed.

But she was alive.

And she was here.

Why was she here?

"Because you, like the goddamned fool you are, decided to abandon me in the hospital and run away instead of facing this problem together," her voice was icy.

I blinked. Had I said that out loud? My brain was scrambled eggs, tryin' to keep up with the emotions ragin' through me. I opened my mouth to say somethin', but no sound came out. Justine rolled her eyes and sighed, but when her gaze found me again, I saw she was close to tears.

"Please come here and hold me," she said softly.

It broke my heart, and in two steps I was across the kitchen scoopin' her up in my arms. I stuck my nose into the crook of her neck and inhaled her familiar scent. She was fresh oxygen and I'd been underwater for far too long.

I felt her release a breath and then hot tears were fallin' on my cheek. God, I'd missed the feel of her. But she was here. Safe and whole in my arms.

I set her down and pulled back to kiss her. Her lips were greedy, drinkin' me in as her arms wrapped around me. Her body melted flush with mine and relief flooded through me. Suddenly, I was cryin' too. I needed to be closer to her. I needed her to never be apart from me again.

I kissed her deeper, somehow. I was searchin' for my soul in her lips, and, with every whimper and little moan she gave me, I found it.

It wasn't until I heard a delicate cough from behind us that I remembered we were in my parents' house. We broke apart and the prettiest blush rose on Justine's face as her glazed eyes struggled to focus.

I laughed sheepishly and wrapped an arm around her waist to turn her around to meet my folks.

"Ma, Pop, this is Justine Wilkson."

"Pleasure to meet you both," Justine breathed, still a bit muddled from our kiss. The possessive part of me crowed in victory at that.

"You are just as gorgeous as Greggy said you were," Ma gushed, rushin' forward to wrap Justine up in a hug.

If she was surprised, it only showed for a moment before she was huggin' my mother back like a child starved of attention. Ma held on a bit longer than she maybe needed to, but Justine seemed to soak it in. Pop held out his hand and smiled when he received a firm handshake from Justine in response.

"You're a good woman, comin' up here to beat some sense into his thick skull," Pop said, his eyes twinkling.

"Well, someone has to have the sense in this relationship," Justine sighed.

"Darlin', you've gotta understand –" I started.

She silenced me with a look and a delicate hand on my arm. "Time and place, Gregory."

Ouch. Gregory. So, she was still mad.

"Are you hungry? We just finished up breakfast, but I can whip somethin' up," Ma offered.

"Oh, thank you, ma'am, but I ate when I came through town," Justine smiled.

All of my blood rushed south hearin' the word "ma'am" come out of Justine's prim little mouth.

God, I'd missed her.

"Ma, Pop, Justine and I have some things we need to talk about," I said, givin' Justine's side a gentle squeeze. "I'm gonna show her around the property. We'll be back for lunch, I promise."

Ma gave us a big smile and pulled Justine in for another hug, while my Pop was watchin' me carefully.

He had never known me to have a woman like this in my life, and when I'd shown up on their doorstep three weeks ago, I was broken. An absolute wreck. I hadn't told them much of what had happened, and I think he assumed I'd broken her heart, or she'd broken mine. The truth was much darker. We'd been broken apart through no faults of our own. But now she had tracked me down. I was drownin' in her, and I knew my Pop could see that. He'd always been able to see through me.

Instead of sayin' anythin', he just grabbed hold of Justine's single suitcase and turned to haul it up the stairs. They'd put her in a separate bedroom, but I wasn't lettin' her sleep anywhere but with me.

"Let's go, darlin'," I whispered into her hair. "Momma, dishes are all done and dryin'."

"Good boy," Ma crooned, pattin' my cheek before she went and opened the front door for us. "Be home soon. I can't wait to talk more with you, Justine."

"Likewise, Mrs. Hudson," Justine said softly.

I took her hand and led her down the porch steps.

It was still pretty early, the sun barely over the horizon. I'd helped Ma and Pop buy this place a few years ago. They'd been in a tiny apartment in town since they'd lost the farm, and I knew they missed havin' property. So, I'd found them a little four-acre parcel just outside of town. It had a barn and a big pasture. It wasn't an active farm, but they had some chickens and a couple goats to keep them busy. Pop still had his job in town at the local butchers, and Ma worked for the library.

It wasn't a big piece of land, but it was peaceful. One corner had a copse of trees that surrounded a little pond that was nice to swim in durin' the heat of the summer. I started to lead Justine that way when she tugged me towards the barn.

I was confused but followed.

She was silent. The only communication was her fingers lightly squeezin' mine when we entered the barn, and she slid the doors closed. She turned to face me, and I saw fire in her eyes.

Here we go. I thought.

"Justine," I started.

She held up a single finger, silencin' me.

"Do you know how it felt to wake up in that hospital room and see Bell when it should have been you?" Her voice was taught, and she was shakin' with the effort to hold back her anger.

236

I wanted her to get angry with me. I wanted her to scream and yell, show me how hurt she'd been. I wanted her to show it all to me so that I could take the beatin' and beg for her mercy.

"I had to go, to keep you safe," I said softly, takin' a step toward her.

She backed up, but I kept advancin' until her back hit the barn door. She couldn't go anywhere.

"I can't imagine how much it hurt," I whispered, raisin' my arms to brace myself against the door. She was bracketed between my arms, and her eyes were flamin'.

"Just know, it hurt me too," I said. "Every single second away from you was pure torture, Justine. But I had to go. You were hurt because of me, and I couldn't stand it if the next time Kelly succeeded in her mission. She wants to kill you to keep you away from me."

"That doesn't mean you disappear while I'm unconscious," she snapped, glarin' at me.

I leaned in until we were nose to nose. I loved the way she flushed when I got this close, but I wanted her breathin' to be heavy from yellin' at me.

"How mad were you? How much did it hurt?" My eyes flicked between hers, urgin' her to tell me the truth. "Where did the anger live?"

Her chest was heavin', and her eyes were startin' to tear. Any big emotion and she cried. I knew she hated it about herself, but I loved it. She was so expressive. So responsive.

"Tell me," I commanded. "Yell at me. Make me hurt like I hurt you."

Without warnin', her hands shot out and shoved my chest backward. The surprise sent me stumblin', and when I looked back at her she was seethin'.

"You left me," she growled. "Alone. I was all alone. You promised."

"I did, I know," I said carefully. "I broke my promise, and I'm so sorry, darlin'."

"You're sorry?" she stalked forward, her hands curlin' into fists at her sides.

I nodded, but didn't speak, standin' my ground as she came chest to chest with me.

"Fuck your sorry, Gregory," she spit. "You left me *alone*. I was never supposed to have to be alone again. And you left."

Tears were flowin' freely down her cheeks now.

"It doesn't matter why you did it. If you did it to protect me. You broke my heart. You made me track your ass down and come to the middle of bumfuck nowhere to find you," she snarled, takin' another step into me, forcin' me backwards. "Do you know what I did to get here undetected? I had Bell rent a car for me, and now he's hiding out at his dad's until we get back. I've paid for everything in cash this entire trip. I have timed recordings for my house, timers on my lights, all to trick that psychopath into thinking that Bell came to visit you and that I'm still home recovering. I hid my face from all traffic cameras, all gas station cameras, everything, the entire drive here. The last few weeks have been hell. Hell I shouldn't have had to walk through alone."

She backed me up until my knees hit a bench. I stumbled backward over it and landed on the pile of hay we kept stocked for ground cover.

Layin' on the hay, lookin' up at her, I was harder than I'd ever been in my life. Arousal and guilt warred in my head. I shouldn't find this so hot, but dear God I loved when she lost control.

I knew I'd hurt her, and I wanted all her anger. I wanted to absorb it all so that she didn't have to hold it anymore. And then I wanted

238

to show her that I hadn't really left. That my heart was always going to be hers.

She climbed over the bench and lowered herself on top of me, straddlin' my lap. Apparently, I wasn't the only one with conflictin' feelin's goin' on.

"But you want to know the most painful part of the last few weeks?" She was shakin'.

I let my hands move to her hips to grip her in place. "Tell me."

Her eyes searched my face, and I saw the moment she fully understood what I was doin', takin' her rage. Her hands landed on my shoulders as she hovered over me, eyes borin' into mine.

"I couldn't stop loving you," she whispered. A hot tear fell onto my cheek, and I squeezed her hips, pullin' her into me.

Her eyes fell shut and her head dropped.

"So weak, and foolish," she muttered. "You broke my heart, left me alone, and all I kept thinking about was how to get back to you. You've ruined me."

"Justine, you are so much stronger than me," I breathed, reachin' up to cradle her face with one hand. "Look at me."

Her eyes opened and focused on my face.

"You don't need me," I said fiercely. "You choose to keep me in your life, and it's a choice I am thankful for every goddamned day. But you don't need me. You would be fine without me. You would be safe. I was going to find Kelly and take care of all of this, and then I was gonna come back to you and beg you. *Beg* you to take me back. I'm gonna spend every day of the rest of my life showin' you how much I can't live without you. Because you don't need me. But I need you. I can't breathe without you."

Her eyes flashed and she ground her hips angrily against mine, makin' me shake with desire.

"You think you feel more for me than I do for you?" she growled. "This goes both ways, Gregory. Equal. I can't see color without you in my life. Food has no taste. Pain is nothing. You are not a choice. Not anymore. You are my everything."

Her nails dug into my shoulders, and then her mouth was on mine. Consumin' me. I slammed my hips against hers, makin' her feel every hard inch of me as her chest fell to mine and her hands tangled in my hair.

There was nothin' gentle about this kiss. There was no part of me that was in control. Her fingers scraped my scalp and yanked at my hair as she ground on top of me, seekin' somethin' from me that she'd been missing for weeks.

Then, she was gone. Standin' above me. I watched as she stripped her shirt off, and then her pants. Her eyes were hard, and she gave me no warnin' before she was on me again, flickin' open my pants with her deft little fingers.

She released my cock without pushin' my pants down and stroked it quickly to bring it right back to attention. She straddled me and sank down in one go.

A strangled cry escaped my lips, and my eyes crashed closed as her hands landed on my chest. She moved slowly on top of me, settin' a languid pace that was churnin' fire in my stomach.

Her eyes never left me, watchin' me bein' eaten alive by her ferocity. When I opened my eyes, she dropped onto my chest, nose to nose with me.

"Make me a promise, Gregory," she whispered, her lips movin' against mine. I just wanted to kiss her, but when I tried, she pulled away and stilled her hips.

A growl pulled out of my chest, I gripped her hips and whispered, "I promise you everything, Justine."

She chuckled darkly and shook her head. "You know what I want you to promise me. And if you break this promise, I will make your life a living hell."

Death threats shouldn't be so sexy, but her pussy clenchin' around me told me she didn't mean it.

I looked deep into her eyes, tryin' to touch her soul.

"I won't leave you alone again. Ever. I promise."

There was a long moment where I wasn't sure if she believed me, but then her eyes welled, and she dropped her head to my neck and began movin' her hips.

She bounced up and down my shaft, my hands guidin' her but letting her set the pace.

Soon, she was mewlin' and whimperin' into my skin. I knew those sounds meant she needed more. She was close, but it wasn't enough.

My grip on her hips tightened and I started meetin' her with thrusts of my own.

"I'm right here, baby," I whispered to her as I pumped into her. I let one of my hands drift to her clit and rub it lightly while we writhed together.

Hay was poking into my back, scratchin' me, but I couldn't concentrate on anythin' except the tremblin' woman in my arms.

"I was wrong to run away, even if I thought I was doin' it for the right reasons," I moaned, thrustin' faster as her whimpers turned to cries and her fingers sank into my skin as she held on tightly.

"I love you, Justine. I will always love you. You are my breath. My life. I will never leave you alone again. You're mine."

My words pushed her over the edge, and she convulsed around me. I captured her cries with my lips and pumped twice more before my own release washed over me.

She collapsed on top of me, and I talked her through the last crests of her orgasm, makin' promises I knew I'd damn well die before I broke.

It took a few moments, but she finally came back to me with an earth-shatterin' smile.

"I missed you, Greg."

My heart swelled hearin' that fall from her lips.

"I missed you too, darlin'," I sighed, stealin' a kiss before I grabbed a blanket from the bench next to me and wrapped her in it. I flipped us so that she was layin' down with the blanket between her bare skin and the hay and covered her face in kisses.

I found her clothes and helped her get dressed, lovin' the knowledge that I was gonna be dripping into her panties for the rest of the day.

"C'mon," I said, helpin' her up once she'd gotten her legs back. "Let me show you the rest of the property, and then Momma'll kill us if we're not back for lunch."

I tucked her under my arm, and we stepped out into the sunlight. And for a moment, everythin' was right with the world.

Chapter Twenty-Nine

Justine

I stayed at Greg's parents for three days. It was a perfect escape from the insanity our lives had become.

His parents were amazingly kind and welcoming. His mother treated me the way I'd always imagined a mother would if she was able to show her love for her children. Not that my mother couldn't, she was just much less outwardly affectionate. It was oddly healing to be doted on by Irene Hudson. And Greg's father, Hammond, was like my father in that he was a quiet man with a great presence. But in his eyes danced warmth and mirth, instead of judgment and disappointment. He seemed happy that his son was happy. A completely foreign concept to me.

I liked it there. It felt like having Greg's arms wrapped around me all the time. It felt like home.

Of course, we had to go back.

I felt slightly guilty for leaving Bell trapped at his father's while I reunited with Greg, but that guilt washed away when he called Greg to let him know that my house had been vandalized again. Just some spray paint on the driveway that simply said, "Whore". How wildly unoriginal.

That did its job of bursting the bubble that Greg and I had managed to build for ourselves on the small plot of land that meant so much to his family.

On our last night there, I laid out the plan Detective Harold and I had come up with.

"Absolutely not," Greg protested. He was pacing around his childhood bedroom while I sat on his bed. "I'm not putting you in danger."

"I won't be in danger, weren't you listening?"

"Your plan is to have me make some grand gesture in public to draw out Kelly. That's puttin' you in danger, Justine."

"The plan is to do the grand gesture in public surrounded by about ten undercover cops," I sighed. "Kelly won't even know they're there, but you and I will be completely safe the entire time."

"Kelly Dimas is a certified loon." His accent always got a bit thicker when he was emotional, and I tried to hide my smile. "We've got no way of knowin' what she'll do or how she'll react."

"I have a pretty good idea," I said, trying to calm him down.

"How could you possibly know what she'd do?"

"Greg," I reached out to him, but he brushed me off and kept pacing. "Gregory." My voice was harder, and it made him stop.

He sighed and ran his hand over the back of his neck. He sat heavily on the bed next to me and dropped his head into his hands.

"I'm sorry, darlin'," he muttered. "I just can't stand the thought of you bein' exposed like that."

"I won't be alone," I said firmly. "You'll be right there, and so will most of Hartworth PD."

"But –"

"And I know what Kelly is going to do because I know how I would feel if I saw you propose to someone else right in front of me," I said softly.

His pained eyes found mine and widened in surprise.

"Propose?"

I nodded, watching him carefully. This was the part that the entire plan hinged on. I knew it would have to be something that would completely tear apart Kelly's soul. So, I'd thought about what would kill me. If Greg didn't love me, and I saw him tell another woman that he wanted to spend the rest of his life with her. It would gut me. I wouldn't be able to stop whatever emotional reaction I'd have. I was counting on Kelly to be just as in love with Greg as I was. She'd been obsessed with him for eight years. It felt like a pretty safe bet.

"Justine," his voice was tight.

"I know." I soothed a hand down his arm. "But it's the only thing that will make her completely snap."

He was silent for a long time, staring into space.

Finally, his hand came up and took mine.

"If you believe in this plan, then we'll do it," he conceded.

"Thank you."

"But I need you to know that this proposal doesn't count," his voice was hard.

I blinked, a bit confused.

A sly smile stole across his face, and he leaned in, placing his lips against mine as he whispered, "When I propose to you for real, it will be intimate. Special. Just you and me, darlin'. The start of our forever."

***

"These are officers Hitchins, Dobson, Hawkes, LaRoux, Ali, Jackson, and Krantz," Detective Harold introduced the people who were standing around the table in the conference room at the precinct. "They'll be in plain clothes no less than ten feet from you at all times."

Greg looked at me. I knew he was still unconvinced that this plan would work, but I had to have faith that it would.

We'd made our way back to Hartworth separately. I'd dropped the rental car off at Bell's and stayed the night there. His dad had dropped him off in the middle of the night, and the next morning Bell had gone out and taken his truck off the jack after replacing his tire. That had been the ruse we'd used as to why he would have needed a rental car to drive to see Greg. Then, I'd hidden in his backseat, and he'd driven to my house, presumably to check on me. The whole ruse felt absolutely ridiculous, but I couldn't be sure that Kelly wasn't watching all of us. So, it was better to feel ridiculous than end up dead.

Greg had flown back into town a few days later and crashed with Bell. He looked like Hell. His lie was that he'd been on a bender out of town, torn up over the guilt of the accident and leaving me. It wasn't a hard sell; Greg *was* a wreck about all of that. And he was anxious about the plan. So, looking strung out and exhausted wasn't difficult.

We gave Kelly a week with all of us back in our normal routine, except that Greg and I weren't speaking to each other. This was the hardest part of the plan. We didn't know where she was, so we couldn't risk seeing each other at all.

Greg and Bell continued working on the brewery. It was coming together. We'd be ready to open in a few months' time. This whole Kelly thing and the accident had delayed us, but the boys were getting things back on track. I had been coordinating with Detective Harold, and finally the day had come.

"You'll both be wired up, so we can hear everything you hear, and you'll be able to hear me," the detective was saying.

Greg's hand tightened in mine.

"We'll have six unmarked cars within a mile range of your location. As soon as we have eyes on her, you'll know. Gregory, I'll cue you when to approach Justine. It must be when Kelly is within earshot, so she can hear the proposal."

I could practically hear Greg's teeth grinding.

"Then, all you have to do is have a big public apology and proposal," Detective Harold finished. "It should be enough to drive Kelly over the edge, and with any luck she'll make a move in the next few days. We'll have undercover officers watching you both for the next week, in case it takes her a bit of time to enact her revenge plan."

"Thank you, Detective," I said softly.

"I'm sorry this is happening to you both," she said, casting her eyes down. "The department should have responded much more quickly to the stalking reports, and for that you have my apologies."

"As long as this is all over soon," Greg mumbled.

"It will be." The edge in her voice left no room for argument.

She took us to separate rooms to get mic'd up, giving me a talk about how to hold myself so I didn't muffle the audio. Then, she led us out two separate entrances that would spit us out heading to opposite ends of the downtown strip.

We were supposed to go about our business, Greg going back to the brewery, and me going to a coffee shop that I frequently worked out of.

After an hour of pretending to work, I packed my things and started to make my way to the parking garage on the other end of downtown. I had to pass by the brewery. As I rounded the last corner, the building came into view and a voice chirped in my ear.

"We have visual confirmation," Detective Harold said. I knew Greg was hearing the same thing in his earpiece. "Kelly Dimas is in

247

the crowd right next to The Bell Tower. Gregory, head out. It's time, kids."

Something about her matter-of-factness took the edge off my anxiety.

For Kelly to believe this, it had to look completely real. I had never been a good actress, so I was a bundle of nerves.

I stepped onto the sidewalk by the brewery and felt someone grab my arm.

"Justine," Greg's voice was insistent. Urgent.

He spun me around and gripped my arms with both hands.

"You're okay," he breathed.

I swallowed. This was just what we'd rehearsed. That this would be the "first" time Greg had seen me since the accident. But the genuine relief in his eyes startled me.

Then, he went to pull me into his arms, and I remembered I was supposed to be angry. I yanked myself backwards, glaring at him.

"I am okay, no thanks to you," I spit.

My heart tore when I saw the anguish on his face. It wasn't real. I had to keep reminding myself. But I also knew how much Greg blamed himself for everything, and that to him it probably felt real.

"Just…leave me alone, Greg," I said, maybe a bit louder than I'd meant to. I took a step back and said over my shoulder, "You're good at that."

"Justine!" he called, stepping quickly in front of me.

"Target is moving closer," Detective Harold's voice said in our ears. "Keep it up guys, she's hooked."

"Justine," Greg said, bringing my focus back to him. "I had to leave. I couldn't see you like that, not when it was all my fault."

I knew he was being truthful. Honest. This had to look real.

It wasn't real.

But it was. The emotions it was stirring up were completely real.

248

"You were supposed to protect me, and instead you just left," I said angrily, tears welling in my eyes.

"Darlin', I know I messed up," he spoke thickly. "But I realized over the last few weeks that I can't live without you."

I could tell we had the attention of the crowd now. Hopefully, Kelly was included in that.

"What do you mean?" My voice shook.

"I can't live without you, Justine," Greg's voice was firm. His hand slid down my arm and gripped my hand, squeezing it comfortingly. A reminder. He was real. His love for me was real. "I don't want to. I want you to be my entire life for the rest of my days. I don't ever want to be apart from you again. Justine, I love you."

My heart rate kicked up when he sank to one knee in front of me. That this was supposed to be a fake proposal seemed to have been lost on both of us. His eyes were shining in the way that used to make me so angry but was now what I lived to see. And the adoration coming from him wasn't fake.

"Justine Wilkson, I have loved you since freshman year of college," he started. "There was never anyone else for me. It was always you, and it will always be you."

My free hand came up to my mouth as tears spilled onto my cheeks. For the first time, I wasn't ashamed to be crying in public.

I was vaguely aware of the murmurs of the crowd, the light gasps and swoons of the women and the faint encouragement of the men.

"Justine, please make me the luckiest man on earth. Forgive me. And marry me."

It wasn't a question. It was a command, as so many of Greg's statements to me were.

A smile split my face, and I opened my mouth.

Before I could say yes, a feral shriek came from somewhere in the crowd.

Then, it was a blur of movement.

"Get down!" Detective Harold's voice shouted in my ear.

Greg reacted first, yanking me down and cushioning my fall with his body just as a crack rang out.

There was a beat of stillness.

The crowd parted, and people screamed.

In the middle of the madness stood Kelly.

Her blonde hair was wild, her eyes bloodshot and bulging. She was panting, the gun shaking at the end of her outstretched arm.

A bullet was lodged in the brick wall right where my head had been moments before.

She was staring at me, tears streaming down her face. She was vibrating with anger, and I saw pure heartbreak in her eyes. We simply stared at each other for a long moment. There was an understanding that passed between us.

I had been right. Seeing Greg profess his undying love for another woman had been too much for her to handle. It destroyed her, just as I knew it would have destroyed me.

I understood. I wished I didn't.

Then, two officers tackled her to the ground, and just like that it was over.

They took her gun, handcuffed her, and took her away.

With any luck, I would never see Kelly Dimas again.

***

Days later, I couldn't stop thinking about the look in Kelly's eyes just before she was brought down.

There was so much pain. So much hurt. Even confusion had flashed across her face. It didn't look like she wanted to hurt me. It looked like she was being gutted, and the only solution was to remove the source of her torment. That just happened to be me.

I was trying to sleep, but her eyes plagued me. I tossed and turned until finally Greg woke. His arm snaked around my waist, and he pulled me into his chest, his chin resting on my shoulder.

"You still thinkin' about her?" His voice was thick with sleep. I shouldn't have moved so much. He should be sleeping peacefully instead of awake with my thoughts.

"I can't stop," I sighed.

He kissed my shoulder softly and nuzzled my neck.

"What's keepin' you from lettin' this go, darlin'?"

"I don't think she had a choice, Greg," I whispered. It felt strange to say the thought aloud.

"What do you mean?"

"I mean," I paused. What did I mean? "I mean that, I don't think Kelly could stop herself from obsessing over you. I think there's something in her head that just couldn't let you go, and she built an entire life with you in her mind. When reality threatened that life, and she had to rectify it."

"Like, she's got a mental disorder?"

I shrugged and turned to face him, letting my fingers trail over his chest. "I'm not a psychologist. But there was no malintent in her eyes. When I saw her, she was hurt and confused. Not vindictive. I think she needs help."

Greg was silent for a long time, his eyes watching me. I held his gaze, trying to keep the heat that swirled through my veins every time he looked at me at bay.

Finally, the smallest smile graced his face.

"You're an amazin' woman, Justine," he breathed, dipping his head to kiss me gently. "After everythin' she put us through, put you through, and you want to help her?"

"I don't think prison is the right place for her," I whispered.

Greg nodded. "I think you might be right. If she does have something deeper goin' on, prison would just hurt her more."

I nodded, and he gripped my waist tighter for a moment before letting his hand drift up my back.

"Go to sleep, Justine," he whispered, pressing a soft kiss to my forehead.

I nestled into his chest, relieved that when I closed my eyes all I saw was darkness.

Chapter Thirty

Greg

There are only a few moments in life that I believe really define a man. His first kiss. His time behind the wheel of a car. His first drink of liquor. His first heartbreak. But nothin' was a more life-definin' moment for me than the day I proposed to Justine Wilkson. For real, that is.

The weeks followin' the sting and capture of Kelly Dimas were a whirlwind. Givin' testimony to the police, handin' over all the notes and evidence so they could build a real solid case against her.

They say the system moves slow, but a month after they arrested her, Justine and I were called to the courthouse to testify in her trial.

"We're going to make sure she can never get to you," the DA told us.

We were in a conference room a few hours before the trial. The attorney was givin' us the lowdown, even though we'd been goin' over all of this for weeks. I knew Justine was ready for it all to be over.

"Did you talk to her attorney about my suggestion?" Justine asked, her eyes sharp as she watched the lawyer fidget.

"Well, I wasn't sure it was prudent –"

"My apologies." Justine smiled in a way that showed no remorse. My hand tightened on her thigh. I loved watchin' her go in for the kill. "But I don't particularly care for your thoughts on the matter. I want the offer of a life sentence to a mental health facility put on the table for Kelly. High security, obviously, but the girl doesn't need prison. She needs help."

"The crimes she's committed –"

"Were brought about by a delusional attachment disorder. Prisons are not equipped to handle the type of disorder Kelly has been diagnosed with. I, as your client and the woman that she attempted to murder not once, but twice, demand that you bring her attorney in here right now so we can put this offer on the table."

The DA looked furious with his arms crossed. He didn't move.

Justine sighed. "I don't particularly want to get on the stand to relive some of the worst moments of my life. I'm fairly certain her attorney will jump at the chance to keep his client out of prison. You are the District Attorney, so the decision to level a plea deal is entirely within your jurisdiction. Add to that the fact that I've told you this several times before, and you're testing the limits of my patience. Bring him in."

Glarin' daggers at my girl, the DA disappeared. He came back a few moments later with a disheveled public defender trailin' behind him.

"My clients have persuaded me to put a new deal on the table," the DA sighed.

"A new deal?" The other attorney's eyes flicked between the three of us.

"Lifetime confinement to a high security mental health facility."

Silence fell over the room as Kelly's lawyer struggled to process this information. He began pacin', lost in his own thoughts before he scanned the room. Finally, his eyes landed on Justine, who had been watchin' him patiently. She smiled softly, as if she could read his mind.

"I know it might seem strange that this is coming to you so close to trial," she said. The only sign she was nervous was her palm in mine, shakin' slightly. "I've been asking for this offer to be made for weeks, but the DA's office didn't think it was prudent."

I smirked hearin' her throw the DA's words back at him.

"I've read the official diagnosis from Dr. Brent," Justine continued, "and from my limited interaction with Ms. Dimas I have to say I agree. She's sick. Prison won't help that. They simply don't have the resources, and frankly I worry what kind of person she would become being locked up like that. I don't want her to ever be able to be a menace to the public again, but in a good facility with good security, I believe Ms. Dimas could find the help she needs."

More silence, and then a relieved sigh.

"Ms. Wilkson, thank you," the public defender looked like he might cry. "I'll take this to my client, but I am confident she will accept this deal with no addendums."

***

Kelly ended up in a place in Vermont. It was far enough away that Justine felt comfortable, and it was tightly run. She would get the help she needed there.

With everythin' that had been goin' on, gettin' The Bell Tower ready to open had slowed down. Bell had been a rock for us through the whole thing, and he was just as relieved as we were that it was all said and done.

The space was nearly there. A few plumbin' issues had cropped up, so we were gettin' those taken care of, and we needed to order all the restaurant supplies. Aside from the stupid stout glasses. I was remakin' the brews that Kelly had drained, and they were nearly ready.

Bell and I had invited Justine over to see the first official lightin' of the dinin' space now that all the electrical was finished and the bare bulbs were hung over tables.

I walked into the warehouse, the lump in my pocket gettin' heavier with each step I took. She was already there, her arms restin' on the bar that we'd ended up puttin' exactly where she'd envisioned.

God, that felt like ages ago, takin' her to the hospital with a board stickin' out of her hand. Back when she was still pretendin' to hate me.

"Darlin", I have no idea how you manage to make a pantsuit look so damn sexy," I growled as I reached her and grabbed her waist, spinnin' her around and into my arms.

She giggled, a sound that I knew I'd never get enough of, and wrapped her arms around my neck.

"It's not sexy, you just know what's underneath," she purred, pressing her body against mine.

Heat flared from the base of my spine all the way to my hair. Before I could say anythin' else, the master lights went out, leavin' us in the dim light from the front windows.

Bell.

Just like we'd planned, soft music started playin' over the speaker system we'd installed. Somethin' sweet and folksy floated down around us as Justine looked around, confused.

Then, the dinin' room lights came on. Warm and soft, they turned the space into somethin' akin to magic. The light played with the glow on Justine's skin, and she'd never looked prettier.

Her eyes went wide, and she stepped away from me to look around and take it all in. She did a slow circle, her mouth open in wonder. When she excitedly turned back to me, her hands flew up to cover her mouth.

I was on one knee, ring box open. My hand was shakin' and my throat was so tight I wasn't sure I'd be able to actually speak.

"Greg," she breathed, tears wellin' in those beautiful eyes.

"It took us years to get here," I finally choked out, my own eyes startin' to water. "Justine, this one's for real. I love you. I always have. I can't do this life without you. You make me happier than I ever thought I'd deserve to be."

Her tears spilled over, so much love pourin' out of her that I thought I could drown.

"Marry me, Justine Wilkson," I whispered.

"It's never a question," she muttered, almost to herself, before givin' me a smile warmer than the sun in July.

"Is that a yes, darlin'?"

"Of course, it's a yes," she laughed loudly and launched herself at me as I stood.

Her arms wrapped around me, and we spun in a full circle. Her lips found mine, and every cell in my body sparked.

She said yes.

She was mine.

Forever.

Epilogue

Justine

I was getting married.

Eventually.

Greg and I were happily taking time to recover from everything, letting ourselves enjoy just being together. Going on dates, spending our nights and mornings tangled in each other. Finding a rhythm in our everyday lives.

The Bell Tower launch had taken another few months to put together, but it was a massive success, just as I knew it would be. All the locals fell head over heels for the intimate yet accessible feel of the place. It was taking off. Greg's brews were the talk of the restaurant circuit. He was making plans to set up a distribution system, now that he had a big enough brewery to make them on a larger scale. The boys were living their dream, and I couldn't have been prouder.

With the restaurant so successful, our latest adventure was helping Bell navigate his feelings for a girl he'd met. In all the years I'd known him, he had never actually wanted a relationship with anyone, so it was a surprise to all of us when Adelaide happened. He was in that sweet spot of miserably happy, and we had to let them work through it on their own.

Now, I had to do something I'd been dreading for months. Telling my parents I was engaged. I'd waited too long, I knew that, but every time I thought about picking up the phone to call them a knot of anxiety landed in my chest. But, as Greg kept reminding me, they should hear about it from me before they got the save the date in the mail.

So, here went nothing.

"Hello, Wilkson residence," Loretta's voice sounded on the other end. Loretta had been our maid from the time I was six years old. She was professional, but warm and kind-hearted. She was my first friend, and hearing her voice sent a wave of nostalgia over me.

"Hi, Loretta. This is Justine. Are my parents available?"

"Yes, of course, Miss," she sounded happy to hear from me. "Let me get them for you."

"Thank you, Loretta," I smiled into the phone.

There was a brief pause, and then my father picked up.

"Justine, what a pleasant surprise," his deep voice actually sounded pleased. "I've got your mother with me. Is there something you need from us?"

Of course, he thought I needed something. As if I hadn't been completely self-sufficient for years.

"No, Papa, I don't need anything. I just have some news to relay," I took a deep breath. "I'm engaged."

"Engaged?" My mother's voice was confused. Rightly so. I think I'd mentioned months ago that I was dating someone, but our calls weren't frequent.

"To be married, yes."

Silence hung over the line, and then I heard an excited giggle from my mother.

"Justine!" she gushed. I could tell that she'd grabbed the phone from my father and was beginning to pace the room. "What wonderful news!"

"We haven't met this young man," came from my father.

"No, Papa, you haven't," I grit out, trying desperately to keep my tone jovial.

"But you know him and love him, yes?" from my mother.

"I do," I smiled softly, thinking of those warm green eyes.

"Then that's all that matters," her voice was firm, and I knew she was glaring at my father. "When is the wedding?"

"We haven't planned that far yet," I laughed. At least Mother was excited for me. "But we were thinking of flying up for the holidays so that you can meet him. His name is Gregory. He's…well, I think you'll come to like him, at any rate."

"Of course, please come home. It's been too long since we've seen you," Mother's voice had gone sad.

A pang of guilt rushed through me. I liked my mother. Our relationship was considerably less contentious than with my father. I knew she missed me. I missed her too. I needed to get home more.

"We'll plan on staying for a week or so, how does that sound?"

"Splendid! Oh, there's so much to plan. Loretta," she called, then she was back. "I'll let you go, sweetheart, but I am so excited to meet this man of yours. All my love, darling."

"Love you, Mama," I said softly.

The line didn't disconnect, so I knew it was just my father and me.

"He didn't ask," he finally said after a long beat.

"He asked me."

I heard his frustrated sigh and knew he was tapping his fingers against his desk.

"Justine," he started and then stopped.

"Papa, I know what you're going to say –"

"You don't," his voice was firm. My mouth clicked shut and I waited. "You've done remarkably well for yourself. You have an excellent career, a beautiful home, and a bright future. Is this young man ready to step up to the plate and meet you where you are?"

"Yes, he is," I said. "He owns a brewery here in town that is quickly growing. It's going to be very successful, especially with my help. He's intelligent and kind. He makes me laugh. He loves me."

I closed my eyes. My father and I didn't have emotional conversations. This was uncharted territory for us.

He was quiet for another long moment.

"Then I'm happy for you. Truly."

Something swelled in my chest, and I felt tears poking my eyes.

"And, Justine," his voice was hesitant. "I know I've been…relentless, in my insistence of your excellence. You have surpassed every expectation I have ever set for you. You are an incredible young woman, and I'm sorry if I haven't said that more to you. I'm proud of you."

That opened the floodgates. Tears streamed down my cheeks as the eight-year-old inside of me jumped for joy.

"Thank you, Papa."

He coughed once, the only display of his own discomfort.

"Call more. Your mother misses you."

I bit my lip to stop myself from smiling, even though he couldn't see it.

"I will."

"Goodbye, Justine."

"Bye, Papa."

The line went dead, and I felt frozen.

The relationship wasn't fixed, by any means, but the words I'd been working towards my entire life had just been said to me. And I found that they didn't matter half as much to me as I thought they would.

I had built my life. Not because of, but in spite of, my father's insistence.

I had found the love of my life, pushed him away, and found my way back to him, all on my own.

My happiness was the result of *my* hard work. Of my love, and who I was.

My happy ending was all mine.

The End

Afterword

Wasn't that fun?! Honestly, I love Greg with every bit of my heart, and writing the contrast between him and Justine was so fun for me. I hope you enjoyed their love story! I think exploring the concept of feeling deserving of love when you have other goals in life is something that isn't necessarily talked about a lot, but it's definitely something that resonates with me. The closer I get to thirty, the more the world keeps telling me that without a partner I'm incomplete. That there has to be something that I compromise in my career or creative goals in order for there to be room in my life for love. But I don't believe that's true.

I think that when you are fully yourself and your life is full of things that fill you with joy and contentment, then you become a magnet for the person that complements that life. Justine learns that throughout this novel. That you can, in fact, have it all. Focusing on your career shouldn't mean that you have to give up on love. And falling in love shouldn't derail your professional goals. As with everything in life, there's balance, and the right person will help you find more balance.

Acknowledgements

Eleven-year-old Becca is ecstatic right now. There were so many years that I was sure I would never finish a full manuscript, and here we are with three full books under our belt!

As always, a huge thanks to my Mom and Dad and sister for always believing in me and encouraging me to follow the things that make my heart sing. The entire rest of my family, who always support me in everything I do and are easily my biggest fan club.

Thank you to my friends; the ones who let me live with them and the ones who let me live through them. And to the ones who hounded me every time they saw me. "When is the next one coming??" You all motivated me more than you'll ever know!

And, as always, my main gal Evie, for suffering through my many mental breakdowns with only partial judgment.

The Bell Tower Series

Want to spend more time in Hartworth and fall even more in love? The Bell Tower Series are all standalone novels that can be read in any order and without having to have read the others. Although, we see several side characters recurring throughout the series, and get to see the evolution of everyone's favorite brewery, The Bell Tower!

Truly & Deeply, the story that started it all (not chronologically), follows Addy and Bell. As Addy works through the aftermath of her attack, she struggles to accept that someone could love her. Bell is persistent, patient, and pining for Addy. This book explores what it means to move forward, and the overwhelming acceptance that love brings.

Utterly & Madly is Raelynn and Johnny's time to shine! This reverse engineered relationship was topsy turvy from the beginning, so check this one out to see how two such fiery, independent people ended up falling head over heels in love.

About the Author

Rebecca has been a storyteller as long as she can remember. She loves bringing people's stories to life and giving voice to things that might not get talked about that often. With a background in acting, she loves diving into new worlds and new characters. She believes in fairy tale endings and happily ever afters. She is happily chasing adventure wherever the wind takes her with her cat, Evie.